LET THE DEVIL IN

Jeff Haws

Let the Devil In

Printed in the United States of America

First Printing, 2019

ISBN: 978-1-945768-08-8

Publisher: Shifty Squid, LLC

P.O. Box 170392

Atlanta, GA 30317

Visit the author's website and blog at www.jeffhaws.com

1

Zac threw his weight forward, his foot landing square in Benjamin's chest. He watched Benjamin tumble backward, his legs flying wildly into the air and his head bouncing off the wood floor in the dimly lit, dank basement as his legs flew into the air and landed hollowly at his side. Zac crouched down and straddled him, their faces inches apart.

"Is this where you want to be? On your back? Helpless?" Zac's voice raised an octave, his arms spread, looking around at the other men. "One boot to your chest, and you're on the floor, exposed. I could *kill* you right now if I wanted to. Easy. Your head's pounding. Your limbs are useless. You're fucking hopeless. One kick. *One.* Is this who we are? Is this who Alessandrans are?"

Seven men stood around them, their eyes shifting between each other and the scene on the floor. Benjamin was rubbing the back of his head, his eyes wide as he looked up at Zac, who stood up straight and swung his leg over the prone body as he stepped away.

"You're all so fucking enamored with *freedom*," Zac sneered. "It's a trap. A lie. A goddamn placebo for the human condition. It's the empty balm weak leaders peddle to even weaker followers. You want *real* freedom? It's there outside the walls Audrey built when she led this town. Go out there, and you'll find freedom, but you'll also find a bleak world ravaged by the virus. Death. Disease. Starvation. You want freedom? You get to be back at the bottom of the goddamn food chain again. You're a fucking caveman. That's what you want? Then get the hell out of here and walk out of those gates now! Nobody's gonna stop you."

His eyes wild, voice at a fevered pitch, Zac looked around at these men he'd brought together. This all seemed so obvious to him, but it was like no one else saw it. Everyone fetishized freedom, but look where freedom had gotten them—as far as they knew, they were the last organized colony of people left on Earth, and it was a struggle every day to survive until the next.

Under Audrey's leadership, the virus stayed out of Alessandra, she kept the hospital running through all the turmoil, built the wall to keep them safe, and made the difficult choices a leader has to make in challenging times. The most consequential choice she made was to require everyone to wear steel rings around their waist when in public in order to prevent the physical contact she believed spread the virus. That also meant banning cohabitation, separating families, and dissolving marriages. It had been a drastic move, and the studies showing contact as the chief means of spreading the virus proved questionable, but the results were clear—H6N1 never breached those walls.

Audrey certainly cut some corners and wasn't always perfectly honest, but everything she did was in service of the town's survival, and it had largely worked. Zac might never forgive Audrey for what she did to his family, but he had to acknowledge grudging respect for her unyielding focus. Even her brother Paul, while he might have gone overboard at times, killed the people he killed because he felt like they endangered the citizens of Alessandra.

And now, too many people looked back in disgust at their leadership, as if it was a bad thing to stand up against the forces that threaten to tear you apart. Tough times call for tough people. Being in the military had taught Zac that much. He wanted to get the rest of the town to see that, too.

He considered what had become of Alessandra in the five seasons (roughly fourteen months, but calendars were more difficult to track than the seasons these days) since Stephanie and Michael took on leadership responsibilities in the wake of Paul being murdered by a mob and Audrey disappearing, and he worried about where the town was headed. These two weak-willed people thrust into illegitimate power didn't seem to understand that this wasn't a world of fucking butterflies and puppy dogs anymore. Call it nihilism if you want, but the times call for what they call for. Perhaps the day would come when granting people total freedom to live their lives as they wish would be viable, but this harsh, resource-stricken world required rules and the discipline to follow them. And that required leaders willing to do more to enforce those rules than saying "Pretty please" a lot.

You can't alter reality, but it can certainly alter you. Zac knew this was hardly the time to worry about what the people wanted; they had to think about what the people *needed* instead. This was war with nature itself, uncaring and indifferent. Fuck your feelings.

His fists clenched, arms ramrod straight at his sides, Zac scanned the room, looking each man individually in the eyes. None of them blinked. None of them moved for the door.

"If you're gonna stay, then we need to get to work. Look around. Is this the town we want it to be? We've lost a lot over the past year, and it's time we start to get it back. It's time we assert who we really are. We need to speak our minds and refuse to be shouted down."

The men still looked hesitant, but he could sense their confidence growing as they moved in closer. His message was resonating. He was getting through to them.

"For now, go home. Okay, guys?" Zac nodded, and he saw the gesture mimicked around the room. "Nothing's gonna change overnight. First, we need to understand what it is we're fighting for, then come up with a plan to get it. It's gonna take time and pressure and persistence. A concerted effort. Some of you will have visible roles in this, and I'll need others to work quietly, helping to spread our message in living rooms and on the street. I'm not gonna lie to you and tell you this will be easy. It won't be. We'll face resistance. From people we call friends and neighbors. And there's a good chance not all of us make it to see this through. But if we stay together with one mind, one mission, by god, we'll fucking get there."

A cry of solidarity rose from several of the men, their fists thrust high over their heads. One of them reached out a hand and helped Benjamin to his feet; he stood and nodded at Zac.

"Go rest up, fellas," Zac said. "There's lots more work from here on out."

2

"So what do we do, then?" Stephanie asked, standing up from her couch, raising her arms in an exaggerated shrug.

Michael shook his head. "Look, I think we both knew discipline and enforcement was gonna be one of the tougher parts of this for us. It's not like we have a court system or a...fucking Council of Elders or whatever to make these calls."

Stephanie rolled her eyes and began pacing the room. "Ignoring it isn't an option, though. Right? We have to do something. What William did was assault, in any damn court of law that used to exist. Hank's in the hospital. What should we do? William was one of Audrey's top officers, and we've always figured we have to watch those guys. But now there's no prison to put him in."

Michael shrugged. "Maybe there should be."

"We've talked about this. The further we head down that road, the closer we get to becoming Audrey." Stephanie ran her fingers through her black hair, yanking strands tight against her scalp. "That's not a direction I want to head in."

It had been hard for Stephanie and Michael since they led the overthrow of Audrey's oppressive regime, then had to rebuild a functioning community in the wake of her disappearance. That vanishing act did help in that they didn't have to figure out how to deal with her, or what threat she might pose to Alessandra going forward. Where their former leader was now—alive or dead—was anyone's guess.

It seemed like a natural fit having Stephanie and Michael fill the leadership vacuum for the town, but neither was willing to just take on the mantle without the explicit consent of the citizens they'd be governing. So, after weeks of cajoling by several people, Stephanie agreed to be a candidate for the town's leader if they organized a vote.

Six weeks after Audrey fled town, Alessandra's citizens descended on the town square, where dozens had been murdered a year and a half earlier on the order of Audrey's brother Paul, to cast their votes for the next leader. Among the 141 voting-age people still living in Alessandra, just sixty-five voted, and fifty-nine chose Stephanie.

She appointed her ex-husband, Michael, as her co-leader, with equal decision-making power. The idea was that they had different strengths and weaknesses, and they'd complement each other well. Instead of moving into Audrey's mansion on the hill on the east side of town, Stephanie and Michael lived in modest homes alongside the other townspeople. The mansion and the surrounding compound was locked and boarded up, but could still be seen looming over the town from the square.

As the transition was happening, Zac lay in a hospital bed, carried there after Stephanie found him lying on Audrey's bedroom floor, unconscious with a fractured skull. All they could tell was that he had apparently slammed his head into Audrey's bed post.

Stephanie knew Zac could be dangerous, but she'd taken an oath as a doctor to help anyone who needed it, and there were few things she believed in more than that. She checked in on him as often as she could until he was finally healthy enough to walk out of the hospital and live on his own, months later. He shook Stephanie's hand on his way out the door that day; that had been a good moment for her. He said he didn't remember anything about what happened that day in Audrey's room.

By this point, she'd seen how difficult this job was, balancing the town's need for leadership with her lack of experience with government. Very little in her career as a doctor had prepared her for dealing with all the competing interests that confronted her every day. What size should the rations be? What jobs need to be filled? What needs to be built or fixed? They'd lost a number of people in the ensuing months, life spans shrinking in a world without modern medicine. Babies were born occasionally, but pregnancy and giving birth also carried extra risk, even with a hospital in town. The population was shrinking, and she worried about that. Sometimes, Michael was helpful to bounce ideas off of; other times, he seemed disinterested. Typically, he'd shrug and go with whatever Stephanie's decision was. But she didn't want or need a Yes man. She needed someone to challenge her, and Michael didn't appear to have that in him.

Stephanie wondered how much being taken and nearly killed by Paul and his men before Stephanie saved him had affected Michael emotionally. She'd given him the space he needed at first, but he wasn't the same. The confident, assertive man she'd married nearly ten years earlier wasn't here anymore, it seemed. But she didn't have time to deal with that. Too much was at stake.

And now, when she needed someone to push her to do something drastic, she didn't have that person. Sometimes, it made her envy Audrey's ability to just throw ethics to the wind and do whatever she deemed necessary. But Stephanie had vowed she was going to govern differently from Audrey in virtually every way. In some situations, though, that put her in a tough position.

"Okay," she said, crouching in front of Michael, who was

slumped on the couch. "We need to talk to William. One of us does, anyway. I need to go to the hospital and see if I can help Hank. Can you go talk to William?"

He draped his arm across the back of the couch.

"I guess so? I wouldn't say I'm enthusiastic about it."

"Michael, I really need your help here. I can't do all of this by myself. I need you as a partner. I need someone I can trust, and count on here. We've been through a lot together, haven't we? And we've come out the other side. We're here. Right now. This is a tough job, but it's the position we're in. We have a responsibility."

Stephanie looked deeply into Michael's eyes, and he stared back. After several seconds, he closed his eyes and nodded slightly.

"Great. Thank you." She slapped her hands against his knees. "Get his take on what happened. I'm gonna talk to Hank, see how he's doing. We'll figure this out."

3

Zac rapped his knuckles against the house's front door, then waited, his eyes wandering down the length of the house. Once a canary yellow, the paint was crusting over into a dingy black and brown; the siding was flaking off in several places. Years earlier, there's a good chance there would have been a flower bed out front, maybe some gardenias or tea olives that would have given off a nice fragrance on a late spring day like this.

But there were few signs of much of that as Zac stood on the porch and surveyed the drab, dilapidated neighborhood. While a few people in the town had continued to do upkeep on their yards, most couldn't find the time and energy when they were fighting every day for survival. It had been more than two years since the virus struck, and the world had shifted under their feet in what felt like the blink of an eye. Billions dead, civilization thrown back practically into the Stone Age, and it was these sorts of little things that Zac occasionally missed. He wanted that world back again. But if he couldn't have it, he wanted to do what he could to make the one he was stuck in better, whatever that meant he had to do.

The door swung open, and Zac turned in that direction. "Is it done?" he asked.

William nodded. "Should work for what we need."

Zac glanced over both shoulders, grimacing.

"We can't do this shit on the front porch. Gonna invite me in?"

"Didn't realize you were gonna wait for an invite." William stepped to the side and swung his arm toward the living room. Zac stepped in and sat on the red linen couch, and William settled into a leather recliner. Zac leaned forward and put his arms on the coffee table.

"So, did he make it to the hospital?" Zac asked.

"Sure. No problem." William shrugged. "Benjamin dropped him off for us. If anyone saw him on the way, he was gonna say he found Hank on the sidewalk like that. Hank wasn't doing too well when he left."

"You didn't have to kill the guy. This wasn't a hit."

William rolled his eyes. "When you tell me to beat the shit out of a guy, you get what you get, man. But Hank's not gonna *die*. He'll be fine. You were worse off than him, and you're sitting here talking to me right now."

"Yeah, well. I come from good stock."

"I'm sure that's the explanation."

Zac laughed. William got up and began pacing the room.

"So what's next? What's the plan from here? I put a guy in the hospital for you. Fine. I want to know how this helps us get back to the way things were. There's still no Audrey. She's gone."

William stopped talking and swallowed hard. "It's not right the way she was done," he finally said, his eyes fixed on the floor at his feet. "She wasn't perfect. But who is? Show me a man who can say he never makes mistakes, and I'll show you a fucking liar. What did they expect her to be? She's human. Fucking sue her. But she was the best damn thing to happen to this town. Do you think any of us would even be alive without her stepping in and instilling order? The virus would have wiped out the lot of us. And now she's the one who's gone. It's not fair."

Zac crossed his legs. "She earned a lot of that. Do you even know what all she did? I'll admit, she did a lot for this town—good and bad—and people didn't appreciate the good as much as maybe they should have. That's why it's time to right some wrongs. Let's just say this is the beginning of that. But if she were standing in front of me right now, I'd still punch her in her fucking face."

William lifted his head, alarmed. "I know it's complicated with you and her, but you've just gotta tell me something. I mean, I believe in what you're saying, so I went through with this. Now you have a good reason to trust me. Give me a reason to trust you."

"Let me ask you a question," Zac responded. "What do you think about Stephanie and Michael?"

"They led the entire overthrow. I know they killed Paul. And, for all I know, they killed Audrey and dumped her body somewhere. They're the reason we're in the mess we're in today. And, as far as I'm concerned, they should be run out of town."

Zac smiled. "This is why we like each other."

4

"You awake?" Stephanie said, poking her head into the room.

Hank squirmed in bed and groaned. "Yeah. Tough to sleep with broken ribs after the meds are worn off."

She pushed the door further open and walked inside. "Need me to call someone to get you a refill?"

"Nah, it's fine for now. Don't wanna get too loopy while we talk."

"All right." She pulled a chair up close to the bed so he wouldn't feel like he had to raise his voice for her to hear. "I won't take long."

He grimaced and nodded.

"So, what can you tell me about what happened?"

"It's weird. I really don't get it," Hank said, shaking his head. "I mean, I know Officer Greene. Plenty well enough to I.D. him anyway. And he just…attacked me. I don't know how else to describe it."

"What were you doing when he jumped you?" Stephanie asked.

"Nothing. Really. Nothing." He pushed his head up on the pillow, obviously struggling to get comfortable. Stephanie figured she didn't have long before his pain became unbearable. Broken ribs were no fun. "I was walking down the street toward my house. Suddenly, I saw a flash of motion out of the corner of my eye; then I felt something hit me in the back of the head. Hurt like hell. I guess I went into some sort of defensive crouch, and that was when I saw his face, clear as day. It was right in the middle of the morning. He looked me in the eyes; then there was another hit into my side, and he took my legs out from under me. Once I was on the ground, I'm honestly not sure what happened. I woke up here."

"You don't know who brought you here?"

"No idea. Nobody's told me. I honestly thought he was gonna kill me. I seriously did, Stephanie."

She put her hand on top of his and rubbed it as she stood up. "I'm so sorry this happened, but you did great to identify William. How certain are you that it was him?"

"Hundred percent. I think he wanted me to know, to be honest."

"Any idea why he would do this? Did you two have a disagreement?"

He paused for a moment, thinking. Then: "Not a one."

"Okay, Hank. Thanks. Get your rest. I'll tell the nurse you need more meds on my way out."

"Great," he winced and adjusted his position. "Maybe make it a double this time."

She smiled. "That can probably be arranged. Thanks again."

Stephanie walked out and closed the door quietly. She flagged down a nurse in the hall and told him Hank needed twenty milligrams of morphine, then kept going toward the stairs that led down to the exit.

It was hard for her to wrap her head around what happened with Hank. Why would William do that? She wasn't aware of there being any issues with him in the previous year. She knew William in the way you know pretty much everyone in a small walled-off town with fewer than

200 adults, but he wasn't someone she was particularly close to.

And, then, there was the memory that was seared in her mind: *"William…Kill the girl first. Stand by for the next name."*

William was the man with the gun, expressionless, shoulders slumped, blithely obeying the orders of a sociopath while Stephanie watched her best friend obliterated on a grainy television screen, Michael tied to a chair, watching the same screen. Paul was toying with her, using William as his trigger man. And when Paul gave the word to put a bullet in Anna's head, precisely because he knew that would impact Stephanie the most, William hadn't hesitated. The image was hazy in the shadows of the night on the town square, still soaked in the blood of so many people, with only Stephanie and Michael watching on. But there was no mistaking it. She'd never forget it, emblazoned deep within the recesses of her soul, attacking her in quiet moments when she'd begin to feel safe and peaceful—William's arm rising dutifully, a marionette on Paul's strings. No moment of wondering whether or not this was just. Whether Anna deserved this fate. He never asked. He didn't want to know. He just raised the gun to the back of her head and fired, and Stephanie's best friend since childhood was gone in a puff of smoke. Then the echo of the gunshot reverberated up the hill to the compound seconds later, an exclamation point on Stephanie's scream.

Beyond an occasional passing glance, that was all she knew of William—he was a thug who was useful to Paul specifically because he'd follow orders without question, even if that meant putting a bullet in an innocent woman's head. That was the kind of man she was dealing with.

She shivered at the thought. Did the town have a cold-blooded hitman on its hands? Was that what this was? If he'd kill Anna and attack Hank for no reason other than he was told to, what else might he do on the right (or wrong) command?

And all this led to an even scarier question—If William did, in fact, do this on command, whose orders was he following?

5

Walking down the street, Michael was thinking William's house was just a couple of doors away. He was also thinking this wasn't what he wanted to be doing. Not today. Not with his life in general.

When he'd pushed for Stephanie to help him expose Audrey's corruption, this hadn't been the outcome he envisioned. He really hadn't thought much beyond feeling betrayed by a woman he'd trusted, and wanted to see justice served to her. He was willing to take some risks to do that, and he knew Stephanie could help make it happen. Eventually, it did—but the costs had been more than Michael was ready to bear.

His best friend, Nick, had survived the trauma of months in Audrey's quarantine camp but, since they escaped, he wasn't the same man. That was even more true for Nick's girlfriend, Rachel, who struggled for months after they helped storm Audrey's mansion, killing Paul and ending Audrey's reign as town leader. Neither Rachel nor Nick wanted to talk about what they'd seen within those fences, but the descriptions from those who went in afterward were horrifying—dead, emaciated bodies, swollen legs and abdomens, skin flaking off, shackled to poles inside tents no bigger than a closet. At least one corpse appeared to have been severely beaten, his tent splattered with dried blood.

Because none of the survivors were talking, it was unclear how much of that they had been aware of, or how much they might have participated in themselves. There needed to be a full accounting of the quarantine camp, but Michael hadn't been able to get it out of Nick in over a year, so he didn't expect anyone else was going to have much luck with the others.

When the prisoners were first freed, Michael figured they'd be fine; Nick and Rachel, imprisoned for sharing a bed one night, had even tried living together for a while. But something just always seemed wrong. Nick wasn't his usual wisecracking self, and was far more irritable; snapping at the least provocation instead of tossing a good-natured insult Michael's way. When Michael would see Rachel, her behavior was even more erratic than Nick's; her eyes never stopped darting left and right, with sudden jerks of her head almost as if she expected someone to attack her from behind at any moment. Michael thought—hoped—there was something like love there somewhere, but hope really was all it was.

That light was extinguished six months after Audrey was overthrown, when Nick was seen sprinting down Kimsey Street at 2 a.m., wearing nothing other than a pair of damp grey socks and a white T-shirt ripped off his left shoulder. He was screaming something unintelligible. Michael didn't know what it was, but he knew the voice as soon as it woke him up. He'd never forget the sound, the sheer helpless panic careening through the night air.

Others heard, and came out on their porches, some lighting candles to try to see better what was going on. Michael sprinted down the stairs from his bedroom and threw open the front door. He couldn't see well, but he knew Nick was coming toward his house. Michael leaped off the porch and ran into the street, trying to stop him and understand what was happening.

When he got out there and Nick was just a few feet away, arms pumping and legs churning hard, Michael could see the T-shirt was soaked through with blood from his collar to his navel, and his face was splattered with spots of crimson. Nick tried to veer around him, but Michael spread his legs and grabbed his friend's shoulders, his eyes wide.

"What happened, Nick? What's going on?" Michael leaned in, trying to make eye contact.

Nick's head rattled back and forth, and he tried to shake free; Michael wrapped his arm around Nick's neck and pulled him close into his chest. Nick hit Michael in the sides, nearly knocking the air out of him, but he wasn't about to let go. Not then. Not ever, he hoped. He just squeezed more tightly.

After a few seconds, Nick stopped thrashing, and his legs went limp. He slumped to the street, chest heaving, tears streaming red streaks down his face. Michael fell alongside him.

"It's over," Nick said, his eyes rolling back as he laid his head on the pavement.

"What's over? What happened? Where did all this blood come from? Are you hurt?"

Nick exhaled in something approaching a laugh, but coming out as a wheeze, then a deep-throated cough.

"You don't get it," he finally said. "Nobody *fucking* gets it."

"Okay, Nick. You're right. I don't get it. Help me understand. What's going on?"

Nick rolled his head to his left and looked Michael in the eyes. He was lying right next to him, but he looked further away than Michael ever remembered feeling from another person. He was physically there, but there was nothing tangible behind those eyes. No life. No humanity.

"It's over. It's finally over." Nick sighed.

Michael's chest began to tighten as he tried to will himself to be wrong about what Nick meant.

"What's over? Nick, you have to tell me. Enough with the bullshit. This is me. Michael. Whatever it is, we'll get through it, okay. *What* is over?"

Nick bit his lip and took a deep breath.

"Rachel. Rachel's over, Michael." Then his head slumped lifelessly to its side.

Months later, Nick was still alive, and he seemed to be improving a bit, but Michael worried about him becoming reclusive. Imagine that—Nick, the handsome, popular football player, big man on campus, shutting himself off from the world. Michael felt like he was fated to live this life, though it wasn't what he wanted. But it had been his stubbornness that had pushed Audrey out, and then it was Stephanie who had to save him from being beaten to death by Paul and his men. And now, here they were, leading the town almost by default. He supposed he could walk away from the role, but where was he going to go? It wasn't like he could move. Alessandra was home. There *was* no place else.

But the memory of a bloody Nick telling him Rachel was dead—it appeared to be a suicide, but all sorts of rumors still swirled, as they do in a small town—was never going to leave him. And now he had to go check in on an alleged assailant to get his story.

"Expecting someone?" Zac asked, looking up at William after a knock came from the front door.

William shook his head and kneeled down close to Zac on the couch.

"What do you want me to do?" William whispered. "Just ignore it?"

"No point. It's either nothing, or Hank's identified you, which is kind of the idea, right? No, just face it. You know what to say. Feel ready?"

He shrugged. "Do I have a choice?"

"Not much of one." Zac nodded toward the closet on the far wall. "That a safe place for me to hang out?"

"Yeah. Just keep an ear to the ground in case shit goes south."

There was another set of knocks. Zac scrambled to the closet, and William went to the door. When he looked through the peephole, he recognized the face on the other side. He took a deep breath and opened the door.

"Michael…Good to see you. How are things?"

"Not too bad. You mind if I come in?"

"Be my guest." William opened the door wider and gestured toward the couch. "Have a seat."

Crouching in the closet, Zac could hear the words well enough, even if they were a little muffled. His view was likewise decent, through the horizontal slots in the wooden closet door. It was warm and cramped inside, with a few coats hanging down, draping across his back and head. Even if he had wanted to, he wouldn't have been able to stand up without banging into either the coat rack or the shelf above it. So his knees were pulled up underneath his chin as he peered through the slats.

He saw Michael sit on the couch, and rub the back of his neck as if he'd been sweating. But it wasn't hot outside.

"How can I help you?" William said as he sat down in the recliner.

"Did you hear about what happened to Hank?"

"No. It wasn't anything bad, I hope."

Michael leaned forward. "He was pretty savagely beaten. Right on the street."

It looked like William flinched a bit, rocking back in his seat, grasping the armrests. "Really? That's awful. When did this happen? Where?"

"Just this morning, in broad daylight. Not far from here.

Over on France. Two or three blocks from here, maybe?"

William shook his head and looked down at his feet. "Well, that's terrible news. Do we have any idea who did it? Is there someone violent on the loose? If you came here to see if I'd help find out who did this, I'm all yours. We don't have a lot of trained police in the town anymore, and you know I'm willing to chip in where needed."

There was a sincerity to his voice that Zac liked. Until a few months earlier, he'd only known William by his reputation as a loyal and competent, if not particularly exceptional, police officer both during and before Audrey's administration. He'd been under Danny Bray's command until Danny was killed during what Paul described as a failed mutiny that Danny tried to lead alongside the people in the quarantine camp. Paul said they might have succeeded, but he saw it coming and got the jump on them, killing Danny while letting the rest live.

And Zac assumed that had left Paul as the de facto police chief, so William was willing to take whatever orders came down from him. That was the main trick with him, convincing him that you had the necessary authority to make commands—once you did, he was yours. That was his reputation, and that made him someone Zac knew he could make use of.

Benjamin—who had been married to William's sister before the virus killed her a few years earlier—was a logical choice for Zac to enlist in helping to bring William into the fold. The fact that he'd already been a part of Audrey's police force told Zac he had at least a certain level of sympathy toward authoritarian rule and strong leadership, and he figured the right push would get him on board.

Once Benjamin convinced William to come to a group meeting and get a feel for what they were proposing, Zac knew he had him. Stephanie and Michael had foolishly not put his skills to use at all, choosing to eschew even the idea of law enforcement in favor of what they called "community management," essentially letting the people of the town sort out disagreements and misbehavior with social consequences. They'd let William sit around feeling bored and unnecessary. All Zac had to do was give him a purpose again, to tell him he mattered to someone, to *something*. That there was a cause he could be a key part of achieving, and that it would make him a hero to the people of Alessandra. He wanted a legacy, and Zac was the only one willing to give it to him.

"William, what were you doing at ten this morning?" Michael said, and Zac thought he looked annoyed.

"What was I *doing*?" William shrugged. "There's not really that much to do around here. I was just sitting around at the house. Why do you ask? You don't think I had something to do with Hank, do you?"

Michael absent-mindedly scratched his forehead. "He identified you as the assailant. He's said flat-out that you did it. Why would he do that, William?"

Zac stifled a chuckle at the idea of a college drop-out with no police training trying to play cop against the real thing.

"Wish I could tell you." William shook his head. "I can't read a man's mind for you. I've seen a lot of shit in my time as a decorated police officer, though, and sometimes people who go through traumatic events can struggle to make sense of it. I saw him recently; maybe his mind just superimposed my face on someone else's. Maybe he took a blow to the head, and he's simply mistaken. I really couldn't tell ya. But if you're accusing me of something, let's get it out in the open now."

Michael looked away from William and squeezed his leg tightly, his shoulders appearing to tense up. After a few seconds, he turned back.

"This isn't how we have to play this. If you tell me you

did it, we can work something out. We just need to know, and see you're contrite."

William leaned forward, his elbows on his knees. "Good fucking luck, then. Now, please get out of here so I can take a nap. This has been tiring."

6

Stephanie leaned against the wall in her living room, her head tilted against the hard plaster.

"So, he has no idea how he even got to the hospital?" Michael asked.

"None." Stephanie rolled her head back and forth against the wall.

Michael sighed loudly. "Is it possible he's wrong about William?"

She pushed herself off the wall and walked over to the couch to sit next to Michael. "I just don't know. He didn't have any doubt about it, I'll tell ya that. He was dead certain. If it wasn't William, he sure as hell was fooled into thinking it was."

They'd been talking about this for a while, trying to figure out their next steps. Nothing like this had happened previously during their time leading the town. In such a small community, people tended to be cooperative; in a real sense, they had to be in order to survive. Petty issues could be dealt with by the parties involved, and Stephanie had hoped that'd be enough to carry them for a while. It had, but it appeared their time was up.

The question now was what to do. The only precedent they had in post-apocalyptic Alessandra was when Trevor Kites was murdered, after being confronted for flouting

Audrey's rules about wearing a steel ring in public and not maintaining personal-space boundaries with others. When Audrey found out that Trevor also attempted to rape Rachel, she declared that Nick was the murderer. Michael had good reason to think Zac was the killer, but when he tried to convince Audrey, the conversation flew off the rails quickly.

Without DNA, fingerprints, and cameras, they were limited in the types of evidence they could even hope to have. As far as forensic science goes, they were thrown back into at least the nineteenth century, if not earlier in some respects. Stephanie had hoped maybe William would cave if confronted with the fact that Hank had identified him. Now, though, it was one man's word against the other, with no witnesses they were aware of.

They couldn't just let this go. It was too much of a threat to the safety of the town. There was too much work that needed to be done every day—from sourcing crops to gathering water from the lake to general maintenance checks on the solar generators, buildings, the wall, and many other jobs—for people to be scared to leave the house. With people able to work together again, Stephanie had divided the labor among everyone in the town rather than having it limited just to the small group of people Audrey had approved to work without the rings around their waist. That meant everyone had some kind of responsibility. It takes a village to run a village.

That also meant it didn't take that much to throw off the timing Stephanie had set up. There was already the constant threat of sickness looming over them, and that wasn't just the pandemic virus that had nearly killed them before; it was a steady barrage of other viruses and infections that hadn't been a big deal prior to the apocalypse, but were a constant threat now. She required everyone to get a basic set of vaccinations, but those vaccines wouldn't last much longer.

In fact, they were largely expired already, with shelf lives that varied between fourteen months and three years. And that three-year mark was approaching fast.

Most of the medicine they'd had when the world went sideways was either used or expired. So the clock was ticking there. No new drug shipments were pulling up to the loading dock behind the hospital. Once the remaining antibiotics expired, even a basic cut on a finger could be a death sentence if it got infected. Ethanol had potential as a disinfectant, but harvesting it entailed distilling it from fermented fruit or grain, and doing that in a large enough volume to stave off major problems was another challenge.

These were some of the problems that kept Stephanie up at night. If people got sick or died, the balance of her system would be thrown off. If the people were worried that someone randomly violent was loose among them, it could impact their job performance and their confidence in Stephanie's leadership. But what were her options? There was no court system, no prisons, no organized method of establishing guilt or punishment beyond basic crowd control. She had no experience building a system like that. The simplest way was to assume the decision-making power herself, but that brought her far too close to being Audrey than she was comfortable with.

"So what, then?" Michael asked. "If William did this, there need to be consequences. But if we can't prove he did it, what can we even do?"

"Who haven't we talked to? Surely, *someone* saw *something.* It'd be ideal if we could find someone who'd say they witnessed the beating, and would positively identify William. I'm confident he did it. Hank doesn't have any reason to lie. It was in broad daylight. It's not crazy to think there could be a witness."

"Sure. But we've talked to a few people already, and

nobody's biting. William's a former cop; there's a good chance he was pretty careful about this. What if there *is* no witness? What's next?"

Stephanie turned and looked out the window. A white oak stood tall, swaying silently in the breeze, green sprouts starting to poke out from their blooms. There was something calming about how nature marched on. People would come and go, births and deaths, marriages and divorces, the good and the bad, it all rose and fell with the backdrop of nature's unceasing consistency. That oak was there long before anyone in Alessandra even existed, before they were the last people on Earth, and it would probably be there when they were all no more. Just keeping time. Unyielding to the problems that plagued them.

"There's nothing else," she said. "We find someone. That's all there is to it."

7

Benjamin frowned and looked back over his shoulder at the other men, Zac sitting in front of them, shaking his head.

"Yes, we're sure about the numbers, but polls are never per—"

"Well, they're not fucking good enough, are they?" Zac said, lifting his eyes up and boring them into Benjamin's. He bent his legs and pushed himself into a standing position, then turned his back and walked slowly away from the men, looking at the ground at his feet.

This was not what he needed to hear. His plan to erode confidence in Stephanie and Michael's leadership had begun taking shape, but he hoped the end result would be him taking over the town. He had so many ideas of how best to push Alessandra forward; even Audrey herself hadn't been assertive enough in some ways. She'd needed Paul—and, at times, Zac—to carry out some of the less politically correct work she knew needed to be done. To Zac, whose Marine sniper training taught him the importance of discipline, patience, and chain of command, that sort of insulation from responsibility was anathema. He was confident he'd be the kind of "The buck stops here" leader he'd always respected, taking pride in making those difficult decisions and doing what's best for his people—even if it wasn't what they wanted.

To do that, though, he needed the total confidence of the people of the town. Or, at least, the total confidence of enough of them to justify silencing those who insisted on dissenting. And, at this moment, Zac was finding he didn't have anywhere near that sort of support.

He'd sent some of his followers around town to talk to as many people as they could about their support of their current leadership, and their opinion on Zac. He wanted to know, if an election were held that afternoon, would they consider voting for someone other than Stephanie, and where would Zac fall on that list?

What they found was that emotions were still raw from Audrey's tenure, and Zac's unpredictable demeanor tainted peoples' opinion of him. In a small town, the path away from your sins was a long one.

Zac did seem to get some credit for being a veteran, and there was some sympathy for his time spent recovering from a serious head injury and the loss of his wife as part of the group of women and children Audrey sent on a doomed march into the backcountry alone, but those who were asked found little interest in seeing Zac take over as the town's chief officer. Many felt he was too volatile to trust with that sort of responsibility. Not everyone was thrilled with all of Stephanie's decisions, but most seemed comfortable with her steadiness and intelligence. After the erratic years under Audrey, that calm had been a welcome change for many, though it was a slow evolution that still wasn't fully complete for plenty of the townspeople.

Zac knew there was sufficient dissent out there, even if much of it was seething under the surface. How could there not be? Everyone suddenly had to work, sometimes doing backbreaking labor for hours at a time. There was no real form of justice for those who committed crimes. And what, honestly, was protecting them from a return of the virus?

Stephanie had even begun letting stray people who wandered up to the gate come into the town to have a home. She sent them to the hospital to be examined first, but what if the virus was too fresh to be detected? What if they weren't exhibiting symptoms yet? What if she was marching in the Trojan Horse that would kill them all? There was no telling where these people had been. And they certainly weren't Alessandrans, no matter how you tried to dress them up, and where you let them live.

He needed to find more of that dissent, and give it an environment in which it could fester and turn into something bigger. His plan was moving in that direction. The problem, though, was how to turn around people's opinion of *him*. How to convince the people of Alessandra not only that it was a death sentence to keep Stephanie as the town's leader, but that Zac was the right person to replace her. He wanted to think that he could talk his way past her, but he wasn't convinced of that. He didn't have any experience with campaigning. He felt confident about firing up a group of people who were already with him, but he feared his rhetoric wouldn't be as effective with those who wanted leadership more in Stephanie's style.

"We need to change some minds," Zac said, turning to face the men from across the room. "There has to be an appetite for our message out there. There simply *has* to be. Help me find it."

"How do you want us to do that?" Benjamin asked.

"Talk to people, damn it. Preach. Testify. To anyone you can. Plant the idea in their head that Stephanie's a fucking disaster, and let's see where it goes from there. Then we'll regroup. In the meantime, the plan's going forward. That should help drive this home. I care about this place more than she does, and people are gonna see that. We're gonna *make* them see it."

8

Nick shoved his back door open and slid inside sideways, holding a metal pail at the end of his outstretched arms, water sloshing over the sides.

The screen door flung shut behind him; he shuffled to the kitchen sink, set the pail on the floor and hunched his back, lungs pumping, trying to catch his breath. Rationing meant that everyone had a designated day of the week to collect three gallons of water from the city's wells for personal use—with water pumped in from Lake Chatuga, on the west end of the town—and this was Nick's day. If you ever lost track of which day it was, you could always walk down to the Square, where Stephanie had a sign set up that displayed the day of the week. There were people almost constantly collecting and boiling water over a fire in order to place into recycled gallon jugs that you could pick up at the old warehouse in the middle of town, but that was considered drinking water. What you gathered from the well didn't necessarily meet the same purity standards; ingesting it was risky, but it was useful for bathing and washing clothes.

While most people would make multiple trips and there were small pull wagons around for those who needed them, Nick always wanted to do it in one, which meant lugging about twenty-five pounds' worth of water a half mile back to his house, trying to conserve every drop. It never felt that heavy at first, but it seemed like the pail was full of lead by the final stretch. The more he did it, though, the longer he found he could carry it before losing his strength. He figured one day he'd walk in that back door with a smile on his face, pail hanging effortlessly from his hand.

He gripped the pail's handle and crouched behind it—he never forgot his Dad barking "Lift with your legs, son" whenever they'd move something heavy—then pressed his knees up, hoisting it onto the counter beside the sink. He stuck a stopper in both drains and poured the water in; he'd found that the two-basin sink could handle three gallons almost perfectly, so he kept the water there to use throughout the week.

Once both basins were filled, Nick cupped his hands and dipped them into the water, then leaned down to splash his face. Nick rubbed his hands up and down, massaging the cool water around his neck, then running his hands through his dark brown hair, which spiked up where the water stiffened it. Some trickled into his mouth, and he spat it back into the basin. On this warm spring day, the splash of water felt heavenly, his sweat neutralized by the coolness of the water brought up from deep in the earth, a jolt of energy that was worth the half-mile haul.

These were little pleasures, but little pleasures were all Nick had left. Prior to the virus striking, he had been known as a bit of a fuck-up, but a lovable and generally well-meaning one. He'd grown up alongside Michael in town, both graduating from Towns High, playing on the football team, competing with each other for girls. Neither was ready for the real world after that, but Nick tried to pretend, marrying one of his high school sweethearts three weeks after graduation. But she told him she wanted to see the world, to experience more than what Alessandra could offer. She said there was so much more out there for them to do, but Nick didn't want any of that. This was his home, and he wasn't going anywhere. They were divorced before they hit six months.

Two more marriages—one because the girl was pregnant, though she stopped trying to get child support out of him years ago—ended in divorce, and he was already feeling like a balding has-been by the time he was thirty, bragging about the time he took an interception back for a touchdown or that hit he laid on a defenseless receiver. He spent the next decade picking up work where he could get it—construction where it was available, some odd-job contracting to scrape together some cash to spend at Walt's Bar on the weekends—and sleeping his way through the women of Towns County before the virus struck and changed everything.

Once Audrey banned cohabitation and forced everyone to wear those rings whenever they were out in public, Nick didn't know what to do with himself. So much of his work depended on connections he'd forged, but it was hard to keep those going in a world of such physical and mental isolation. And all touching was banned, meaning even those fleeting physical connections he found himself craving more and more were gone, figments of his past. He'd spent so many years eschewing love in favor of lust that he thought the latter was all there was. By the time Rachel walked into his life, he'd given up on both. And now she was gone, too.

Nick was aware of the reputation he had. He knew people thought he'd lost it. Maybe they were right. If you were crazy, would you be too crazy to realize it? He had once been considered one of them, a loyal lifelong Alessandran who knew everybody in town. He could charm anybody, and get just about any girl he wanted. He may have been past his prime, but there was something magnetic about Nick, and he knew it.

Now, nobody wanted to see him, much less sleep with

him. The magnetism, if it had ever really been there, was gone. He was a pariah. Sometimes, he thought he might as well have the virus; people seemed to believe the crazy was just as contagious.

As water dripped from his face, he wondered if maybe they were right when he heard a knock on his front door. Nick couldn't remember the last time he'd had a visitor.

"Nick, I know you're in there." The voice was muffled through the door, but it was unmistakably Michael's. "We need to talk. I think you might be able to help us."

9

Derrick ran a rag across his brow and stuffed it into his back pocket, then lifted a large bag of compost onto his shoulder, the end of it sagging against his back.

When he'd come to the gates of Alessandra six months earlier, legs wobbly from a walk he guessed—but had no way of being sure—was at least three hundred miles over the previous few weeks, clothes torn and reeking of sweat, shoes nearly worn through, Stephanie had asked him one question. She didn't want to know where he'd come from, or what he'd been doing. She didn't want to know how he'd gotten there, or how he'd survived this long. She wanted to know if he was willing to work. Would he put in the labor to earn the shelter, water, and food he'd get in exchange? His legs on fire, he nodded, and his knees crashed to the ground. He wept, his head cradled in his hands as Stephanie gently patted his back. This was a promise he was never going to break.

He was one of a handful of men and women who had found their way to Alessandra over the previous year. He still remembered the astonishment he felt when he saw those walls rising out of the forest floor, an oasis in a vast and unyielding sea of nature's ambivalence. He wasn't even sure why he'd kept walking, or why he'd come in this direction rather than another one. He didn't have a compass; he just wanted to find some water and set up camp nearby. Through debilitating blisters and back-aching fatigue, he kept going, day after day. It had been easier during the winter; walking was one of the only ways he could drive some warmth into his body. But if he didn't find some abandoned structure to sleep in at night, he had to worry about hypothermia—you sweat, you die. It had been a constant reminder to him that nature was unforgiving. His life was his own responsibility.

When he first saw the walls of Alessandra in the distance, he thought it was probably a hallucination brought on by sheer exhaustion. Or it was some town that was long ago abandoned. For months, he'd wondered how many people were left on Earth. He couldn't remember the last time he'd seen anyone at all. Through all those miles, all those months of walking, he didn't see a single soul. The birds chirped from the trees. The squirrels scurried around him. The threat of bears was always on his mind; without a gun, he was prey and not predator. But no humans.

The evidence that humans had once existed had been frequent—small abandoned towns, crumbling eight-lane highways, neighborhoods turned to ruins, trash left behind by people before him. Whenever he saw a crumpled potato chip bag—which was surprisingly often—he'd pick it up and see if there was anything left inside. Sometimes, running his fingers around the inside and scraping out the salt provided him with the energy to get through the rest of the day. But his only company had been his thoughts. With no maps to be found, Derrick was convinced it was God's work that led him to Alessandra, because luck just wasn't an adequate explanation.

In his pre-virus life, he'd owned a landscaping business in a small town just north of Valdosta in South Georgia where he was born and raised. After studying geosciences and botany at Valdosta State University, it'd been a natural fit to use his education to serve the community. He bought all the equipment he thought he'd need from a local hardware store, slapped "Derrick Digs Landscaping" on the side of a pickup truck, and started driving around town, telling family and friends he was open for business. It didn't take long for them to put him to work, building vegetable gardens, pruning trees, moving flower beds. Within five years, he was pulling in nearly $1 million in revenue, and had a team of ten men driving five trucks to jobs in the area.

He was also married, to the girl he told his mom he was going to marry the morning after their first date in eleventh grade. They'd gone to see a movie, then grabbed a couple of tacos on the way home. When Tameka touched his hand as he drove and their fingers interlocked, he felt an electricity run up his spine. It was like a new sort of life was injected into him for the first time, that feeling of connection, like God was telling him Tameka was the one.

They'd gone to Valdosta State together; once they graduated, there was no question that they'd be heading straight to the altar. It was a new beginning for both of them, making a life in their hometown, him with a new business, Tameka starting her career as an elementary school teacher. Eight years and two daughters later, Derrick's landscaping team with more work than they could handle, there was nothing more they could even think to want out of life.

Then the virus struck. At first, it was sad seeing a few people die so suddenly. Quickly, though, it became scary, as more fell ill and then died within days of showing symptoms. It all happened so fast, the world descending into chaos. He wondered how the stability he'd thought he had could just be the veneer over something so fragile. People started quarantining themselves in their homes and wearing masks in hopes of staving off the virus. Some threw everything in a vehicle and fled, hoping to get somewhere without people before they fell victim.

But Tameka refused to leave. She said they'd get through

it, that this was their home. Besides, where else would they go? Derrick wanted to take the kids and just drive, but Tameka said you only had to watch the news for two minutes to know the virus was out there, no matter where you went. You couldn't run or hide. The Center for Disease Control was recommending people lock their doors, close their windows, and stay inside. They didn't know how the virus was spreading, but they were working on it. Derrick yelled and lashed out at Tameka, but she held firm. She and the girls—4 and 7 years old—were staying. She hoped he'd stay with them.

And he did, right up to the moment when he was holding Tameka's head in his lap, pressing a cold washcloth to her forehead that felt like it had just come out of the oven, her arms and legs bubbling with boils. He'd told the girls to stay in their rooms, and not to even come near the stairs without him saying it was okay. The house was so quiet. Tameka wasn't making a sound; for a few hours, there'd been pain, but it was like a light switch had flipped. Her eyes shut, her lips parted, and she was still. Peaceful. The line between life and death was just that—a line. Once she crossed it, he knew she was in God's arms and not his.

When he went upstairs to explain to the girls what happened, he could tell before he even entered their room what he was going to see. Death had a stink. See enough of it, and you start to feel it in your nostrils before it's even there yet. And, in the previous weeks, he'd seen more than most encountered in a lifetime before the virus struck. The stench was practically wafting out of their bedroom, an invisible, insidious cloud threatening to rip an even bigger hole in Derrick's life. He broke into a sprint and burst through the doorway, where he saw both girls sitting on the floor beside their beds, crying and rubbing their arms, red bumps forming, the same ones Tameka had started feeling the night before.

His throat tightened, and tears wanted to come, but he fought to choke them back, not wanting his girls to know how bad it was. He walked over and sat between them, holding out his arms for them to slide over against him. He embraced them both, squeezing their bodies tight to his sides, their heads resting on his chest. As he told them not to worry, that everything would be okay, he said a silent prayer that the virus would take him—in place of his daughters if possible, but assuredly either way. And, judging by the virus's rapid and furious spreading, he figured this was a prayer that would be answered by morning.

But when the sun came up, his daughters limp on the floor beside him, Derrick had no boils, no bumps. He awoke aware and seemingly healthy in his home that stank of death. He kissed the girls' cheeks, still lukewarm, the memory of life fading into the distance, then sat on their bedroom floor, legs spread in front of him, arms hanging limp at his sides. What was there to do? What reason did he have to go on?

He had no idea why God had chosen him to survive, but the only reason he started walking was because he believed there must be some higher purpose to it. He hadn't done anything to earn the gift of life in a world full of destruction. He'd lived an unremarkable existence of imperfect morals. He'd had a brief affair a few years earlier, with a woman he met at a bar—he wasn't proud of it, but it happened. Sometimes, he drank too much, and ended up weaving his truck home, hoping Tameka wouldn't smell alcohol on his breath again. He had impure thoughts, and his faith wavered regularly. His temper could be short, and he wasn't as forgiving as he wished he were.

Still, God had singled him out, and Derrick thought there must be a reason. He didn't believe in coincidences. There must be more for him to do with his life.

And so, he packed a small bag and began walking.

Through the eerily quiet streets of the town he grew up in, that same stink emanating out of every door, window, and alley. The stillness made him shiver as he looked at the Christmas decorations hanging from the light poles, ribbons and wreaths that may never be pulled down by human hands. At first, he didn't go far, finding other small towns, hoping to find other people, then raiding their homes and stores for supplies. He'd stay in one place for several weeks before moving on. Eventually, though, the towns depressed him; it was like sleeping on graves. If he ran across one, he'd gather what supplies he could and move on quickly.

That led him, ultimately, to Alessandra. This was where he believed God had wanted him to be the whole time. He still didn't know why, but he was confident this was the place where he could make a real difference. This was, for better or worse, home.

He loaded another bag of mulch into the wheelbarrow and grabbed the handles, pushing it toward the garden in the back yard of Father Philip Hayden's home. Father Hayden's church was the only one in town, so Derrick embraced it even though he wasn't Catholic. He found Father Hayden to be a kind and gentle man who was skilled at reading people, and he enjoyed getting the chance to help him out; he was working on a small garden next to a shed he was building for him against the house. It was maybe three-quarters done, and he figured he could knock the rest out in another week or so. He stopped the wheelbarrow by the empty garden bed and lifted one of the bags of mulch, splitting it open with his knife and spreading the mulch evenly between the lumber boards. He picked up his shovel and buried it into the soil, beginning to move and fold it over itself.

Then he felt something hard slam into the side of his head, and he hit the ground.

10

"Oh, shit, man," Zac said, standing over Derrick's body, lying limp in the garden bed, his face half buried in the still-moist soil. "What did you do?"

"Nothing. I mean, just what you said," said William, glancing up at the first hints of light from the sun sneaking up on the horizon. "I surprised him. One hard blow, and he went down. You said you didn't want him to identify me this time, so I had to make my one shot worth it. It's not like I can go down to Wal-Mart and buy a ski mask."

"Goddamn it, William. I'm sure you could figure out a way to cover up your face if you felt like you needed to. Shit. Is he dead? He better not be dead."

"Nah, he's got a pulse. But he may not have one much longer if we keep talking about it rather than getting him help."

"Oh, for fuck's sake…Broken ribs. Fingers. Maybe a collar bone or something. He looks like he's got a cracked fucking skull. That wasn't our deal. We're not cold-blooded murderers. We've got a mission. When the mission is to crack skulls and kill, I'll tell you that. Got it?"

"He hit his head on the wooden board when he fell. I couldn't help that. But whatever. We need to get him out of here, and do what we can to clean up that blood."

"Just help me get him onto the gurney. The hospital's just

a couple of minutes up the road on my bike. I can drag him up there and drop him. It's still early and dark enough that nobody should see us. Turn that board so the blood isn't showing. And don't fucking wake up Father Hayden."

William nodded and lifted Derrick by the shoulders, while Zac grabbed his feet. They carried him to the gurney Zac had taken from the hospital's storage space, and laid him down there, fastening the straps over him so he'd stay in place. Zac had tied a rope to the front of the gurney, so he could drag it rolling behind him as he rode.

Derrick's consistency had made him a nice target for them. After watching him for several days, they knew he arrived at Father Hayden's house each morning before dawn. It looked like he was building a vegetable garden, small shed, and doing some other beautification work in the back yard; they didn't know how long the job would take, so they knew they needed to pounce while his schedule was set.

Now, William was hoping Derrick would survive, as he watched Zac ride off toward the hospital, where he'd drop the body out front. Then he'd stash the gurney in some nearby bushes so they could retrieve it late that night or early the next morning. Afterward, Zac would take the long way home, so it wouldn't be apparent he'd been at the hospital if anyone saw him. He could just say he was on a bike ride, which also gave him a decent alibi for the attack.

William walked back to the garden bed. He could see a smattering of crimson on the cinnamon brown wood, along with an indention the shape of a head in the mulch. He pushed around some of the soil to smooth it out, then grabbed the wood and turned it so the blood spot was facing into the ground.

He looked around and didn't see any other signs of a scuffle, because there really hadn't been one. He hadn't expected Derrick to go down so easily. This was a confrontation he had been worried about. William was built reasonably well, but Derrick had the forearms of a man who lugs 100-pound bags of mulch around all day. William knew the element of surprise was essential so he could get the jump on Derrick, and he'd done that well—maybe a little too well. The plan had been to daze him, then take his feet out from under him and get some good blows in while he was down. Then he had a syringe with Midazolam from the hospital to inject him with if needed; it wouldn't completely knock him out, but it would make him very lethargic, and he almost certainly wouldn't remember being dropped off at the hospital.

While they were fine with William being identified for the first attack on Hank, they didn't want any trace of this one to exist, beyond Derrick's injuries. The hope was to sow confusion about what was going on. Did William really attack Hank, or was Hank mistaken? What would his motive be? If not him, who was doing this? Let that worry linger over the town like a cloud. Let people not trust one another. And let Stephanie and Michael be powerless to stop any of it. That would hopefully provide Zac the opening he needed. Hank and Derrick were just unfortunate collateral damage in a war for the soul of Alessandra. Hopefully, they'd both be fine in the long run. If not, though, William knew as well as anyone that sometimes people had to die in order for progress to be made. That was just reality. You could either spit with the wind or against it. William knew what his choice would always be.

He stood up from his crouch and scanned the area around the garden once more. As far as he could tell, it looked exactly as it had when he arrived earlier. He nodded and turned to walk toward the street when he heard a noise from behind him. It was a high-pitched creaking, like a hinge that needed oil. He stopped, afraid to look back. Should he just run? But if there was someone there, he wouldn't be hard to identify, even from behind. This was something he had to face.

"Officer Greene?" He heard Father Hayden's voice and cringed, shaking his head. "Is there something I can help you with?"

William took a deep breath and slowly turned around, gripping the syringe in his pocket as he walked back toward Father Hayden.

11

Looking around as he sat down on the couch, Michael couldn't remember the last time he'd been in Nick's house. Years ago, they used to spend plenty of nights there, drinking beer, watching football, talking about women. It all came to such an abrupt end.

It's one of the weird parts of civilization crashing. There's no buildup—or, at least, none that you can see. The virus builds silently, while you're going to work, watching TV, and picking your kids up from soccer practice. It was there the whole time, gaining strength, morphing into something that would kill them all. A time bomb ticking, waiting for its moment to explode.

If they'd known the last night they sat in front of the TV and pounded Bud Light while watching the Falcons game was actually *the last night*, would they have treated it any differently? Would they have done anything to acknowledge that? It occurred to Michael that, for everything you enjoy doing, that you do regularly, there will be a last time you do it. And, in all likelihood, you won't even know when that last time is.

Looking back, Michael couldn't even remember when it was. It felt like lifetimes ago. There was no way they could have imagined what was coming. The virus had struck in the spring, so Michael assumed it had been sometime that previous winter when he and Nick had last sat here, just being friends. With the typical nonsense to bitch about, sure, but nothing compared to now.

He could remember it all—the creaky wooden floors, that eleven-pound trout Nick had mounted on the wall, even that familiar scent emanating from nowhere in particular. It was like being transported in time. Back to when nothing was perfect, but everything sort of made sense. The world was on its axis. The memories in this room were so thick, they had a physical being, like he could reach out and touch them. But Michael knew he needed to be in the present.

"You think I can help with something?" Nick said, sitting down in a ragged loveseat opposite Michael and Stephanie.

"Yeah, we do," Michael said. "Have you heard about what happened to Hank?"

"Don't think so." Nick shrugged. "I don't tend to hear the town gossip these days."

"Right," he said. "I get it. Well, Hank was jumped by someone yesterday morning and beaten pretty badly—"

"Is he gonna be all right?"

Michael took a deep breath, and Stephanie jumped in.

"Yeah, he should be okay. I visited him and talked to the doctor. Broken ribs, several bruises. They were still worried about internal bleeding, but they said he was stable, though they were having to manage a lot of pain."

"That sucks," Nick said. "Hope he gets better soon. Do we know who did it?"

"Well, that's sort of where you come in," Michael said.

Nick narrowed his gaze and sat forward, nearly coming out of his seat.

"Wait. You think I did it? I may or may not be crazy, but I'm not—"

"No, no," Stephanie said, waving her hands in front of her. "Nothing like that. We know you weren't involved."

He settled back into his chair. "Okay," he said, unease in his voice. "What, then?"

"Well, Hank identified his assailant," Michael said. "I think you know him a bit. William. Officer Greene."

"Yeah." Nick sucked in a deep breath, and paused for a moment. "He's one of the ones who helped drag me off to quarantine, and he cuffed me to take me down to the square for what was supposed to be my public execution. Then it turned into the mass execution of a bunch of other people instead of me. I know you guys say he was just following orders, but I've never been comfortable with anyone from Audrey's crew just living among the rest of us, like it's no big deal what they did."

"I hear you." Michael nodded. "Maybe you can help us put an end to that."

"How?"

Michael looked at Stephanie and raised his eyebrows. She ran her fingers through her hair, the strands pulling tight against her scalp.

"What were you doing yesterday morning, a couple hours after sunrise?" she asked.

"Nothing." He shrugged. "Sitting here, I guess. I never really know how much time has passed. But unless I'm doing some job for you, digging a ditch or clearing a gutter or whatever, I'm pretty much here. Where else would I go?"

"The assault happened just up around the corner there," she said. "I don't think you could see it from inside your house, but is there any chance you were taking a short walk around that time?"

Nick lurched forward again. "What are you asking me?"

"Basically, it would be very helpful to us—and, we think, to everyone—if you saw something. If you could attest to William being the attacker. We don't have forensic tools, Nick. This isn't *CSI: Alessandra*. We have Hank saying it was

William, and we have William denying it."

"And you want the crazy guy no one likes to be your star witness?" he asked.

"We need someone we can trust," Michael said. "You've been my best friend since we were kids, man. I know you're not going to screw us over. As you know better than anyone, William's a follower. An order taker. We think he did this, and we don't think he just did it on a whim. And that means we don't know who we can trust right now. But we know we can trust you. We know you'll try to help us."

"Help you by…lying?"

"Look, Nick. It's a big ask. I get it," Stephanie said. "But don't think of it as lying. We *know* he did it. We just can't *prove* he did it. And the people of the town deserve certainty, so we can give them justice. We can't let this crime go unsolved. It'd tear the community apart, out of fear and distrust. We need to deliver a swift, decisive verdict. You can help us with that, *and* you'll get to condemn someone you know is a bad guy anyway."

"All right," Nick said. "What's the plan?"

"We'll let you know when we need you," Michael said, standing up and extending his hand. "Thanks, man. I knew we could count on you. I haven't turned my back on you yet, and I'm not going to. Ya hear me?"

Nick nodded and shook his hand, then pulled him in for a hug.

12

William walked up the steps to Zac's front porch and knocked, but didn't hear anyone inside. He wondered if Zac had run into any problems dropping Derrick off at the hospital. That definitely wouldn't be good. They knew it was risky for Zac to drop the bodies off with these jobs, but he didn't trust anyone else with that part of the work. It seemed to William like he was getting his hands a little dirtier than they needed to be for this plan to work out, but he wasn't going to be dissuaded.

Zac wasn't the perfect leader by any means; William much preferred working for Audrey, who was a better balance of strength and calm. Both Zac and Paul were too volatile for his taste, and too prone to violence. But you go to work with the leader you have, not the leader you want and, in William's mind, Zac was a better option than either Stephanie or Michael.

Stephanie was smart and confident, but Zac was right that she didn't have the toughness to be the leader of a town in such dire circumstances. She had this idea in her head that Alessandra could have something like a democracy, and William thought that was madness. This was the end of the world. Might was going to prevail. The meek were destined to rot. She didn't have to like that, but she needed to accept it. As long as she wouldn't, William was more comfortable giving a shot to Zac, who would at least do the dirty work that needed to be done.

Michael was just incompetent, pretty much all the way around, as far as William could tell. He'd been a useful stooge for Audrey until they had a falling out. Then he helped lead that disastrous coup that accomplished nothing other than getting a bunch of innocent people killed and chasing Audrey away. She was too smart to let them lock her up or anything; William was sure of that much. He was also sure that she was still alive somewhere, and that they'd never see her again. Audrey loved Alessandra, but she wouldn't be able to handle seeing it like this.

William caught some motion out of the corner of his eye and looked around down the street to see someone approaching on a bike. He started walking toward the street.

"What the *fuck* are you doing here?" Zac hissed through clenched teeth, as he threw his bike down. "You're connected with at least one violent assault. I'm not supposed to have anything to do with it. What if someone sees you on my porch? You think that won't raise some eyebrows?"

"Oh, it's fine. I could be over here for anything. And we have a bigger problem to deal with."

Zac's eyes went wide. "What bigger problem?"

"Remember how you told me not to wake up Father Hayden?"

Zac looked away and mouthed the word "Fuck," then closed his eyes tightly. After a moment, he looked back at William.

"What'd you do with him?"

"It's fine. I gave him the Midazolam, so he should be out for a—"

"Wait…How long ago was that?"

"Well, let me just check my watch." William mockingly lifted his left arm and looked at his bare wrist. "Hmmm…I guess it's 'How the hell am I supposed to fucking know?' o'clock."

"Jesus Christ, you idiot. How long do you *think* it's been? Did this happen right after I left, or did it take a little while before you ran into him?"

"I cleaned up the scene. Turned over the board, like you said. Started to leave, and then I heard him come up behind me. Immediately injected him, then took him back inside, tied him to his bed, stuck a pillow case in his mouth, and waited for the Midazolam to kick in. Sat there for a little bit trying to decide what to do, and figured I should come get you."

"You *sat there* for a little bit? For fuck's sake."

Zac stood his bike up and straddled it, then hopped on the pedals.

"Run as fast as you can to Father Hayden's," he said, as he started pedaling. "I'm riding on ahead."

Zac turned the corner onto Father Hayden's street and slowed to a stop; he scanned the area, listening for anyone talking or noises other than the spring birds chirping in the trees. There wasn't a lot of time to waste, but he also didn't want to be seen snooping around Father Hayden's house on this particular morning.

After several moments, he was confident no one was outside; someone might still be watching from a window, but that was a chance he'd just have to take. After William fucked things up, he really didn't have any other choice at this point.

He left the bike in a bush three houses down so that nobody saw it lying in front of Father Hayden's house and wondered why, then he walked the rest of the way. He decided to go around the back so he wouldn't be seen strolling in the front door. Nobody locked their doors in Alessandra, but he was wondering if that was about to change.

Zac walked past the garden and pulled the screen door open, then stepped inside. He'd never been inside Father Hayden's house, so he needed to find the bedroom. His feet tapped on the linoleum floor as he walked down a small hall into the kitchen, balsam wood cabinets to his left and right, a small dining table a few feet ahead, with two white chairs sitting slightly askew.

He walked as briskly as he could while making as little noise as possible, staying on the balls of his feet as he almost hopped through the house. Two black faux-leather couches sat in the living room, next to a red brick fireplace that looked like it'd been used recently, with gray ashes scattered along the top of a pile of black ones.

Zac's guess was that the bedroom was on the second floor, so he headed toward the stairs. On the wall next to them hung a black cross with Jesus nailed to it; he tried not to look at it as he hurried past.

The stairs moaned unmercifully as he stepped, despite his best efforts to step lightly. He got to the top and looked down the hall in front of him. Three doors, plus another door straight ahead that he assumed was a closet.

He walked toward the first room, reaching into his pocket to pull out a switchblade. The door was open most of the way, so he could see inside. It looked like an office, with a mahogany desk and dozens of papers scattered haphazardly across the top. The room was quiet and empty.

He proceeded to the second door, which was slightly ajar. The sun shone through the room's large windows and cast light through the open door crack, throwing it against the hallway wall as one large, jagged streak. Zac's shadow erased the light as he stepped up to the door and peered inside another nearly empty room. He could see a conspicuous dust-free rectangle on the floor, where it looked like a bed had been before it was moved. The curtains had been removed from their rods, and a dingy lamp with a ragged, torn shade sat on the floor in the corner furthest from him. Father Hayden was not there.

That left one room remaining, just a few feet ahead to his right. The door was shut. Zac's first thought was to be annoyed William had closed it, but then it occurred to him that may have been smart—If Father Hayden woke up tied to the bed, making him worry about who might be lurking on the other side of that door would be a good thing.

Zac got to the door and put his hand on the knob. At this point, there was little sense in being circumspect. If Father Hayden was still out, he wouldn't hear Zac enter the room. And if he was awake, there'd be nowhere for him to run. So, Zac turned the knob and shoved the door open.

13

His eyelids struggling apart, Father Hayden woke up, his head like a hammer swinging into an anvil. He moved to rub his eyes, but panic rose in his throat, and he vomited, trying to turn his head away from his body as he did. Most of it splattered across the bed, the stench rising into the room around him, making him more nauseated than before.

His arms were tied to the headboard with bed sheets, and they were both completely numb from being suspended above his head. He had no idea why, or who might have done it, as the room spun, seemingly picking up speed as he racked his brain for answers. He kicked his legs and thrashed his arms, a thousand pin pricks knifing their way through each nerve. He wanted to scream, bellow for someone to come untie him, to get him somewhere safe.

But then he stopped, his muscles stiffening in place as the realization struck him: this was his own bed, and his bedroom. He was home. And the door to the room was shut tight. His heart raced.

How was it possible he didn't know how he got there? Had he been drugged? He was trying to think of what the last thing he remembered was, but his mind seemed blank. He remembered going up to bed the previous night. Did he ever even wake up? Yes, he thought so. But he wasn't sure, trying to recall like trying to grab ahold of flames as they leaped and danced above a pile of wood.

All he could say with certainty was that someone tied him to the bed, and it was likely that person had bad intentions. If they'd wanted to kill him, though, they could have already easily done that. So there was some reason he was still there. Was there someone standing guard on the other side of the door, waiting on…something? Or Someone? He listened for noises. A creak of decades-old floorboards. A muffled cough. Conspiring whispers. Anything. But the silence hung like a black cloud, ominous and heavy above him, amplifying every sound he made.

Between his earlier thrashing on the mattress and the squeaking of the bed springs, anyone who was in the house would have easily heard him. That'd be particularly true if they were right outside the door. But in an otherwise quiet house, he was confident you'd hear that plenty well even if you were sitting downstairs. Yet, a couple of minutes later, not only was no one rushing into the room, he didn't even hear any stirring. No footsteps coming up the stairs. No shadows moving from underneath the door. Had the person tied him to the bed and then left? Was he alone in the house?

If so, there was a very real possibility that person would be back. God had protected him from the worst thus far. Now, it was time to take the next step himself.

Writhing a bit, he noticed the bed sheets weren't tied especially tightly around his wrists. He guessed this had been a case of making do with what was available, or the person would have brought rope or something else stronger to tie him with. Father Hayden twisted his arms so his palms were downward, and pressed them as close as he could to the mattress, then pushed his torso toward the headboard.

He was able to stretch just enough to get his wrist and head to meet. Wrenching his neck to his left, he bit down hard on the sheet, grinding his teeth and rattling his head back and forth, like a dog attacking a bone. He could feel it loosening a bit, and he dug in deeper, tasting the fibers as they tickled the back of his throat. He spit it out of his mouth and coughed, then dry heaved over his arm, his stomach contorting into a knot.

He took a moment to catch his breath, then began shaking his left arm, wiggling it against the ripped bed sheet. He grabbed it with his teeth again, fighting back the nausea and trying to work it loose. Then, finally, he could feel the fibers were separating enough to where it couldn't hold the knot; he bit hard once more and pulled, then yanked his arm free.

With his left arm out, the right one became far easier, though he had no reason to think he had unlimited time if the person who did this to him was indeed coming back. As quickly as he could, Father Hayden pulled at the other bed sheet, now turning his body and facing the headboard, sitting up on his heels for more leverage. While he picked at the knot with his left hand, he shook the entire sheet, flailing his arm up and down, trying to stress the sheet beyond what its knot could handle. Then he felt that loop loosen, and it fell off his wrist, limp. He was free.

Adrenaline had made him forget about his pounding head, but it couldn't overcome the dizziness that came from looking up after getting himself untied. He was on a Merry-Go-Round, the world whizzing by him while he sat still. Whatever they'd given him, it was powerful. He was fighting a nearly overwhelming temptation to just flop back down on the bed. That was what his brain wanted. Just lie back down and sleep. Putting his feet on the floor felt impossible. Now that he was free, all he wanted was to be locked back up again, safe in the arms of sleep.

Then, a creak. Footsteps. Two. Three. His eyes danced as he listened, still as a stone. Now he heard nothing. Had he really heard footsteps, maybe that back screen door opening? How sure was he? Sixty percent? Seventy? It didn't really matter. He needed to act like it was 100 percent, because he doubted the guy was coming back to do some Bible study.

Quickly, he surveyed his surroundings. Anything that could be used as a weapon? His bedroom was pretty sparse. An old dresser and a mirror. There was a desk lamp that he didn't use much anymore; maybe that was heavy enough to be a rudimentary weapon, but it certainly wouldn't accomplish much if the guy had a gun.

Another footstep. No doubt this time. Someone was leaving the kitchen and walking into the living room. What little chance there was that this was just one of the members of his church looking for him—*Wait…What time is it? What day is it, for that matter?*—dissolved as the person remained silent. Any well-meaning person would have been yelling his name. This person was trying to be as quiet as possible, but there was only so much you could do in an old house to silence the creaking in an old house.

Father Hayden figured his chances of winning a man-to-man fight with a person who was likely armed—while struggling against lethargy, dizziness, and nearly crippling bouts of nausea and cramping—were nearly zero. If this man walked through that door with the intention of killing him, he might as well start introducing himself to God now. Father Hayden needed to hide or escape. Now.

Then he glanced at the window to his left and had a thought—*How close to the window is that shed Derrick's building?* Carefully, he slid off the bed and tapped his feet to the floor like it was a frying pan on the stove, trying desperately to avoid making a noise that would alert the intruder that he was awake. He shuffled to the window and shoved his fingers underneath it, pressing up to get it open. He stuck his head out and looked down.

It would be far from a perfect landing. The roof was about a six- to eight-foot drop from the window. He'd either hit right on the pitched top, which would hurt like hell, or he'd hit one of the sides, which would probably do little more than just glance him off to the ground below. It also wasn't directly below him; it was a bit to his right, which meant if he wanted the soft landing in the garden dirt rather than the red-clay ground, it would take a bit of a sideways leap. And, then, he also knew the shed was still under construction. Was it even sturdy enough to take his 185 pounds falling on it, or would he just crash right through?

He heard a foot land in the hall outside his bedroom and assumed he only had seconds left before the door opened. There was no more time to think or try to gauge the odds. It was time to act.

Father Hayden took one more glance back and jumped.

14

Without breaking stride, Stephanie shoved open the front door to Saint Francis Hospital, her long legs pushing her forward with a purpose, shoulders up, eyes searching for Doctor Frank Lawry. Following Doctor Giles' retirement shortly after he issued the H6N1 virus report that justified Audrey's edict forcing everyone into steel rings and dissolving the town's family structure, Stephanie and Frank had become the co-chairs of the hospital's research department. She'd been passionate about the work they were doing—her mom had been a big part of building Saint Francis into one of the best research hospitals in the Southeast before she died—and she loved the job. She'd given that up to provide the leadership she knew Alessandra needed, but that decision was getting to be even more fraught with challenges than she'd anticipated. Now Frank had sent word that another man had been attacked. This time, it was one of the refugees Stephanie had admitted into the town.

She saw Frank coming down the stairs toward her, and he stopped.

"How bad is he?" Stephanie said as they walked up to the second floor. Michael was a couple of steps behind.

"Well, the good news is he's awake and somewhat responsive now, though he's in a good deal of pain we're trying to manage. Eyes are reacting to sound, he has flexion withdrawal, and he can speak, though his words seem a little confused. He took a pretty good blow to the head."

"And he got here the same way Hank did?"

"Just lying out in front of the hospital, yeah."

They stopped in the hall outside Derrick's room.

"And nobody saw anything?" Michael asked.

Frank shrugged. "As I'm sure you know, we don't exactly have a huge staff here these days. We're lucky someone even spotted Derrick lying out there. We used to have cameras, but we have to prioritize energy resources elsewhere now. It's all we can do just to take care of our patients and still work through H6N1 research."

"Nobody understands the challenges you deal with every day more than I do, Frank," said Stephanie, flashing a quick glare at Michael. "We all appreciate that you're doing what you can. You said Derrick has been speaking. Has he been able to tell you anything useful?"

"Like, who did it?"

"Right. Or anything at all, really."

"He hasn't said much. We *did* find Midazolam in his system, though. Pretty good amount too."

Stephanie's eyes widened, and she stood up straight. "Same as with Hank. How much of that stuff do you think somebody got ahold of?"

"We're fairly sure they got around twenty to thirty milligrams."

"Shit," she said. "That's enough to do this several times."

"And Derrick's only number two."

Stephanie nodded. "Are you okay with us talking to him?"

"We're fine with it. Just don't push him too hard. But whoever's doing this, we need to figure it out. So get what you can."

Frank continued down the hall, and Stephanie led

Michael into Derrick's room. His head had a large bandage wrapped around the top, and several wires connected him with beeping machines behind the bed. His eyes were pressed shut.

Stephanie pulled a chair out and motioned for Michael to sit down behind her; she leaned over the bed and softly laid a hand on Derrick's arm.

"Derrick? Are you awake? It's Stephanie."

His eyes fluttered open.

"Oh, hi." He winced as he turned his head in her direction. "Thanks for coming. Sorry I'm a little…groggy."

"It's totally okay. I'm so sorry this happened to you. It's not what Alessandra is supposed to be about. We'll figure out who did this."

"I know. For the most part, people here have been great." He closed his eyes and took a deep breath. "My head feels like it was put through a blender."

"Yeah. Unfortunately, it may feel like that for a day or two. But the doctors here are the best. You're in great hands. They'll take care of you, and you're gonna be fine."

Derrick nodded slightly, then grimaced as he tried to hold back a yawn.

"Do you remember anything about what happened?" she asked.

His shoulders slumped. "Last thing I remember before waking up here is working in Father Hayden's garden. I think. It's all just…fuzzy. No, I'm almost certain it was Father Hayden's, because I remember the partially built shed I've been working on for him. I was shoveling, moving dirt in the garden, still maybe a half bag left to dump, and then suddenly the lights went out."

"So you have no idea who attacked you?"

"Clearly, my head took a hard shot. But no, I don't remember anything else."

Stephanie looked back at Michael, who mouthed the words *"It was fucking William"* and shook his head, his eyes narrow.

"Okay. Thanks," she said, turning back to Derrick. "Get your rest. We appreciate you taking a few minutes to talk."

"Sorry I couldn't be more help. It's just hard. Maybe in another day or two, I'll remember more."

She nodded. "Sure. If you do remember anything, tell a doctor, and they'll come get me. I'll come back any time. Day or night. Understand? Whatever you need, we've got you."

A slight smile curled across Derrick's lips, and he closed his eyes. Michael stood, and Stephanie walked ahead of him out into the hall. As she did, she saw a nurse sprinting in her direction.

The nurse, draped in dark blue scrubs with white elephants dancing across them, was gasping for breath by the time he reached her.

"Doctor Sloan!" he yelled. "George is in the lobby. He's been looking for you."

Stephanie looked at Michael, who frowned. If the head of gate security was looking for her, it was rarely good news.

"Do you know what he wants?"

"He just said it was urgent."

Stephanie thanked him and broke into a half-jog, her feet hitting each stair like a tap dancer doing a routine. She saw George Yates waiting for her at the bottom.

"What's so important?" she asked.

"There's someone at the gate, Stephanie. We need you out there."

"It's *really* bad timing, George. Can't you put them in holding for a little bit until I can break away? Give me a day or so."

"This isn't your typical refugee case. You're gonna want to deal with this *right now*."

Exasperated, Stephanie leaned forward, her arms thrust outward.

"Why?"

George sighed, then spoke in a low voice. "It's Audrey. And she's not alone."

15

The door swung open, and Zac stepped inside the room. Curtains billowed, fluttering wildly next to Father Hayden's bed, knotted and torn white sheets with one end tied to the headboard hanging limply, a handmade quilt rumpled along the end of the bed. The stench of vomit hung in the air, almost making Zac's eyes water. Father Hayden wasn't there.

Zac looked around the room. *Surely, he wouldn't have jumped from the second floor*, he thought, scanning for someplace he might be hiding. A closet to his left caught his eye, and he quickly shuffled over to it. It had a brown folding wooden door with several large slats. It would have been a good place for Father Hayden to sit and see what was going on in the room, but a pretty bad—and obvious—place to hide. But if he was desperate enough, he might have just settled for whatever option he had. Zac pulled the door open, and the light crowded out the shadows inside; there was nothing there except clothes hanging neatly on hangers: a few sport coats, some polos, several black cassocks. Four pairs of black dress shoes were lined up perfectly along the floor. Father Hayden wasn't there with them.

Zac pivoted toward the bed, sliding down to his knees and lifting up the bed skirt. He didn't have a lot of light, but he could still easily see there was no one under there; it was spotless. Not even a collection of dust balls lingered.

Frustration welled up inside Zac's chest as he stood back up, seeing the vomit splattered across the sheets. Even without looking closely, he could tell it wasn't dry. He doubted it could be more than a half hour old. That meant Father Hayden woke up nauseated, probably a little disoriented, and not very long ago. So where the hell was he?

How could William have allowed this to fucking happen? First, he nearly kills a man we just wanted to rough up. Then, he gets the attention of Father Hayden, one of the last people we wanted to get the attention of. And finally, he lets Father Hayden escape, with no idea how much he remembers seeing, or what shape he's in.

The fact that Father Hayden wasn't there suggested he was at least well enough to walk out on his own, even if he wasn't at 100 percent. Could he have awakened quickly enough to simply walk down the stairs and away from his house? How poorly was he restrained if he could get out of it in a drugged-up state?

As Zac tried to decide what to do next, he heard the front door shut, and then footfalls on the stairs. For a moment, he thought it could be Father Hayden coming back, but then he heard the voice.

"Zac? Are we good?" William bellowed.

Zac took two large steps toward the door, then yanked it open and stepped out into the hall.

"What the fuck?" Zac gestured wildly with his arms. "He's fucking *gone*, man."

William stopped, and his eyes widened.

"What do you mean, 'Gone'?"

"What do you think I mean? He's fucking gone. Out of here. Disappeared into the air like dandelion spores."

"But that…" William stumbled over his words, pushing past Zac into the room. "That can't be. He was out like a light. And I had him tied to the bed."

"Yeah, good job with that, by the way. You might use

rope next time."

"Where was I gonna get goddamn rope? I wasn't expecting to do this shit. This was supposed to be a quick job. I didn't know I'd have to be ready to tie a priest to his bed this morning. That wasn't in the job description."

"Yeah, well, maybe it needed to be," Zac said, scratching the back of his head. "Look, you need to get your shit together or this plan is gonna fall completely apart. Hell, with Father Hayden who-knows-where, it may have already fallen apart. Can he identify you?"

"I…I mean, I don't—"

"*Can he fucking identify you?*"

"I don't know!" William screamed, his arms raised toward the ceiling. "Of course he saw me, but how the hell am I supposed to know how this drug works? You're the one who gave it to me and told me how great it was. Why don't you tell me, doc?"

Zac stepped directly in front of William, staring into his eyes.

"You intimidate a number of people around here because you're kind of big, and you're a *former* cop. I've got news for ya: I don't give a shit. You're useful, or you're not. Right now, we have to operate under the assumption that Father Hayden knows you did this, and that the clock is ticking before he tells someone who matters. Being identified by one guy wasn't that big a deal. We can explain that away. Getting identified by Father Hayden too pretty much proves you're guilty of both of these. And then the attention goes from 'Stephanie's not tough enough for this job' to 'William needs to hang.' And then you might just give me up in order to save your sorry ass. That's not how this is gonna go down, okay? Are you up for this? Because I need to know right now if you're not."

William swallowed hard and nodded.

"Good," Zac said. "Let's go find this fucking priest before he gets too far. You go toward the lake. I'll head toward Stephanie and Michael's place."

"What do I do if I find him?"

Zac closed his eyes and shook his head.

"Kill him," he said, his voice crisp and sharp as a blade. "Take him someplace quiet, and kill him."

At the mercy of gravity, Father Hayden landed barely on the right side of the shed's peak, a dead-weight bag of meat and bones crashing into the tiles and tumbling wildly over the eave before a final manic fall into the garden's loose mulch, arms flailing, the world refusing to stop turning.

He squinted and shook his head, then blinked several times. He didn't know if the man had entered the room in time to see him leap out the window. But, even if not, he figured the man had noticed he was gone by now. And it wouldn't take him more than a minute or so to know for sure that there was no Father Hayden there. That meant time was short. Father Hayden knew he needed to get moving.

He tried to quickly assess if he had any injuries. His head was still pounding, and he didn't feel very steady, but he didn't think he was any worse there than he'd been when he woke up. Sitting, he rolled over to his right side and then his stomach, beginning to push up to his feet. As he did, lightning shot up his left arm, from his wrist to his shoulder, crashing him back to his knees. The pain knocked the breath out of him, and he had to pause on all fours, damp mulch flaking off his clothes.

Father Hayden carefully lifted his left hand off the ground, his wrist a noodle dangling over the edge of a boiling pot. Straightening up on his knees, he used his right hand to slowly bend his left wrist, and the pain shot through him again, a knife sinking deep into his arm and twisting. He figured he must have broken it during the fall. That'd have to get dealt with, but he knew he didn't have time to worry about it now. He needed to go.

Out of the corner of his eye, he saw movement inside the house. From the garden, he could see through the screen door straight through the kitchen to the front door, which opened as someone stepped into the living room. Another man? He only glanced quickly, and he didn't have a great view through the screen, so he couldn't make out who it was. It was someone fairly big, and he looked kind of hunched over, wearing a khaki-colored jacket. Father Hayden didn't dare take another peek; he could hear just well enough to tell the man's footsteps were going up the stairs, so he got his feet on the ground, steadying himself with his right hand, and began running.

Just as he got a few steps away, he heard the man yell something he couldn't quite make out. Did he recognize that voice? It was too muffled for him to be sure. And, at this point, it barely mattered. He needed to make sure he lived through this before he started worrying about who did this to him. If they caught him and killed him, whatever voice he heard wouldn't matter much. He needed to get moving, through the thumping head, through the stabbing wrist, through the nausea roiling his stomach. Whatever aches and pains and bruises he had needed to be tossed aside so he could keep his momentum going forward.

But, in his state, going forward quickly wasn't the easiest task. He kept having to correct himself from lolling to one side or another as he ran through his neighbors' backyards. Was he even getting further away? He felt like he was swimming in the ocean, the waves lifting him and dropping him but the scenery never changing around him—everything was blurred, like he was looking at the world through a thick filter. He wanted to head to the hospital, but which direction was it in? Father Hayden had lived in Alessandra for almost thirty years, but it'd never looked less familiar, a foreign planet he'd been dropped upon.

Stumbling clumsily, several long steps took him to his right and slammed him sideways into a house, dropping him hard, where he threw up on the ground. On his knees, he stared at the grass, his chest heaving with deep, raspy breaths. Where was he? How far had he gone? How much further could he go? He had no idea.

His body began to shake, softly at first but growing in intensity. His teeth rattled, and it felt like his brain was swelling inside his skull, desperate to break free. He could feel the energy sucking out of his body, as if it were being exorcised, a demon escaping from its cage. He was a mere husk, still upon the cold ground, his stomach contents staring back up at him.

The call of sleep was too much to resist. There had been no time in his life when he wanted one thing but needed the exact opposite as desperately as in this moment. His survival instinct implored him to put one foot in front of the other, to keep moving to stay alive, but his body refused. There was nothing there. He was an engine without fuel, gears grinding to a halt.

With his back against the wall of some house he didn't recognize, Father Hayden slept.

16

Stephanie could see the gate up ahead. Just hearing Audrey's name still gave her chills, but knowing the woman who brought Alessandra to its knees was not only still alive but standing merely feet away, asking to speak with her, Stephanie thought her legs might crumble beneath her for a second and she had to steady herself.

Every season that had passed since Audrey fled in the wake of the coup, Stephanie had become more convinced that Audrey was dead. She'd probably snuck away when everyone was distracted in order to avoid facing the wrath of Stephanie and the rest of the town, but then what? She didn't have any bush survival skills. How long could she possibly have made it on the outside of these walls by herself? A few days? A week? Two? Humans could be resilient creatures, but anything beyond that seemed like wishful thinking for Audrey.

But now, as Stephanie strode toward the gate, flanked by George and Michael, the woman who built it somehow stood on the other side, more than a year after they'd last seen her. How had she survived this long? And what did she want?

They reached the gate and stopped.

"All right. Open the gate, George." She nodded in his direction, then turned to Michael. "I think I should go out there alone."

"The hell you are. I'm a part of this too."

"You know Audrey a lot better than I do. You worked for her; you trusted her. You feel personally betrayed, I know. I just don't want you to do something you'll regret."

Michael took a deep breath. "I'll be fine. She's not my favorite person, but he says she's got what? Three large men with her? I don't think a round of fisticuffs works out in our favor. And, more importantly, we both know what she's capable of, and who the hell knows what she's like after whatever she's been through for a year and a half?"

"Okay, fine," Stephanie conceded. "You're right. Having you and George backing me probably isn't the worst idea. I'm doing the talking, though. Got it?"

They heard the gate start to creak, and it slowly swung open, gradually revealing the outside world. They left the walls infrequently enough that it was easy to forget the rest of it existed. Besides the large gardens some Alessandrans tended on the north side, there was nothing the townspeople needed out here. Stephanie virtually never left the safety of the walls except to greet the rare visitor who found their way to Alessandra, typically looking for a place to settle. Alessandra certainly wasn't a rich town, but in this world, they were a fortunate one. They didn't have everything they wanted, but they had everything they needed to sustain a small colony.

It was good that they did, because they knew the dangers lurking outside those walls. And, of all of them, the biggest was still the virus. H6N1. The World Killer. Was it still active somewhere? Were there still carriers who could be the Trojan Horse for it? Saint Francis could test for it, so people inside the walls could be screened. But outside the walls, there was no way to be certain someone was healthy. There was the possibility of carriers who didn't exhibit symptoms—at least, not for a while—so it wasn't smart to take chances.

George handed Michael and Stephanie surgical masks, and they put them on as the gate swung open far enough to reveal Audrey and her men. Even though Stephanie had known Audrey was going to be there, it was still a jolt to see her for the first time since that final night at the compound, Audrey running down the hall with a crowd of people she'd had locked in quarantine, Nick wielding her knife as they charged toward Paul, Stephanie jamming a knife of her own into Paul's side before he could get off a shot at the mob that was coming for him.

In those final moments, Audrey had recognized some level of responsibility for the awful events that had happened. She helped the people who'd been tortured in the quarantine pen escape, and exact their vengeance on her brother. She'd shook Stephanie's hand and apologized. Seeing Audrey now, standing there in tattered, clay-streaked garments, her face lined with far more than a year's worth of age since that night, Stephanie wondered if maybe Audrey had changed. Had she learned her lessons? Was she still evil? Had she ever really been?

Walking through the gate, Stephanie found herself studying the men Audrey had brought with her. Two had dark complexions, and the third was lighter, with scars that crossed his face and arms. Each wore pants made from the dark brown fur of an animal she couldn't identify, the tufts of hair spilling onto the ground. They wore no shirts, exposing chests rounded and bulging from years of labor, their arms taut and thick as logs. Strapped diagonally across each man's chest was a black band with red trim that appeared hand-woven, the handle of multiple blades jutting out from pockets along the length of it. Their faces were stone and ash, expressive in their lack of expression, giving nothing away in their tight lines and still eyes, nary the hint of a curl on their mouths.

Stephanie stopped ten feet in front of Audrey, with Michael and George to her left and right, just a step behind. She'd been pondering what to say since the moment George told her Audrey was there, but that had all been in theory. This was real. Audrey was real. In the flesh. There was no mistaking it now.

"You'll forgive me if I don't shake hands," Stephanie said. "We can't know where you've been or what you might be carrying."

A wry smile formed on Audrey's lips as she nodded lightly. "You'll remember I stood in your shoes many times. You're smart to stay where you are."

"Then you should also know that I'm very busy, so I'd like to get right to it rather than waxing nostalgic about the past. I don't see much in the way of supplies on you, so I'm guessing it's not trade you're after. What is it you want?"

Audrey turned her head left, then right, looking at her men, whose faces didn't change.

"Our colony collapsed. Various reasons I don't feel the need to go into, and you're probably not terribly interested anyway. So—"

Stephanie's eyebrows raised, and she glanced back at Michael, who shrugged.

"Wait…You're saying there's another organized colony *within walking distance* from here?"

"Well, several weeks of walking, yes. South, southwest, by the sun. Not far from the old Atlanta. A great place exists called Graysburg. It *used* to exist, anyway. The culture wasn't sustainable over the long term. It was unfortunate. We're the only survivors I know of."

"Was it the virus that killed them?"

Audrey paused and looked at the ground, then raised her eyes back to Stephanie and shook her head solemnly. "No." She took a deep breath and swallowed hard. "No, I think we're past that. We've seen a lot of this land, and I see no sign of the virus today. I suspect it's been starved from a lack of remaining hosts. This world is practically dead, and we're all practically dead along with it. When we left Graysburg, I told the men here that I knew of a place that was alive if we had the perseverance for a journey. When I found Graysburg, it was by chance, running into a fellow traveler who knew where it was, and led me there. I thanked him many times for saving me, as it was truly a savior for me. I had been near giving up before the people of Graysburg gave me purpose. Now, I wanted to return that favor to the few who I still could—these men who made this trip with me. I wanted to lead them somewhere to show them there were places of light still left in this world."

"It sounds like you've come a long way," Stephanie said, her head tilting slightly. "I doubt you've ventured this far just to show them our pretty wall."

"It is a magnificent wall, isn't it?" Audrey smiled. "Building that was such a project. You helped with it. So did you, Michael. And George. We were all part of making Alessandra what it was and is. I'm glad to see the town still has smart leadership. I was confident it would still be standing strong as ever when we arrived."

"You still haven't told me what you want, Audrey. What were you expecting at the end of this long walk?"

Audrey sucked in a deep breath and cleared her throat, then brushed some glistening sweat off her forehead.

"Well, you're right. I didn't drag them all this way just for a round of show and tell or a trip down memory lane. We're tired. Exhausted, really. Everything we have, we rationed to get here. This is the end of the line for us. We haven't eaten more than a few stray berries for three days, and clean drinking water has been nearly as hard to find. If you turn us away, we'll be dead within a week. Maybe two. All we ask is for some temporary shelter inside your walls. And we're not asking for charity. We're willing to do more than our share of the work that needs to be done. As you can imagine, each of these men can do the physical labor of three to four average men. They're real assets. We'll earn our keep."

It was the request Stephanie had expected but hoped against. Her mind swirled.

"The *fuck* we'll let you inside and ruin everything we've built again!" Michael's voice exploded from behind his mask as he stepped forward with emphasis. Stephanie pivoted a bit toward him and put out a hand, motioning for him to stay calm. She didn't want this to turn violent.

"Surely you can understand our skepticism," Stephanie said. "After everything that happened."

Audrey nodded. "Of course. I did some things I'm not proud of. That's my cross to bear. I can't change the past. I wish there was something I could do to turn back the clock. If my past mistakes are what keep us outside those walls, that'll be a heavy burden, but it's an earned one. I can't say what choice I'd make if I were in your position. Remember, though, that I let the quarantined prisoners out. I led them back into the compound to take out my own brother. If not for me, more people would have died."

"Why did you leave?" Stephanie asked, her hands clasped across her waist.

"I was ashamed." Audrey's head hung low, her eyes fixed on the dirt at her feet. "I'd done what I could at the end, but I just couldn't face everyone in town after my brother had ordered the murder of so many, and I was the one who'd let that snake into our midst. The guilt was too much. I knew that leaving was likely a death sentence, but it was one I probably deserved. But God gave me a pardon in the form of Graysburg and the wonderful people there. I don't know why, but he did. And now I'm here before you, asking you for another one. Just a few days, Stephanie. And put us to work. Then we'll be on our way. That's all we ask."

Stephanie's stomach tightened, and she stared straight ahead.

17

The clouds were gathering, and a bitter wind began to cut across Zac's skin as he walked past Stephanie and Michael's empty houses, cinching his light bomber to his chest, his desperation growing deeper as icy blades sliced him into pieces.

If Father Hayden was thinking clearly, Zac figured the two most likely places for him to head were east—to find Stephanie and Michael and tell them what happened, or to the hospital to get treatment. The latter depended a bit on how bad of a shape he was in.

If the Midazolam worked as it should, Zac was pretty sure Father Hayden wouldn't be able to do much physical activity just yet. From what he remembered when it'd been given to him a couple of times while he was in the military—as a sedative for doctors to deal with injuries—it was pretty potent stuff. You certainly didn't wake up and sprint half a mile to a hospital.

Was it possible the Midazolam was old and had lost some of its potency? Or that someone stumbled upon Father Hayden and helped him get out of the house before Zac arrived? He couldn't completely rule out either of those possibilities yet, though the vomit suggested the drug had at least had *some* effect. Still, Father Hayden might have been ratting them out right at that moment, as drops of rain began to tap the top of Zac's head.

This wasn't the time to seek shelter, though. Zac had been through worse, crawling through swollen, muddy bogs, soaked to the bone with water that stank of rotting weeds and dead carp, then fighting off shivering for hours on a nearby hill because the shaking trigger finger is the finger of a dead man.

The rain's intensity picking up, Zac scurried under the crumbling awning of what had been a candy shop years before. The blue vinyl was tattered and dirty from years of neglect, but it provided just enough cover for him to duck beneath in order to buy himself a few moments to think.

Assuming Father Hayden didn't get help—only because, if he did get help, all bets were off at that point—where might he have gone? Zac still thought the hospital was the best direction to look. And if the drug's effects were still hitting him, this downpour would slow him down even more.

Zac darted out from under the awning, staying close to the row of abandoned buildings whenever he could, letting the gutters stuffed with leaves above shield him from what it could as he ducked his head and churned his legs, running toward Saint Francis, six blocks away. The wind rattled the windows and knocked twigs off the trees, bouncing off the pavement. It was one of those springtime storms you get in the North Georgia mountains, winter's touch seeping through, another reminder that you're always at the mercy of nature.

Two blocks before he reached the hospital, Zac swung into a doorway and pressed himself into it, soaked cold but briefly out of the worst of it. Sheets of rain fell diagonally like curtains being swept shut as he watched.

If Father Hayden had made it all the way to the hospital, there wasn't much Zac could do about it. It wasn't like he could just walk in and ask for him at the receptionist's desk.

But, standing here, Zac knew Father Hayden wasn't along the most direct route to Saint Francis. If he had been disoriented at the time, who knows what sort of circuitous route he might have taken.

Zac took a deep breath and counted to three, then ran out and around the building, circling to the back and running through the grass. Puddles were forming all around him, making each step a hazard for soaking his feet even further as he sprinted away from the hospital, back toward Father Hayden's house.

He turned the corner, back into the residential area, passing through the backyards of houses that used to shelter happy families but were now mostly empty. Propane grills still sat on some back decks, rust flaking off of them as rain pelted the metal. To his right, an old park with the unmistakable metal cage structure that used to serve as a backstop for a baseball field, nature long since having reclaimed the land for overgrown grass and spindly weeds.

Zac's instinct was to keep his head down into his chest to keep the cold water out of his face, but he knew he needed to keep his eyes up and aware. If Father Hayden was out there, Zac needed to find him before anyone else did.

He could see Father Hayden's place three houses away, each soggy step making him long for warming his feet by a crackling log fire. Then, suddenly, he stopped. He looked up, letting the rain run down his face, opening his mouth to take in the water, one cloud-filtered drop at a time.

He lowered his head and turned to his left, a smile beginning to curl across his lips, heart starting to pound. There was a dark mass huddled against the wall of the house, a sun shade above shielding it from most of the rain. He knew immediately it was Father Hayden.

18

Listening to Stephanie talk to Audrey outside the gate, Michael could feel his throat tightening, trying to swallow his rage like a dry pill. He didn't like the direction the conversation was headed, and knew he needed to step in.

"Will you excuse us for a moment, Audrey?" Michael said sharply. "Stephanie and I need to talk about this privately."

"Of course," Audrey said, *appearing* to project patience. Michael wasn't sure how much of it was an act. "Take all the time you need."

Michael put his hand on Stephanie's shoulder and led her several steps away, back toward the gate until he felt like they were out of earshot of Audrey and her men. He didn't want to give anything away, so he knew they both had to *look* calm even if he was anything but. They turned their backs to Audrey and leaned their heads in close.

"You know we can't let her inside, right?" Michael said. "You're not actually considering it, are you?"

Stephanie sighed and rolled her eyes. "It's just temporary. Besides, I really think she's—"

"You are! You're thinking about letting that shark back into our town." Michael clutched his hands behind his back to keep from gesturing wildly. "Do you not remember everything that happened before? And how it was all her fault? The wives and mothers left to die? The broken families? The quarantine concentration camp? The rings? All those lies?"

"Look, I get it. I know all of it. You don't have to tell me. I was on the front lines of this, Michael. I was almost killed multiple times, just like you were. I was just as much a witness to the Town Square massacre as you were. So don't remind me like—"

"Then why? Why would you invite that back upon us willingly?"

Stephanie paused, rubbing her forehead and looking down.

"She made mistakes. But she realizes that. The decisions—"

"Mistakes? She fucking killed—"

"Will you let me fucking finish, Michael?" Stephanie's teeth pressed together in a sneer. Michael stopped and looked up at the sky, seeing dark clouds starting to gather overhead. "She made mistakes. Nothing can change that. But I don't believe she's some purely evil monster. I just don't. I think she got carried away. I think Paul was a bad influence on her. And maybe she got a little drunk on power. But in *this* Alessandra—*our* Alessandra—she'll have no power. No authority. Even if she *had* crazy ideas…whatever. But in the end, I truly think that what she wanted was what was best for the people of Alessandra. She didn't necessarily know about the forged documents. Paul directed that. Who initiated Doctor Giles' murder? Paul. Who ordered everyone killed at the Town Square? Paul. Who ran the quarantine camp? Paul. Maybe she never should have brought him in, but he was her brother, for Christ's sake. That's an understandable blind spot to have. And when it was clear that he had gone all the way to the dark side, *she* led the group that finally took him down, then voluntarily surrendered power. Is that the work of an evil person, or someone who was temporarily led astray?"

Michael shut his eyes tightly, shaking his head. "But Stephanie…how can we just let all that—"

"We'd both be dead if not for her, Michael. It's true. Same with Hank and Dennis. Paul had you three lined up in a row, ready to kill. He wasn't letting any of you go. He would have made me watch all of you get murdered, and then killed me too. You know that's what would have happened if Audrey hadn't gotten there with the people from quarantine when she did. He showed he'd do it when he had William shoot Anna. And I'll always regret not being able to save her. So I've made mistakes too. We all have.

"But I'm not gonna have more blood on my hands, by shoving these people off to their deaths. Not again. This is temporary. Her men are plenty strong enough to be able to earn their keep. They'll work for a few days. Maybe a week or so. They'll earn some supplies to take with them, and we'll send them on their way better equipped than before. I think we have to do this."

Michael exhaled, all the possibilities rattling around in his head. What Stephanie was saying had a certain level of logic to it, but he couldn't forget the past. He couldn't forget the anger and resentment in Audrey's voice when he told her it couldn't have been Nick who killed Trevor; it was almost certainly Zac. How dismissive she was, and how power-mad she sounded, hopped up on the idea that she could just make him go away with the wave of her hand, like reality bent to her will. Who had been the bad influence on whom? Did Paul push her toward authoritarianism, or did she pull him, and then just couldn't stop the momentum once she started it? Maybe the most damning thing was that she ultimately authorized all the terrible things her brother did, or consciously stood aside so she could pretend not to know.

Michael felt raindrops hit his head, and a chilly wind cut across his face.

"I think it's a mistake. Let me just say that," Michael said. "But if you're sure, go ahead." He remained standing with his back turned as Stephanie walked back toward Audrey.

"Okay, we've decided to let you all inside *temporarily*." Michael cringed as he heard Stephanie speak. "That's contingent upon you doing whatever job our teams see fit. If you meet the terms, we'll provide you with some food and supplies so you'll be better equipped when you leave in roughly a week. And, of course, all of this is void if you test positive for anything worse than a runny nose. What do you think?"

"That sounds perfectly acceptable. Thank you." Audrey smiled, and the men nodded quietly as the rain began to fall harder. "I hope we can make you *and Michael* happy you did this."

"So do I," Stephanie said, trying to cover her head from the rain as George and Michael began running for the gate. "Now, let's get going before we drown."

Stephanie turned and sprinted for the gate. Audrey, still smiling, walked calmly behind her, and the men kept her pace.

19

Father Hayden's eyes reluctantly pried open, he began to look around, slowly realizing he was back in his room, in his own bed, his arms tied above him—this time with a gnarly stretch of rope that stunk of mildew and fish. Pain rocketed down his left arm from his injured wrist. A small scream escaped his lips as he tried to contort his body to get his arm into a position that would at least dull the pain.

The bedroom door flew open and a man in a blue surgical mask and hairnet stepped inside. He walked briskly to the side of the bed, his eyes intense on Father Hayden's face.

"What do you want from me?" Father Hayden barely managed to squeak out, the pain still pervading his every thought.

The man just stared, still, unblinking. As Father Hayden squirmed into a position where the pain began to lessen, his eyes scanned over the man, who was wearing a solid-black cassock, just like the ones Father Hayden wore when on duty. He assumed the man had taken it out of his closet, but he had no idea why. The silence was almost as uncomfortable as the pain. Father Hayden shivered; his clothes were cold and wet, as if he'd been tossed into a running shower. The sheets beneath him were soaked with water.

"I…I don't know who you are. I don't know anything," Father Hayden said, his teeth beginning to chatter a bit. "I'm not even hurt in any way that couldn't just be me being clumsy. I fell. That's what happened. I was…going down the stairs, slipped, and fell. Hurt my wrist. Old age, ya know?"

Father Hayden forced a laugh that came out more like a groan, then squeezed his eyes tightly shut. His shivering was causing the rope to pull against his wrist, each jerk like a hammer driving a nail into his arm. He grimaced, and tried to compose himself.

"Just cut me loose and walk out of here. I'll wait…until you're gone. Five minutes. Ten. Whatever you want. Then I can get to the hospital for this wrist. I'm good. I won't tell them anything. I mean, what would I even say? I stupidly jumped out a window because I thought someone was chasing me? They wouldn't even be—"

"The drugs," the man said, his voice startling, a deep growl; Father Hayden couldn't decide whether or not it was done purposefully as a disguise. He definitely didn't recognize it. "The doctors would be able to see you were drugged."

Father Hayden's breaths came shallowly; it was suddenly like he was in a low-oxygen environment. He felt like he was hyperventilating, and his body began shaking nearly to the point of convulsions. He kicked violently, slamming against the bed, his arms yanking at the ropes while the bed creaked incessantly beneath him. He didn't know how long that lasted but, finally, he started to regain control, his breathing still ragged, but his body slightly warmer from the movement. The man hadn't moved, his eyes still boring into Father Hayden's.

"I…um, I don't know about any drugs," Father Hayden said. "But why would they test me for that? I was just a dummy who fell and hurt his wrist. I just need a splint or something, maybe something to dull the pain."

"And the rope burns on your wrists," the man's voice was cold, meticulous, a throat full of gravel, lacking emotion.

"Where did those come from?"

Father Hayden felt his chest tighten, and he jerked his head back and forth. All his jerking around had caused the rope to rub against his wrists, leaving irritated red rings around them. He looked back at the man, still disconcertingly calm as he stood by the bed.

"Um, maniples. I wore maniples for Mass last Sunday. See, they're, um, liturgical handkerchiefs priests can wear around their wrists. I just must have tied them too tightly, ya know? Stupid mistake. Didn't notice until the service was over."

It was the best Father Hayden could come up with on the spot. He'd never worn maniples, but he'd known some priests in the pre-virus world who liked calling back to such old traditions. Thinking back to then brought moments from his old life flashing through his thoughts: late-night Bible reading in the library at seminary; the first time he was fitted for his clerical collar; how proud his Dad was to be in the front row at the first service he led as priest in Alessandra. These last couple of years had been extremely difficult. But, in some ways, they'd been rewarding for Father Hayden, as he'd had so many lost souls to try to keep on the path toward God. In the most trying times, he knew some would be drawn closer, and some pushed further from their faith. He didn't want to put himself on some sort of Jesus-like pedestal, but he did believe there was a good reason he had been chosen to be the priest for one of the only organized colonies left in the world after God cleansed the Earth. He knew none of this had happened without a purpose, and he hoped it would create an opportunity to rebuild a society around His word, and Father Hayden relished the chance to be a significant part of that.

He'd stayed through it all, watching the world crumble around them, but Alessandra found a way to survive. There was so much death and destruction everywhere—people losing family and friends to the virus, seeing the entire societal structure fall apart and having to return to a far more primitive way of life than any of them were used to—and people needed to know there was a meaning to it all. Father Hayden couldn't always claim to know what God's grand plan was, but his trust in God had carried him and his congregation through the most challenging times. Was this to test them to determine the strongest of mind and body? Was God cleansing the world to basically start over? It was easy to look to the Bible to see precedents for it, from the Great Flood of Genesis 6-8 to Sodom and Gomorrah in Genesis 18-19 to the Egyptian first-born sons and the Canaanites under Moses and Joshua.

In the pre-virus world, those stories had been difficult to explain and understand. But after the virus, there was a certain comfort in it—God had found reason to do large-scale cleansings before, and a better world had emerged from its ashes. Trust in Him, and it will carry you through.

Gazing up at this masked man, Father Hayden wondered what God's reason was for placing him there at this moment. Even when it was confounding, it was still easier to find reason in God's work on a mass human scale than it was to reduce it down to one man tied to his bed, another man staring down at him with murderous eyes. No matter the perfection of heaven, everyone begged on their death bed for more time in this earthly hell.

"You can identify us," the man said.

"I—I can't! That's the truth! On my mother's grave, God rest her soul. I have no idea who you are. None. I know you gave me some drug, because I've felt awful this whole time, and I can't remember hardly a thing since I went to bed last night. I have no idea what's even happening. Please!"

The man grabbed the pillow beside Father Hayden and

clutched it with both hands. His eyes never wavered from Father Hayden. Those cold, soulless eyes.

The man climbed onto the bed, straddling Father Hayden's legs. He sat down on them, pinning them to the mattress, then leaned forward, holding the pillow in front of him. Father Hayden quickly realized what was happening and began to scream, but that was quickly muffled by the pillow's weight on his face.

Father Hayden tried to yell, but he couldn't find the breath. And even if he could, no sound was escaping the vacuum the pillow created. He thrashed his limbs. Anything to break this man's hold. He was strong, though. Grip firm. Father Hayden turned his head wildly left, then right, back again, searching for small pockets of air. The man's thick hands pressed hard into the mattress, tight against the sides of Father Hayden's head. He had to lean forward a bit to press the pillow with enough force to cut off the air, so Father Hayden had some space to kick, violently swinging his legs. It felt like the man had nothing on underneath the vestment, which meant he was also unprotected; Father Hayden knew the shot that would really hurt and might save his life, but he couldn't seem to quite connect. Lots of wild shin shots to the man's thighs and butt, but he had the cassock pulled between his legs, providing just enough of a shield for his groin.

Time wasn't on Father Hayden's side; he knew that much. But what was time when you couldn't breathe? Your brain could think of nothing else—just sheer, unbridled panic. Do whatever you can to get the smallest bit of oxygen. Kick. Punch. Thrash. Bite. Could he kill a man? In this moment, there was nothing Father Hayden wouldn't do to taste sweet oxygen on his lips. Suck it deep into his lungs. He couldn't have taken his last breath. It couldn't be. There was so much to do. He had to fight. He wanted his arms free, needed to grab the man by the throat and pull him off. Rip that mask off and find out who would do this to him. And why? What could he possibly have done to wrong this man to the point where he'd want him dead?

He was still kicking, but he could feel the energy draining from his body. How much longer did he have? He didn't know. A part of his brain wanted to play dead, hope that would cause the man to let up. But survival instinct didn't allow it. The only option was to breathe. That crowded out every other thought. There was nothing else in this world.

Suddenly, the pillow was gone, and there was light again. Father Hayden was alone in his church, adorned with his full vestments, standing upright in the aisle between the pews. He looked around; he'd always admired the beauty of the building. The stained-glass windows weren't elaborate, but they cast wonderful cascades of red and gold into the nave during the afternoon, when he'd often sit in there and write. There was Jesus, nailed to the cross behind the altar, where he'd spent so many hours speaking to his congregation, conveying the Word of God. Helping them with their troubles. Offering some small bits of wisdom.

He loved this place. He'd enjoyed every minute there. His hand falling on the back of a pew, he took it all in, glad this was where he could spend his final moments.

Then it all went black.

20

Stephanie stretched and pulled apart tangled strands of her hair as she walked into her living room, where Michael was sitting with a book in his hands.

"Whatcha reading?" she said, sitting down on the couch across from him. He looked up and laid the book in his lap.

"*Nineteen Eighty-Four*. Haven't read it since high school. Thought I'd see how much I remembered."

"Not the lightest read, huh?"

"Yeah." Michael laughed. "How does it feel to be living in your own dystopian nightmare?"

"This shit ain't exactly Orwell, thankfully."

Michael shut the book and laid it on the coffee table. He sat back for a moment, and his eyes wandered around the room. Stephanie crossed her legs, her blue cotton robe draping over her knees.

There was a comfort to being here with Michael. Their history together went back to high school, when they'd both been athletes at Towns High—she quite a bit better at volleyball than he was at football and baseball—then tried to go to college together at the University of North Georgia before Michael dropped out and she transferred to the University of Georgia and then to Emory to work toward a degree in medicine. Eventually, their paths crossed again when she moved back to Alessandra after graduating, and they were married less than a year later.

The rocky marriage led to a divorce, but neither of them left Alessandra. There was some of the bitterness you'd expect following any divorce—they always end badly; otherwise, they wouldn't end—but it didn't linger for too long. Stephanie just wanted to move on with her life, and she hoped Michael would find happiness with someone else. She assumed they both would. But she threw herself even more deeply into her work at Saint Francis, and she never found anyone in Alessandra who could deal with her work hours and met the standards she'd set for herself. She knew Michael dated some women here and there after the divorce, but if any of them were ever particularly serious, she didn't know about it. And, in a town like Alessandra, word about that sort of thing got around quickly.

Stephanie hadn't exchanged more than a few passing words with her ex-husband in years before he walked into her office and told her he thought Audrey was hiding something about the virus study she'd commissioned from Doctor Giles, and he needed her help to investigate what was going on. He didn't know who else he could trust. She'd been pretty dismissive at first; in fact, her initial instinct had been to tell him he was crazy and to peddle that nonsense to someone else. But part of her still saw that boy who confidently asked her out in high school when no one would have guessed he had a chance. The one who had this fuel within him that few seemed to be able to see, but which glowed like a bright white light to her. It was what had attracted her to him in the first place, and she couldn't totally explain it. People told her she was "out of his league," a Homecoming Queen, star athlete, and future respected doctor slumming it with a college dropout who'd be a lifer getting grease on his hands at Alessandra's furniture factory because he didn't have the education to do much more.

But to her, Michael glowed. And so she decided to help him. He'd been right about Audrey, and it led to the downfall of her corrupt administration. After that, it seemed everyone left in the town assumed—Stephanie included—that the two of them would rekindle their relationship. They'd been through such an intense few weeks, nearly dying, and her having to save his life twice in the span of two days. She'd never felt closer to him or more thankful that he was alive than when they had stood there, holding each other, relief splashing over them like a waterfall with Paul lying dead a few feet away and the world finally making a modicum of sense.

They had sex that night, writhing around in Stephanie's bed for hours, a sort of euphoric release of all the energy that had built up over the previous days. It wasn't about love, or even lust. It was the fact that they *could*, without worrying about who might find out, or what the consequences might be if they did. They could feel the touch of another, skin to skin, clothes strewn across the floor, slick with sweat. It was like the world hadn't changed; the world could just be right there, the two of them, their bodies connecting like jigsaw pieces, their eyes locked on one another. Stephanie suspected they weren't the only ones who celebrated the same way that night.

A year and a half later, though, a romantic relationship just hadn't materialized. Part of it—maybe most of it—had been the stress of trying to lead the town, and keep the people safe. So much of their energy was poured into making hard decisions every day that there was little to devote to anything else. And then there was the question of what the point would even be of a relationship. Stephanie had no interest in having kids, and there was nothing preventing them from just having sex every now and then if they needed a physical release. So why make anything official? Let the people have their rumors and their gossip. She didn't care.

They lived in separate houses, and she was fine with Michael hooking up with anybody he wanted to on his own.

At this moment, though, she had bigger issues on her mind.

"Do you really think letting Audrey in was a mistake?" she asked, leaning forward in her chair.

Michael looked down and swallowed hard. "I mean, I want to trust your judgment. And I know that, pretend whatever you want, we're not equal partners in leading this town. I know this is your show, and I'm just a supporting ch—"

"Don't say that."

"It's true, Steph. Okay? It's true. And…It's okay. I get it. You're smarter than me. I'm just another loser dropout in a town full of loser dropouts. You're the local girl who did it all, then came back to serve the community. I can't live up to that. You deserve to be making the final call on stuff like this. There's nobody I'd rather have in that position."

She cocked her head and looked across the room at him, changing position on the couch, curling his legs up underneath himself like she'd seen him do a million times when he was nervous. She knew he was basically right, but she'd wanted to make him feel like he was someone important, to elevate him to a higher plane. He'd done a lot to earn that as they worked to push Audrey out. If not for Michael, none of that probably would have happened, and Alessandra would have been a very different place at this point. Michael was smarter than he—and others—gave him credit for, though. She wished she could make him see that.

"But…?" she said, expectantly.

"But I'm gonna tell you when I disagree with what you're doing. Somebody needs to. I think that's why I'm here. I think that's my biggest role. Audrey didn't have that; she had ultimate power, and the only voice in her ear was trying to get her to take even more. I'm gonna tell you when you're wrong. I'll call you on your bullshit. As far as Audrey goes, you made some good points, and I'll admit it gives me pause. Maybe you're right. *Maybe.* But I'm nervous about it. And now I've got to live in the same town as her again."

"Just for a few days."

"Yeah, yeah. A few days. Sure. Regardless, it's uncomfortable. And potentially distracting, especially with everything else we're dealing with right now."

There was a knock on the door, and both their heads turned in that direction. Stephanie got up to answer it, Michael just behind her.

She opened the door and saw Dennis standing there; a flood of guilt washed over her. She didn't want it to linger so long. He'd told her he forgave her for naming him when Paul forced her to pick the next person to die that final night in the compound. She had refused at first, then watched Paul order Anna, Dennis's ex-wife and Stephanie's best friend, to be the first to die. She and Dennis both screamed and fell to the ground as her body collapsed limply. Stephanie knew if she didn't choose someone, the next victim might be Michael, and she couldn't figure out how to deal with that. So she shouted Dennis's name. She didn't think the shame would ever fully loosen its grip on her, but she was usually able to push it down. Seeing him standing there, though, brought it all back.

She took a deep breath and tried to compose herself.

"Dennis…Nice to see you," she said, a bit lightheaded.

"You too, Stephanie. Michael." He nodded, and Michael did the same. "Have you guys seen Father Hayden?"

Stephanie looked back at Michael, who shrugged.

"No idea. Been a busy morning, to be honest. Why do you ask?"

"Well, a few of us were supposed to meet him at the

church for Bible study, and it's not like him to just blow us off. So I went down the street to his house to see if he was there. Maybe he forgot about it. I walked up to the porch and, before I could knock, I thought I heard something upstairs. A loud bang. Sounded like something big hitting the floor, and then what sounded like voices. Multiple men. At least two. So I knocked, and everything went silent. I tried yelling his name, because I know he's in there, ya know? I'm not hearing things. But…"

It was that moment that the conversation with Derrick rang back in her head. He said the last thing he remembered before he went unconscious was working in Father Hayden's garden. If that was where he'd been assaulted and nearly killed, there was a good chance this wasn't a coincidence.

"Shit," she said, sprinting back toward her room to put on some clothes.

"Is something wrong?" Dennis asked.

"Quite a bit, yeah," Michael said. "The question is exactly what."

21

"Is he dead?" William asked, pressing his ear to Father Hayden's chest. "I didn't want to have to kill him."

"Well, you should have thought of that before you set off his alarm bells after a simple job I asked you to do," Zac said. "You left me with no choice. I had to protect us both. We don't need you being connected to multiple of these things."

"I know that. It's just...he was a good man. He didn't do anything to deserve this."

Zac grabbed Father Hayden's legs at the ankles and swung his body around on the bed.

"Yeah. Life's not fair. Millions didn't deserve to die in that fucking plague. My wife and those other women didn't deserve to be marched out into the wilderness with no food or water. Nobody gets what they *deserve* in this world, William. We get what we get. Father Hayden being 'good' or not doesn't make a damn bit of difference. The world's going to take him at some point just like the rest of us. What we've got to do is make the best decisions for the future of this town, which means executing our plan. And what 'good' was he even doing? Preaching some bullshit about heaven and hell, and how this all happened for a goddamn reason? I'll tell ya what...a god who can't find a better plan than 'Hey, let's put millions through an excruciating and untimely death in order to teach the survivors a valuable lesson' isn't worth worshipping."

William looked downcast. "He gave people hope, Zac."

"More like delusions. Hayden was a bullshit peddler. Plain and simple. A snake oil salesman. You buying it doesn't make that shit any less true. Now, grab his arms."

William stood still, staring at Zac.

"His arms, William. We can't just leave the body here."

William bit his lip and crossed his arms. After a few seconds of silence, he grabbed Father Hayden's wrists. They lifted him off the mattress and carried him toward the door. After a couple of steps, William abruptly let go, and the body crashed to the floor with a thud.

"I'm not doing this," he said. "I've done a lot for you, but I'm not helping you dispose of the body of someone you killed. *You* did this. Not me. *You*. You deal with it."

Still holding Father Hayden's ankles, Zac screamed. "Pick up his arms, William! Right the *fuck* now, or I swear to god—"

"I thought god was just a delusion, Zac."

Zac rolled his eyes and shook his head.

"I'm trying to help *you*, William. You've already been identified as Hank's assailant. You think it's going to take them more than two seconds to figure out that maybe you're the one who attacked Derrick too? And ya know where that puts you? Right in Father Hayden's back yard on the morning he was killed. It's not that—"

They heard bangs from downstairs and stopped talking; Zac dropped Father Hayden's legs to the floor. Someone was knocking at the door. Zac raised his finger to his lips, and neither man moved.

After a minute, the knocking stopped. Father Hayden's room was in the back of the house, so Zac knew anyone at the front door couldn't see movement through a window. But they'd been pretty loud. Could the person have heard them?

"Father Hayden?" the voice carried up the stairs and into the room. Zac knew he must be yelling loudly for them to hear him. Which meant the neighbors probably heard him too. "Father Hayden, are you there? We're waiting for you at Bible study."

Shit, Zac thought. *How many people are in this Bible study group? How many know something weird is going on? This means time is short. We've got to get rid of him ASAP.*

William raised his eyebrows at Zac and pointed toward the body, then downstairs. Zac sneered and whispered, "I don't know. Just wait a second."

They stood still, listening. Then they heard the doorknob rattling, and Zac cringed, though they had fortunately thought to lock the door; otherwise, they might have had another body to dispose of. The question, though, was what the visitor would do when he left. Who would he tell?

They waited—one minute, two. They heard nothing. Zac backed up and opened the bedroom door, then hurried across the hall to one of the other rooms. He ducked low beneath one of the windows overlooking the front yard. Slowly, he raised up until he could barely see a man walking away from the house toward the street.

From the back, Zac couldn't immediately recognize him. When the man got to the street, he turned right, in the direction of the church a block away. Time was ticking. He hurried back across the hall and into Father Hayden's room.

"We need to get him out of here *now*," Zac said. "Grab his fucking arms."

22

Watching George leave, Audrey stood in the living room of her new house and exhaled loudly, her men sitting nearby. With an olive green couch and plain wicker chair lying on its side in the corner, the place was a big step up from what they'd gotten used to over the previous weeks. Her bed was small, and the mattress was a little lumpy, but it would beat sleeping on the cold dirt, or a bug-ridden pile of leaves and sticks. Her men would share the house next door, so she'd get a little bit of space to herself.

It had been a long time since Audrey had lived in Alessandra with no position of authority. She'd spent nearly eight years as deputy mayor to Charles Handy before he succumbed to the virus following a trip to Atlanta for a conference. They rushed him back after he started exhibiting symptoms, but it was too late. He never woke up again. And Audrey was thrust into the role of leader that eventually ended with her self-banishment.

Once she made it to Graysburg, she found the people were living more primitively than those in Alessandra. There was no hospital, no solar or hydroelectricity, no wall to keep them safe. Just a small village of homes, a few wells for water, and a large farm that everyone except for the pregnant women worked to maintain. It was a constant drumbeat of weeding, fertilizing, planting, tilling, rotating, and fighting off pests. Audrey didn't have much expertise in farming—that was one thing she'd left to others in Alessandra—but she was impressed by how efficient and cooperative their system was in Graysburg. And she could also see they could use a bit more sophistication to the way the town worked.

Quickly, she established herself as a well-traveled, educated woman who had a lot of knowledge to share. She worked with them on pickling, canning, and storing they'd practiced in Alessandra so that less food went to waste. She taught them basic navigation skills to help them efficiently get to the river and back, along with fishing and netting practices that would bring them relatively easy protein.

And she offered them training in basic defense, both at an individual level and at the town level. The people of Graysburg had considered themselves safe, but Audrey told them what she'd learned about the virus, and some of the challenges they could have if people saw what they had and decided to invade. There may not have been many organized colonies, but she warned them there were definitely marauders who wanted what they had, and the day would eventually come when they'd have to defend it.

Audrey's knowledge and resourcefulness gained her a great deal of respect in Graysburg. While they didn't have an official leadership position, it was only a few months before she had essentially taken charge. The townspeople looked to her for quick, confident decisions about major initiatives, and they were seeing their food rations and birth rate improving the longer she was there.

As her role became more important, she knew she needed special protection in the case of an invasion, and recruited the three men who were still with her to stand guard over her whenever possible. It was just a precaution, but she felt it was an important one. There was no wall in Graysburg, but she wasn't going to be the first one taken out if a horde came over the hill one day.

That started to become a problem, though. There were no guns in Graysburg and, thus, very limited means of hard enforcement of any rules she laid down. That meant less security, and her paranoia grew that the people might rebel against her, that maybe the threat wouldn't come so much from the outside as from inside the town. Privately, she railed against the people of Graysburg, how they were disloyal to her despite all she'd done for them, that they wouldn't know a garden bed from a hole to shit in if she hadn't shown up. She felt underappreciated, and vulnerable.

Meanwhile, the men's loyalty to her only intensified, though their presence had a way of isolating her. What had once been an open-door policy for anyone in town to come and ask questions or make requests had become a series of appointments and name checks. She lived in a small house and not the mansion she'd had in Alessandra, but she turned that into as much of a bunker as she'd ever had, hunkered down in a back bedroom most of the time, writing her theories on leadership and what she'd do with the town if given the sorts of resources she hoped she'd eventually have.

One night, while sitting at her desk, she heard a woman screaming, then saw people run by her window. She stood, craning her neck to try to see what was happening. Two blocks away, a crowd was forming. At first, she couldn't tell what the commotion was about. Had the invaders she had been certain would eventually come finally made their way into the town? Were they under siege? Audrey was doing an inventory of what she had. She felt she was as ready as she could be. Her men had knives, and most of the townspeople had some self-defense skills, with a few guns scattered here and there. Everyone had a copy of the crisis plan she'd drawn up, and people knew their roles. If they followed it, they would survive, and she'd be a hero.

But the people weren't following the plan. There was Tim, running to the east rather than manning the lookout tower. And Penelope, a statue in the middle of the road instead of grabbing her bow and loading a quiver. Why weren't they doing what they were told? Had they forgotten? Did they not understand the level of threat they were facing?

Then she smelled it. It tickled the hairs of her nostrils and clung like a barnacle to the back of her throat—smoke.

Her bedroom door swung open.

"There's an emergency, Ms. Reese," one of her men said. "The church is on fire, and it's serious."

Audrey shut her eyes and gritted her teeth, balling her hands into tight fists. She stormed out of the room, brushing against the man's shoulder as she went through the door.

"Do you have a plan for this?" he asked.

She stopped and took a deep breath.

"We'll do the best we can," she said, without turning around. "But I'm not sure it'll be good enough."

One of the other men opened the front door for her, and she stepped outside. From the street, she could see it clearly, the flames shooting into the sky, red, white, and blue set against the black of night. In a world that had become so dark, the large fire was like a beacon, casting light across a town enveloped in shadows. A beautiful disaster. Part of her just wanted to stand there and watch it burn, but she needed to join the others.

She sprinted toward the crowd that was gathered in the road. "How did this happen?" Audrey asked Penelope, staring up at the flames.

"Oh, Audrey…Um, no idea. We all just saw the fire and came out to see if there was anything we could do. But there are no firehoses or anything. And even if there were, would it be worth wasting so much water on one building?"

Audrey nodded. "It'll be sad to see it go."

Then she heard a voice from her right: "Look! Another one!"

Her head swiveled to where he was pointing. A house on the next block had caught fire, and the flames were growing. A gasp erupted from the crowd, and some began moving in that direction. Audrey heard noises from near that house, and coming closer. She thought she recognized the sound, but she couldn't immediately place it. It was like pattering on the ground, rapid and picking up the pace. She realized it was the sound of hooves hitting the ground just before she saw four men on horseback, wearing long, dark robes and hoods that obscured their faces. One of them leaped off his mount and stood looking at the crowd. The other men pulled long guns out from underneath their robes.

"We're claiming this village and everything in it," he said, his arms spread wide. He began to pace as the men pointed their guns toward everyone, then unlatched a large red container from the side of one of the horse's saddles. "We'd allow you all to stay under our direction. But, frankly, we just don't trust you. If you move without permission, you'll be shot."

He began pouring liquid from the canister on the ground. It smelled like gasoline, and her stomach pulled taut.

"Everyone, come in a little closer, as if you like each other," he ordered, allowing a small amount of liquid to leak out for each step as the terrified crowd huddled together. "We're gonna need a tight group. There ya go. Good job."

Audrey wondered if everyone else recognized the odor. It had been a while since any of them had probably smelled gasoline, but she figured it was unmistakable. And if she was right, there was no plan for getting them out of this.

She looked around, trying to determine how many people from the town were out there. She didn't know how late it was, but she didn't think it'd been dark for too long. Maybe a couple of hours. Lots of the people who came out had probably been awakened by the commotion, but some were likely still asleep. There were definitely at least a handful of people who weren't present. Had anyone noticed the invaders and grabbed their weapons to fight back? Could those weapons have been effective, if they were making a charge? Or had they merely fled in a panic?

The man completed a circle around the group, the pungent aroma of petrol gathering around them. He held the container in both arms, facing them.

"I don't really have any big speech to give," he said. "But I hope this shit life isn't the only one for you. Best of luck in the next."

He lifted the container over his head and splashed it into the crowd, gasoline soaking Audrey's hair and face and dousing everyone standing near her. A collective scream lifted from the group, as if they were just realizing their fate. Then the man stepped back, lit a match, and tossed it on the ground, igniting a circle of flames to light up around them.

For Audrey, the heat was overwhelming almost immediately, a blowtorch sweeping across her body, like it could strip the skin right off. Sparks jumped and fell, the heat radiating through the group in terrifying waves as the people pulled in tighter, trying to put as much distance as they could between them and the circle of fire. Audrey was frantic, imagining catching fire, burning as brightly as the sky above the church, the searing pain unrelenting as she screamed and begged for mercy, an immolation to any god that might be watching.

Screams reverberated around her, melding into a terrified warbling, seemingly impossible to be coming from the mouths of humans. There was no distinguishing one from another, the men from the women, the adults from the children, sitting atop their parent's shoulders to lift them further from the flames.

Next to her, Audrey felt Penelope begin to gyrate wildly; her long, dusty brown hair was ablaze. She was beating at her head, trying to put it out, but the gasoline intensified its persistence, spreading, engulfing her as she fell to the ground. Three people turned and started pounding on her, trying to beat back the flames. One man stripped off his shirt and pressed it against her, but his gasoline-kissed garment exploded in a blaze of its own, engulfing him as he crouched next to her on the ground.

A guttural scream escaping her lips, Audrey was suddenly yanked by the arm over the fire circle to her right. She felt herself lifted onto a man's shoulder and carried quickly away. She heard gunshots ring through the night as the screaming faded into the distance. She watched the flames around the group grow and multiply, even as it got further away, her head bouncing as her rescuer ran underneath her.

Close to a mile away, they reached the river that had been the lifeline for the town. The man stopped and laid her gently on the ground, the smell of pecans and spring blooms bringing her new life as her head nudged a root protruding from the dirt. She could hear the water gently flowing and bubbling a few feet away.

Her eyes adjusted to the darkness of the forest; she could see enough to recognize the man who knelt next to her, one of her protectors—Nathan, when he went by a name, but they rarely found the need for one. As he leaned in closer, she could see the skin on his face was red and broken in patches. She gasped and reached up to touch it, but he winced and turned away; she scanned down his body and saw his right arm had similar wounds.

Audrey pulled herself up to her knees and began crawling to the water, motioning for him to follow her. She bent forward and dipped her head into the water, trying to rinse the gasoline from her hair. When she brought her head back up, she pointed toward the water.

"You need to clean your face and arms," she said. "Do you need help?"

He shook his head, then cupped his hands and lowered them into the water, bringing it up to his face and splashing it. His head jerked back, but then seemed to relax. He closed his eyes and breathed heavily as he dipped his arms deep into the water, letting it rush over him.

She shuffled toward him and leaned in, careful not to touch his cheeks, kissing him gently on the forehead.

"Thank you," she said. He turned to her and pressed his lips together firmly, curling them in a slight smile and nodding almost imperceptibly.

"The other men are going to meet us here," he said, in a voice barely above a whisper. "What do we do now, Ms. Reese?"

She leaned back on her heels, and pulled on the soaked threads of her hair, lying heavy on her scalp. She looked deep into the woods, into the dark unknown.

"We walk," she said. "And I think I know where."

23

Stephanie banged on Father Hayden's front door, but there was no response. The house was quiet.

"Father Hayden!" she yelled, trying to lift her voice as high as it could go. "This is Stephanie Sloan. Michael is with me. We're just here to make sure you're okay. Please open the door!"

Nothing. Birds chirped behind them, and a slight breeze brushed past, rustling the limbs of the front-yard pine. Stephanie reached for the doorknob and twisted, but it was locked tight. That seemed unusual. Who locked their doors in Alessandra? On the other hand, maybe the person who *would* lock his door was the man who saw his gardener get attacked in his back yard that morning.

Stephanie thought about trying to kick down the door, but she figured it was a lot more difficult than the movies she remembered made it look. So she left the porch and ran around to the back of the house, Michael following behind.

She saw the garden with its fresh soil, lumpy and uneven; it looked like Derrick had been interrupted right in the middle of work, his shovel leaning against the shed he was building. The screen door swung open easily when Stephanie pulled on the handle. The question came to mind: If Father Hayden was afraid enough to hold himself up inside and lock the front door, why didn't he latch the back one?

From what Dennis had told them, the men he heard had likely been inside the house not much earlier. That meant they could still be inside with Father Hayden. Maybe armed. Stephanie looked at Michael and put a finger to her lips, then held the screen door as it slowly swung closed. There was a slight creak as it did, but Stephanie didn't think it was loud enough to hear upstairs.

Stephanie stepped as quietly as she could through the kitchen, and on to the staircase. Behind her, she saw Michael peeking around the corner into the living room. He met her eyes and nodded, mouthing "We're good."

Stephanie stayed on her toes as she took the steps one at a time. There was still no noise; if the men were up there, they were staying quiet, waiting to pounce. She could feel the tension roiling in her stomach, twisting into coils. Who were these men, and why were they doing this? What was going on in her town? How had she lost control of the situation so badly? She hated that she didn't know the answers.

Approaching the halfway point of the steps, she craned her neck, trying to see the landing at the top as soon as possible. If someone was waiting for her there, maybe she could catch a glimpse and prepare herself before he had the chance to attack. Little by little, she could see the floor; with each step, she braced herself to see a sign of a person, some movement, anything. Three steps from the top, she could see across the upstairs hall. It was empty.

Stephanie saw three doors in front of her, and she didn't know which one to enter. But she felt a tap on her shoulder, and Michael pointed to the end of the hall, holding up three fingers. He'd apparently been here before. *I guess he's a better Catholic than I am*, Stephanie thought as she pressed herself against the wall on the side of the hall where Father Hayden's room was, and Michael followed suit behind her. She slowly slid across the wall, staying high on her feet, trying to take advantage of the more secure floor bracings at the wall joint so the boards didn't creak.

There was still dead quiet in the house. Was it possible they'd find Father Hayden merely sleeping in his bed at the end of all this? Just resting after a busy morning? What a relief that would be. Maybe Dennis had mistaken what he heard, or Father Hayden talked in his sleep. Whatever. She just needed him to be safe, but she feared deep within her bones that he wasn't.

Next to his door, she looked back at Michael, and he nodded. She reached for the knob, pulling her arm back quickly to cover and clenching her teeth as she braced for...what? Gunshots? Screaming? A rushing onslaught of large, scary men? She wasn't sure. But whatever it was, it didn't come. The quiet was unbroken.

Stephanie peeked her head inside and scanned the room, largely empty and neat except for a fitfully unmade bed, sheets strewn on the floor, a couple seemingly knotted and hanging off the foot, a dank rotten stench hanging in the air. When she touched the sheets, she noticed they were damp. She walked to the right side of the room, while Michael flanked to the left. She bent down to look under the bed heard him slide the closet open. No Father Hayden.

"Window's open," Michael said, pushing the curtains aside as he peered out. "Little odd. Hasn't been all that warm today. Even rained hard earlier."

"Guess he could have just wanted some fresh air," Stephanie said, joining him at the window and sticking her head out to look around. She could see the top of the half-completed shed; it looked like there was some damage to the roof, as if something heavy had hit it and scraped off some of the shingles. A bird, maybe? Would that be big enough? Or was that just part of it being a work in progress? She thought she'd ask Derrick the next time she got the chance.

She could see down to the garden, and she thought about what had happened there. Derrick said he'd just been working and was blindsided by someone. He said he loaded some mulch into the garden, and then what? She tried to remember. Something was starting to bother her, but she couldn't figure out exactly what. She felt a tingling sensation looking down on the scene. Something wasn't right.

Stephanie thought back to the conversation with Derrick. He said he had put in the mulch, then was digging with his shovel when he was hit. She looked down again.

Then it hit her—the shovel was leaning against the shed. Yet Derrick was working with it when he was knocked cold. So he didn't place it there, unless he was wrong. It was possible the men picked it up and leaned it there after the assault. Why would they do that, though? There was another possibility that came to mind. And it was one that nearly knocked her to the floor.

24

"You're gonna have to repeat that," Zac said, pausing for a moment, then walking quickly toward Andy, who was sitting on the top step of Zac's front porch. Andy's mouth curled in a crooked smile.

"Audrey's back," he said. "Showed up at the front gate a few hours ago. With quite the entourage too, I hear."

Zac pressed two fingers to his creased temple.

"What do you mean, she's 'back'? Did Stephanie actually let her inside?"

"Yeah, she's here. Just a few blocks away, in the old Peterson place on Pine."

"You're sure?" Zac felt almost dizzy. He'd given up on Audrey even being alive, much less returning to Alessandra.

"I mean, I haven't seen her myself, if that's what you're asking. But that's the word around the campfire. When I heard, I came here to tell you. Been waiting for a while. Where've you guys been?"

Zac looked at William, who folded his arms across his chest.

"I've gotta see this shit," Zac said, ignoring the question. "You said she's in the old Greene house?"

"That's what I was told. But I'm not sure you're gonna be able to just walk right up there and bring her a housewarming gift."

"I think I'll do fine." Zac started to walk in the direction of Pine Street.

"Don't I get a thanks?" Andy yelled from behind them.

Zac held a middle finger over his shoulder and never broke stride.

As he walked, Zac's mind tumbled over itself, considering what Audrey's return might mean for the town. And, more importantly, for him.

The last time he saw Audrey, he was straddling her on her bed, his knife gleaming as blood ran from her chin, down the blade and onto the sheets. He had waited for that moment ever since Audrey had forced his wife and two daughters from his home, stealing the guardrails of his life, the people who gave it all meaning. Audrey claimed they were going somewhere safe until the virus was under control, that this was what needed to happen for the people of Alessandra to survive over the long term. Separating them meant that the whole population couldn't be wiped out at once, and they'd be reunited once the virus was eradicated.

He had walked into her room that day holding Paul's butcher knife, wanting to force her to tell him where his wife and daughters had been taken. He had been ready to do whatever he could to get them back. If she'd told him they were 1,000 miles away, he'd have driven the knife into her chest and then started walking until his shoes turned to dust.

But, looking up at him, her arms and feet tied to the bed, she told him the truth—his wife and daughters were dead, along with the other women and children she'd sent off. She said they couldn't produce enough resources for everyone, and she thought the men would be more useful. They had to cull the population, so they left a few dozen women and children alone, miles from Alessandra, with nothing but the clothes on their backs. They had no survival skills. Audrey knew they'd never live for more than a couple of weeks, but she was okay with that. She said her responsibility was to Alessandra, and sacrificing a few to save the rest was a difficult but necessary decision.

In that moment, fighting tears back, rage turning him into a pressure cooker needing a release, all Zac wanted was to make her suffer and then die. What else was left? His wife and daughters—his reason for living—were gone forever. They died a miserable, shivering, stomach-churning death, likely watching others shrivel up and die around them. What had that been like? What terror did they feel as they were left behind, knowing they had no way to get back to town, that they probably didn't even know which direction to go? How long had they survived on scavenging berries, maybe eating some insects and finding a stream to drink from? What had that moment been like when they finally gave up and laid down in the woods, Karen clutching Brittany and Corinne close to her chest, listening to the last breaths of their tragic lives? Had she hoped maybe Zac would come for them? Had she told the girls he was on his way, even if she didn't believe it?

That rage had distracted him, though. All he could think was how he wanted to hurt Audrey, to maim her, then watch the life drain slowly from her body. But she got a foot loose somehow, and struck him between the legs, driving him hard up and then tumbling over the side of the bed. The next thing he remembered was waking up in the hospital, Stephanie changing a large bandage on his head and telling him he was lucky to be alive.

He knew he wasn't the only one. Audrey had escaped him that day.

Was she actually back? He could hardly believe it—not only that she was still alive, but that Stephanie allowed her back inside the walls after everything that happened. Did

Stephanie think she'd changed?

If so, it was just one more piece of evidence that she wasn't fit to lead the town. She was endangering everybody by letting a lunatic inside the walls. Zac knew exactly what Audrey was capable of, and he was ready to pay her a visit.

25

Stephanie pushed past Michael, nearly knocking him off his feet, and burst through the bedroom door into the hall. She hit the stairs in a dead sprint; it was like she was barely touching each step on the way down. At the bottom, she turned the corner to her left and ran through the kitchen to the back screen door, ramming through it onto the small porch.

There was the garden she'd seen from above. When she'd been down there before, nothing had struck her as strange; her mind had been too focused on what might be waiting for her inside the house. But looking down from the second floor, the entire picture came into focus: the lumpy mulch of the garden, the damaged shed roof, and that neatly placed shovel. *Somebody* had done that.

The screen door swung open, and Michael stepped onto the porch. Stephanie was standing next to the garden, and looked over at him.

"What was that about?" he asked, bewildered. "You just about shoved me out the window."

"What?" Stephanie looked back at the shovel, her head beginning to ache. "Oh. Yeah. Sorry about that. I just…come over here for a minute."

Michael approached her and looked at the shovel.

"I don't think Derrick propped that shovel up there," she

said. "He told us he was using it when he was hit in the head. Which means somebody else went out of their way to lean it up like that."

Michael tilted his head and frowned.

"Well, is it possible he's just wrong? He did take a pretty serious blow to the head."

Stephanie exhaled loudly, scratching her head. "It's possible. Something just seems…off."

"Or maybe Father Hayden found it lying there and leaned it against the shed before…well, before whatever."

Stephanie nodded slightly, and they both stood, staring silently at the shovel as if it would start talking, like the mulch still stuck to it would begin reshaping itself into words that would point them to the answer.

"Wait," Michael said. "What about this?"

He walked toward the back of the shed and picked up a mulch bag, seemingly drained dry and flapping impotently in the breeze.

"Didn't Derrick say he still had a good bit of mulch left?" he asked.

Stephanie's heart leaped in her chest.

"Half a bag."

"Do you see half a bag sitting anywhere?"

They both looked around the shed. She met Michael's gaze, her eyes big and the muscles of her neck tightening into a noose; he shrugged.

Eyes still fixed on the garden, Stephanie reached her hands out and grabbed the shovel. She was walking as if in a trance. This couldn't be reality. Her mind needed some way to protect herself from what she might find, from being in this place, and from what she was about to do. She was asleep in her bed, surrounded by a mound of fluffy pillows like she had before the virus stole those creature comforts from their lives. Everything was white, peaceful, the sun cutting bright lines just across her chest, telling her it was time to roll over and hit the snooze button, then get up and put on a pot of coffee. She'd wander back to her room and crawl back into bed for two or three more snoozes before the aroma of roasted Colombian beans wafted in, beckoning her to embrace the day.

But that wasn't reality. In the world she couldn't escape, she was holding a shovel, looking down at mounds of fresh mulch that stank of rotting fruit and human shit, the stench crawling into her nose and settling into her throat. Was there another smell she couldn't quite identify? She wasn't sure, but she was afraid she was about to find out.

Stephanie lifted the shovel, her hands shaking. Michael stood beside the shed, a blank expression on his face. As a doctor, she'd seen some shit in her day; she had stories that still shook her, stories she'd never tell anyone who wasn't a medical professional. But there was something about the comfort of a hospital that made even the craziest things seem like just part of the normal course of events, like there was a bubble around the place that turned the extraordinary ordinary. Within those walls, anything was possible, and everything had already happened.

Standing here in the priest's yard, though, it was all so surreal, like finding an elephant in a punch bowl. It just didn't fit. The world had gone askew. This wasn't what was supposed to happen. Not today. Not in Alessandra.

Stephanie pushed the tip of the shovel into the mulch, piercing it an inch deep, and felt no resistance. She flipped some of the mulch away, and only saw more underneath it. As much as she wanted to resist it, she was going to have to go deeper if she was going to figure out if her instinct had been correct.

She stuck the shovel a bit further down, and thought she might have felt something there. She moved the shovel, and it definitely scraped against something. She closed her eyes and sucked in a deep breath, salty sweat dripping off her forehead and down her cheeks.

With a flick of her wrists, she flung a chunk of mulch to her right, into the yard, and then dropped the shovel, stepping back from a human finger pointing at her from the garden.

26

Lying in bed, Audrey heard a man's voice outside. Muffled and somewhat distant at first, she could tell it was getting closer. He was yelling something, and it sounded like her name was part of it. He didn't sound like he wanted to welcome her home.

She rolled out of bed and slipped her feet into a pair of loafers, then went through her door to head toward the front of her house. As she stepped out of the bedroom, one of her men stepped forward to block her path.

"We may have a problem, Ms. Reese," he told her, as the voice got louder and closer, she thought probably on her block now. "Just stay here. We'll send him away."

She recognized the voice now, screaming her name and demanding she show her face. It was Zac. She remembered well the last encounter she'd had with him; she was surprised he'd survived. When she left him bleeding on her bedroom floor, she thought that was the end for him.

Paul had thought Zac was useful, but Audrey hadn't been anxious to work with him when she was in charge. She felt he was too volatile, unpredictable, and emotionally driven. He didn't think far enough ahead, and would take on more than he could handle because of it. But he probably thought he could run Alessandra better than she could. He was the Dunning-Kruger Effect at work—he didn't know enough to know what he didn't know.

Audrey recognized that she'd caused him a lot of pain, but she still maintained that banishing the women and children was the most prudent decision. It wasn't personal; she hadn't wanted to harm Zac's family specifically. It was all about the greater good. She knew love could blind you, and maybe she couldn't expect him to understand her reasoning in the moment, but she hoped he'd gain a better appreciation over time for the difficult position she'd been in. His shrill screams while marching toward her house suggested that he hadn't.

She stretched to look over the guard's shoulder and see out the front window. She could see Zac approaching the house from the street, and her two other men stalking across the yard toward him. She rocked back on her heels and looked at the man in front of her, the burn scars tracing rivers across his face.

"Let him in," she said.

"Um, Ms. Reese, I think that's a bad idea."

"Audrey!" she heard Zac yelling, right outside now. "Get off me! Get your fucking hands off me! Audrey! If you're in there, come outside! We need to talk. Get the fuck off me!"

"I don't want him screaming his head off in my yard, and I don't want him hurt. Do you hear me?"

He nodded.

She placed a hand on his shoulder. "I suggest you let me go."

He stood still as she brushed past him, to walk out the front door. She saw the two men were carrying Zac away from the house.

"Let him down!" she ordered, her hands cupped around her mouth. The men stopped and looked back, still holding his feet off the ground.

"Audrey!" Zac's feet were swinging six inches from the

grass. "Call off your fucking goons!"

They looked at her, and she nodded. The men let Zac go, but still stood between him and Audrey, arms folded across their chests. She stepped down off the porch and walked across the yard toward them.

"Good to see you again, Zac," she said. "Surprised I'm alive?"

"I might ask the same of you."

Audrey smiled. "What is it you want? Just to see my face again?"

"Yeah. I can barely see the mark from where I cut it open."

Audrey touched her jawline and could faintly feel the scar she'd nearly forgotten was there.

"What are you here for, Zac?"

"What am *I* here for? What are *you* here for? After all this time? After the way you left?"

"We just need a place to temporarily shelter, replenish our resources, and then we'll be on our way."

Zac did nothing to conceal his laugh.

"Oh, the hell you will. Is that the story you told Stephanie?"

"Believe what you want, but it's no story. We were going to die out there. Stephanie knew that, and I appreciate her helping us. We're going to do what we can to repay that, and then move on."

"For fuck's sake. If Stephanie believes that load of shit, I'm even more right about her than I thought I was."

Audrey looked down the street to her left and right. She didn't see anyone.

"I don't want to cause a scene out here, Zac. Would you like to come inside and talk?"

He rolled his eyes and took a step back. "You can't be trusted, Audrey. I guess your street toughs here haven't figured that out yet, but you're a fucking snake. Paul always said he didn't trust you, and neither should I. He gave me the knife I used to cut you, and would have killed you with. You betrayed us both, so I guess he was right. Say what you will about your brother, but that man was singularly focused on this town's well-being. You cared more about your own damn reputation and spinning shit to help yourself than you did making Alessandra better. And now here you are again."

Audrey barely moved as Zac talked, controlling her breathing and letting him finish his rant before she made a move to speak. More often than not, she'd found it was the best way to deal with men questioning her leadership—let them show their cards first. They couldn't help themselves.

"I'm sorry you feel that way," she said, her face belying any emotion. "But I've always only wanted what was best for the people of this town, and everything I'm telling you now is the truth. You're welcome to not believe me, but that won't change anything. I'm sure we'll be crossing paths again soon. Maybe it can be under more pleasant circumstances."

She extended her hand between the men, toward Zac. He looked at it, then up at her, and turned to walk in the opposite direction.

"Go fuck yourself," he yelled over his shoulder.

27

Stephanie picked up a bullhorn from behind a podium on the stage in Alessandra's town square, brushing a light coating of pollen off its surface. She could see the first groups of people walking toward the square in the gathering dusk. Michael came up from behind her and touched her shoulder.

"Hey," she said, turning to look back at him. "How long until everybody knows to come here?"

"Shouldn't be long. Nick and George are helping to get the word out. They're telling people to break off whatever they're doing and come to the square."

"Okay. That's good. Thanks, Michael."

He lowered his hand to her back. "Nervous?"

"Wouldn't it be weird if I weren't?" She tried to smile, but she wasn't sure it looked that way. He gently rubbed her back, a gesture he'd done a million times over the years but still almost gave her chills in the moment.

"What are you gonna say?"

"Oh, I don't know. Father Hayden's dead, there are murderous thugs on the loose, and you're all gonna die. How's that sound?"

"Succinct."

Michael looked out over the front of the stage, and Stephanie followed his gaze. She could see a crowd starting to gather, maybe thirty-five or forty people now. Hank was apparently well enough to get out of his hospital bed; he had the stiff gait of a man whose midsection was heavily bandaged, but he'd made it. She flicked a hand at him in a sort of half-wave and smiled, then looked down at the stage.

"But, seriously…I'm gonna tell them the truth, as we know it. No more, and no less. They deserve to be informed. Simple as that."

"Okay." Michael nodded. "I think that's the right call. People are gonna be scared."

"So am I."

Michael stood and began to walk to the stairs that led off the stage.

"Oh, Michael," Stephanie called after him. "Just be up here with me. When I'm talking. Okay?"

He gave a quick bob of his head and scampered down the steps to the asphalt below.

Placing the bullhorn on the top of the podium, Stephanie looked out over it into the square. The crowd was growing quickly, over eighty people deep. From her vantage point, she could see several of the town's streets, and all of them had small groups of people—couples, families, a few children on their father's shoulders—walking in her direction. She knew these faces, all of them. She'd set their broken arms, given them flu shots, even helped to bring some of them into the world at the hospital. They were an integral part of her life, and had been since the beginning, really. She loved Alessandra, never more than at this moment. She loved that they all came, that they showed her that respect. There was pride there. She hoped that would help to carry them through this, whatever it was.

The people were milling about in the square, some standing silently or sitting on the ground, others talking to friends they might not see as much as they'd like. The square used to be the center of activity in Alessandra, where they'd have farmers markets and craft fairs, festivals and celebrations, but it'd taken on a more funereal feel since the massacre. In addition to all the lives, that was one more thing Paul had taken from them—a sense of place and belonging in a space that should have been their own. He had turned it into a place of mourning. Behind where the crowd was forming, Stephanie could see the wilting flowers and crosses, adorned with scrawled signs, some clearly by the uncertain hands of children, saying "We love u, Sally," "We'll never forget," or "God gained an angel." She noticed people didn't even seem to like looking back there; looking at the memorial forced you to remember, and sometimes it was easier to forget.

As the last stragglers made their way into the square, settling in with the crowd of at least a couple hundred people, Stephanie stepped from behind the podium, holding the bullhorn. Michael came up the stairs and smiled at her, then sat in a chair at the back of the stage.

She drew in a deep breath and looked for friendly faces to gain some comfort. She made eye contact with Hank, who raised his chin and stuck a thumb in the air, then lightly patted his side. She found Nick—looking a bit disheveled, his hair spiked haphazardly, hurrying over to a spot on the outskirts of the crowd—and Dennis, who was staring ahead blankly, standing alone and stiff in the back left corner. Walt—one of the town's oldest surviving residents, who still ran Alessandra's only bar—was predictably there with a glass of something brown in his wrinkled hand. Gathered together in the very back stood Audrey, the three men who came with her, and George; they seemed to be talking and laughing, likely catching up from earlier times.

Stephanie looked up at the sky, which was a bruise blue as dusk approached. It was time.

"Thank you all for coming," she said, her voice reverberating into the air. "I know this isn't something we've done a lot of, but I...*Michael* and I..." She turned to him and smiled. "We thought it was important, given the circumstances.

"As virtually all of you know, Alessandra has been through a hell of a lot over the past few years. We've done remarkably well in surviving a worldwide plague that appears to have wiped out the vast majority of human population. We've pulled together, worked smartly and efficiently, and figured out a way to carve out a new version of our community, one I think we're all very proud to call home. I love this place, as you do. This is where I grew up, and this is where I want to live out my days."

Stephanie closed her eyes and exhaled, her hands clenching and unclenching.

"And that's why it's important that we address this latest threat in a direct and transparent manner. This time, it comes from inside these walls. I don't mean to alarm you, but I do need you to be vigilant—there is someone in the town who suddenly seems to mean harm to others. He—or she—may very well be standing here right now."

A murmur floated up from the crowd, with people looking around and moving restlessly, the nervous chatter growing in intensity. Stephanie raised the bullhorn above her head, then brought it back to her lips.

"I know this is hard to hear. But please, everybody, let me continue. Hank is standing right here near the stage, and he was the first victim, getting jumped out of nowhere two days ago. He suffered broken ribs and a few bruises, but we're all so thankful he's going to be okay. Derrick was next, taking a blow to the head while he was working in Father Hayden's garden early this morning; he's in the hospital, getting the best of care. We don't know if there will be any long-term effects. And then there's Father Hayden."

She lowered her head and looked at the stage, trying to gather herself. In the hospital, she'd told dozens of families and individuals that their loved one was dead. You were taught as a young doctor how to handle it; it never became easy—nor should it—but it was part of the job. Stephanie thought back to her training: *don't use euphemisms, use a comforting voice, look them in the eyes, allow them to grieve.*

But that was almost always with a small group of family members in a private room, where she had hopefully been able to prepare them for the possibility ahead of time. This was standing on a stage, telling an entire town that one of the most well-respected members of their community was not only dead, but had been murdered—by someone who lived among them.

Looking out over the crowd of anxious faces, strained frowns and hands pressed to mouths, she questioned if this had been the best way to do this. She had talked it over with Michael earlier, and they knew you couldn't keep a lid on news like this very long. People would quickly figure out that Father Hayden was missing; then, Stephanie and Michael would have to either lie about it, or tell a few people, letting the narrative get out of their control. There was no easy way to break the news, but at least this way, everyone found out at the same time. There would be no crazy rumors or conspiracy theories. *This* was what happened.

The anguish, though, was more than she'd anticipated. She needed to provide comfort to hundreds, when she couldn't figure out how to provide it to herself.

"I can't tell you how sad it makes me to report that Father Hayden…is not with us anymore. Michael and I found him dead this afternoon, at his home. And we have reason to believe he was murdered."

There were screams and gasps, wailing people falling to

the ground. Stephanie could feel herself go glassy eyed, seeing the chaos she had unleashed. To her right, she noticed some people leaving, hurrying back toward their homes. Among them, she saw Zac and William, breaking into a sprint.

She felt her breath picking up, chest heaving like an accordion, throat turning dry. The crowd was a moving, shifting entity, panicked people trying to come to terms with what they'd heard. She looked over the top of them at the sun set a fiery orange, the horizon slowly swallowing it, darkness not far away.

Then she felt a hand on her shoulder.

"Are you okay?" Michael jarred her back to the moment.

"I—Yeah." She quickly rattled her head back and forth. "I'm fine. This is just too much. I didn't expect this reaction."

"It's fine. You've got this. Just keep talking. Keep them engaged. They need leadership. Give them that. You're the right person for this. Okay?"

Stephanie straightened her back and nodded, brushing the hair back out of her face.

"Yeah," she said, looking at the bullhorn in her hand. "Thanks."

She brought it up to her mouth as Michael took a few steps away.

"Stay with me, people of Alessandra! Please, listen for a few more moments. This is important for you to hear."

The incessant murmur began to die down, and Stephanie saw heads turn. A few people helped to hush others, and eyes gradually gravitated back to her, some people even stopping from down the street and hurrying back to hear. She had their attention. She could feel their pleading eyes, looking for a reason to hope, a reason not to fear for their lives. Begging for reassurance. She knew she needed to dig deep within herself and find it for them; she was the only one who could.

"I know this has been difficult for you to hear. It was

heartbreaking for us to find. Father Hayden was a wonderful man, who helped so many of us through challenging times. He was hard working, selfless, and loving to everyone he came into contact with. He deserved a much better fate. He was one of us. An Alessandran. And justice *will* be handed down to his killer, swiftly and without mercy. I *guarantee* you that."

She glanced back at Michael, who nodded.

"We've weathered storms before, and we'll do so again. Once, it was a virus, and now it's another type—the virus of evil. We never thought it would land here, but no walls can completely keep it away. Evil doesn't have to scale concrete or overpower security to invade your midst. It can lurk in men's hearts and wait for the right time to show itself. Today, we're facing it head on. There's no denying that. How do we fight against it? By banding together, by watching each other's backs and staying vigilant. Continue to live your lives. Continue to do the work that matters so much to all of us. But keep your eyes open. Watch for people who are in the wrong places. Whoever did this dropped Hank and Derrick's unconscious bodies in front of Saint Francis under the cover of morning darkness, and nobody saw a thing.

"So if you see something out there, say something. You can, of course, come to me or Michael, but just get the word out however you can, and to whomever you can. The people who are doing this are hiding in the shadows. They're counting on our population being sparse, and for that to leave more shadows than light. But let's throw up a big fat spotlight on this town. Let's make this the most hostile possible place for evil to live. Give it no oxygen. Strangle it, and it *will* die."

She could see some head nods in the crowd, eyes still fixed on her. The chaos from earlier seemed like it was replaced by something resembling resolve. They were here for this moment, with her, with each other.

"I'm proud of you all. You're responsible for creating the kind of community I know can survive this. There's no group I'd rather face this with than all of you. We pull together in tough times and do what's necessary to defeat the threat. This place, this town, it matters to each and every one of you. And that makes my heart full, looking at your eyes out there this evening, knowing that you've got my back, and I've got yours. Evil may not know it yet, but it picked the wrong fight. Love you all. Thank you."

Stephanie laid the bullhorn down and placed her right hand across her chest, then extended it out to the crowd in a wave. Most of the people applauded, as Michael walked up beside her.

"How'd I do?" she asked.

"I knew you'd nail it."

"Still a lot of work from here."

"We can do it. Together. You good?"

She looked over the crowd as the applause died down.

"Yeah. I'm just gonna sit here and think for a few minutes."

"Sure." Michael started to walk away, then stopped. "Think William's running scared right now?"

She smiled. "If he's not, he should be."

28

"Michael and I found him dead this afternoon at his home. And we have reason to believe he was murdered."

Zac heard the words, and the crowd erupted into a frenzy around him, with shocked gasps and impotent screams into the sky. A woman fell onto her knees at Zac's feet, and he leaped out of the way, bumping into William.

"This is a fucking nightmare," Zac said. "We've got to figure some shit out. Come on."

Zac stepped over the woman, and William followed him through the square and into the street, both of them running to the next block. When they got a couple of houses away, they ducked behind one and sat on the ground.

"What do we do?" William asked. "It took them all of maybe a half hour to find Father Hayden's body. That was a stupid place to bury him, and now—"

"If you had a better fucking idea, you sure as hell didn't bring it up at the time. We had to do *something*. Do you know how long it takes to dig a goddamn grave from solid soil? Would we have been better off just dumping him on the ground somewhere?"

"You know as well as I do there's a small, hidden exit out to the woods behind Walt's bar."

"Yeah. And what? We were supposed to just lug a dead body all the way there in broad daylight without being seen, then squeeze him through? Maybe if you had planned better, we could have gotten him out there *alive*, and *then* killed him. Would have had a lot more options then. But no. He told me he could identify you. Knew exactly who tied him up there, because you weren't careful. You're *never* fucking careful. And Father Hayden's dead because of it."

William brought his knees up to his chest and looked at the ground. His hands clutched the sides of his head, yanking at his hair.

"Oh, for fuck's sake, don't turn into a blubbering mess on me," Zac said, punching him in the shoulder. "There's no time for that. You need to figure out what to do in order to save yourself, and I'm willing to help."

William let his hands fall and turned to Zac. "What about you? You're involved in this just as much as I am."

"William, we've been over this." Zac rolled his eyes. "You're the only one who's identified. They'll easily connect you to Derrick, and then to Father Hayden. I'm clean." He raised his hands and showed his palms to William, flipping his hands around and rubbing them together.

"Stay with me, people of Alessandra!" The voice came barreling in from behind them, and both of them turned in that direction. It was Stephanie, pleading with them to return to the square and listen. What else was there to say?

Zac crawled in front of William and got to the front edge of the house, peering around the corner to see the square. He could see people turning toward the stage, and others who had started to leave scampering back. She'd gotten their attention, and she was speaking again. He couldn't hear it all clearly from where he was, but he could tell she was droning on with some nonsense about how great Alessandra was. Trying to talk about how they were in this together. It was the kind of thing a leader should do.

"I've got an idea," he said to William. "Follow me."

As Stephanie kept talking, they ran around the back of the house and through yards toward the square, coming around the rear of the stage, where the old City Hall still sat abandoned, an edifice Zac thought symbolized Alessandra as well as any other.

They crept along the City Hall's front wall, staying close to it in order to stay out of sight. But Zac wondered if it was even necessary. All eyes were fixed on Stephanie, whose voice was hitting a crescendo. He could tell she was feeling the moment, drawing off the energy of the crowd to try and get them on her side. She was going to basically enlist them all as deputies to try and catch William—and maybe Zac, too. That was going to throw his original plan awry, but he thought he saw an opportunity here to skip a few steps and accelerate it.

"And that makes my heart full, looking at your eyes out there this evening, knowing that you've got my back, and I've got yours. Evil may not know it yet, but it picked the wrong fight. Love you all. Thank you."

Zac couldn't see Stephanie, but he could hear the crowd break into applause and knew she was wrapping up her speech. The time was now.

"Stick right here until I say your name," Zac said. "Got it?"

"Um, yeah. What are we doing?"

"I'm saving your ass. That's what we're doing. When I say your name, come up on stage with me."

"How will I hear—"

But Zac was already focused on his next move, and started walking toward the steps up to the stage.

When he reached the top, he saw Michael was talking to Stephanie. Zac walked up from behind them; neither noticed him before he reached around them and grabbed the bullhorn, then walked past the podium toward the other side of the stage. He heard Stephanie start to say something, but he was already bringing the bullhorn up to his mouth.

"Before you leave, ladies and gents," Zac said, seeing people stop and eyes pivot in his direction. "Can I have just a few more minutes of your attention?"

Zac knew he didn't have the same well of goodwill that Stephanie did with the people of Alessandra. Nor did he have the same gravitas that she was able to summon when she needed it. He didn't have a doctorate hanging on the wall of an office anywhere. He just considered himself a plain old military dummy. But he also knew military dummies could rise to the occasion. He'd been underestimated before, especially by people who thought their formal education trumped his experience in places like Afghanistan, Ukraine, and Beirut. He knew Paul had believed in him, though. And he sure as hell believed in himself.

Behind him, he could see Stephanie and Michael nearly frozen. They were too committed to being "fair" to come yank the bullhorn out of his grip. Paul would have never let the bullhorn fall into someone else's hands; if it had, though, he'd have thought nothing of tackling the person and driving his head into the stage to teach him a lesson. This was another example of what Zac couldn't stand about these two—They *should* have taken him down, but he knew as well as everyone else that they wouldn't. Especially not in front of the whole town. It'd look bad. And that was the last thing they'd want.

"Thanks for sticking around. Why should Stephanie have all the fun today, right? I think you all deserve to hear more than one side of this story. Heck, I'm sure Stephanie and Michael agree. They're fair folks. So, let me give you another perspective of what's been happening these past few crazy days.

"Now, of course, it's terrible what's happened to these men. I'm happy to see Hank is feeling well enough to join us.

I heard you took quite a smack to the head, my friend. I'm
sure that makes it tough to remember everything accurately,
and I know that's gotta be frustrating. The same with
Derrick, who I hope will recover quickly from his own
incident. And, yes, I was as shocked as the rest of you to hear
that our beloved Father Hayden is no longer with us. He
really was a wonderful man. I'm not sure I ever…"

Zac paused, bringing his hand up to cover his mouth and
looking away from the crowd. He pressed his eyes tightly shut
and tried to force tears to come. He thought he felt just a
slight bit of dampness around his eyes, but he wasn't sure if it
was enough for anyone in the crowd to notice, so he swiped
his sleeve across his eyes, then bit his lip hard before bringing
the bullhorn back up.

"I'm sorry. It's just that…Why did it have to be Father
Hayden? His is a void that will be felt in Alessandra for a
long, long time. I know none of us will ever forget how much
he sacrificed for us, the nights he spent ministering to the sick
and depressed, the way he brought God into our lives when
we needed that hope the most. And he's looking down from
a prime seat in heaven, smiling at us right now. That much I
know."

Zac spun and walked to his left, looking at Stephanie and
Michael, still standing together by the podium.

"'Why did it have to be Father Hayden?' is a good
question for those of us still here, though. It's a good
question for Michael and Stephanie, who I guess are the
leaders of this town. Because we all need leaders, right? We
need direction. We need discipline. And we need to feel safe.
Did Father Hayden feel safe, murdered in his own home?
Did Derrick feel safe, just doing his job? Did *you* feel safe,
Hank, walking down the street, minding your own business?"

He pointed at Hank, who stared blankly back at him as
the darkness started to set over the square. Zac stopped

pacing toward Stephanie and Michael, and spun back in the opposite direction.

"Do the rest of you feel safe now? Who's next? Whoever's doing this, why would they stop at three? Michael and Stephanie would like you to think they can find this murderer who shouldn't be allowed to even *live*, much less stay a member of our community. But *can* they? This happened on their watch. Are they the right ones now to clean up the mess? And let me tell you something else. They have a suspect. They have someone they want you to think did it. They're gonna serve him up on a silver platter to you, based upon the word of one man—Hank—who, while I'm sure is honest and well meaning, can't possibly be sure about who hurt him. That suspect is former chief police officer and military veteran, William Greene."

Zac paused, waiting for William to come on stage. He rolled his eyes.

"*Come on up*, William. William." Zac let the bullhorn fall from his mouth and sighed loudly. "Where are you, William?"

Finally, he saw William scampering out from behind the stage and quickly climbing the stairs, walking up next to Zac, who threw his arm around his shoulders.

"Good to see you, William. So, Michael and Stephanie want you all to believe that this humble public servant who doesn't have a violent bone in his body and who has done so much to protect this town…suddenly turned into a murderer? Of a man he greatly admired, and sought counsel from on numerous occasions? William is a devout Catholic. Isn't that right, William?"

Zac held the bullhorn up to William's mouth and nodded to him.

"I'm a devout Catholic," William said, barely audible, into the cone.

"I, for one, think Michael and Stephanie just want to give

you *someone*, and they're willing to badmouth great man in order to do it. And I think we need to wonder if that's what we want in our leaders. Do we want leaders who value the *illusion* of safety, the *illusion* of order, over making the hard choices and actions that result in *true* safety and order? And, as I'm sure most of you have heard by now, Stephanie has allowed Audrey back inside, after everything we went through with her. After all the trauma, all the death, and the mothers, the wives, the children she marched away to die. Does *that* make you feel safer? Does having her here benefit us, or was Stephanie just too weak to turn someone away at the gate?"

Chatter wafted up from the crowd as heads looked around, then finally faced the back, where Audrey was standing and looking straight ahead. Her men pulled into a tighter circle around her, their shoulders and backs stiff.

"Regardless of how her decision on Audrey turns out, is that a chance we should take? Was that the best call *for Alessandra*? As a military veteran myself, I know all about the discipline it takes to run a unit, and to secure a border. And I don't know about you, but I'll be locking my damn door and sleeping with a gun under my pillow tonight for the first time in years."

They were almost out of light, but Zac could see just enough to pick up some nods in the crowd, at least within the first few rows.

"Just something to think about. I didn't mean to interrupt or anything, but I thought this was important, and I wanted to share while we had you all here. Stephanie and I don't see eye to eye on a lot of things, but we definitely agree on this— we love you all and wish you all the best. Now go get some rest. And, above all, *be safe*."

A nervous chatter emanating from the stunned crowd, Stephanie could feel the anger boiling up inside of her. She couldn't believe what she'd heard, but she hadn't seen any reasonable way to stop it from happening. It was a slow-motion train wreck occurring as she watched, and she was helpless to stop it.

As Zac waved to the crowd and William uncomfortably scampered down the stairs off the front of the stage, Stephanie lunged toward Zac and touched his arm.

"We need to talk for a minute," she said, then walked to a darker spot toward the back of the stage next to Michael. She saw a wry smile on Zac's face as he joined them.

"What the *hell* was that?" Stephanie asked. "It was important that people left here feeling *better*, not worse. I'm trying to be reassuring, not scare them half to fucking death. And you *undermine* that? Why?"

Zac shrugged. "Guess I'm more interested in them knowing the truth than in pumping them full of happy drugs."

"What does *that* mean?" Stephanie squinted, her mouth twisted in a grimace. "Telling them they're in danger and we all need to be a part of the solution isn't fucking 'happy drugs.' It's *true*. But it lets them feel like they're part of the solution. Which *they are*. Or they *can be*. You're just telling them 'The world sucks, now go hide in a corner.'"

"Well, maybe the world *does* suck, and maybe they *do* need to hide in a corner for a while," Zac still had this smirk on his face that made Stephanie want to slap him as hard as she could. "And if so, it's because *you* let it get that way."

"*Me?*" Stephanie gestured wildly with her hands.

"Yes, *you*," Zac said, sounding calm. "I know you think you're perfect, but you're not, even with your fancy Ivy doctor degree. Even *you* can make mistakes. And here, the evidence that you made multiple ones is Father Hayden's dead body. Innocent men never died under Audrey's wa—"

"She *marched a bunch of women and children into the woods and left them to die*, for fuck's sake! Your *wife and daughters* were among them! You just talked about this!"

"Come on, Stephanie. I was just using that to make a point to the people. The fact is, that was a tough decision made in the best interests of the town. You can agree or disagree with it. Obviously, the fact that I lost my wife and daughters makes it hard for me to support it. But, no matter how you feel, that's not the same as an upstanding member of the community being murdered in his own bed."

"What could I have done to prevent…" Still incredulous, Stephanie started to speak, but then something struck her. "Wait. What do you mean he was murdered in his bed? Where'd *that* come from?"

Zac blinked, his expression going blank. "That's what you said in your speech."

"No. I never said that. I didn't even *know* that. Still don't. But you sounded like you do."

"No, I don't know anything." He waved his hand dismissively. "If you didn't say it, I must have just assumed since you said you found him at his home. The point is, Father Hayden is dead, and that's *your* responsibility. You also have no idea who did it, and I've heard the rumors just like everyone else that you're trying to pin it all on poor William, despite no real evidence. And, call me crazy or stupid or whatever, but I feel like people deserve to know that. And they *should* be scared. *Damn* scared."

Stephanie pressed two fingers to her temple and closed her eyes. "Look, Zac." She shook her head and exhaled loudly. "I know we've got a complicated history. You let yourself be a hired goon for that Paul, who just wanted to kill everyone who got in his way. You came after me that night in the hospital loading dock, and I had to subdue you. And still, I saved your life. I nursed you back to health after we found you with your skull practically cracked open on the floor of

Audrey's bedroom. I did that because I believe people can change, and life is to be respected. I could have left you to die there, but—"

"Maybe you should have."

That smug smile was back.

"What?"

"Maybe you *should have* let me die. Here's the thing, Stephanie. Say what you will about Paul, or Audrey. But they never would have saved me in your position. They would have recognized that I was a threat. That people who stalk you into a dark room with ill intent are not people you should extend a hand to. When you let the devil in, you invite the evil in with it. Paul and Audrey knew that. That's a lesson you've yet to learn, and that's why we're all in danger right now—Your lax leadership gave rise to an atmosphere ripe for someone to do something terrible without fear of consequences, and that's precisely what's started happening. Who knows where that ends? But I'll be damned if I'm gonna stand by and listen to you pretend like this isn't on you. It's *completely* on you. I just hope you realize that before it's too late. You too, Michael."

Stephanie began to respond, but Zac spun on his heels and walked briskly away.

Zac smiled as he stepped back onto the square, thinking he'd left Stephanie flat footed from his ambush. It'd be interesting to see what her next move would be. He already had his planned out. Now he just needed to meet William.

He walked down the street to the house where they'd waited outside earlier in the evening, and went around the side. To Zac's relief, William was sitting there waiting, as instructed once Zac's talk was done.

"That took longer than I expected," William said. "I was starting to think you weren't coming."

"Doing that much damage takes time, my friend."

"What damage?"

"Doesn't matter. The point is, that went even better than I'd hoped. And it set us up really well for the next part of the plan."

"And that is…?"

"I need you to check yourself in to the hospital," Zac said, placing his hand on William's shoulder. "Like, *now*."

"The hospital? What for?"

"I don't give a shit. Make something up. Something they can't easily detect, and just have to run a bunch of tests. Chest pains. Bad headache. Fucking…sore throat. I don't know. Just get your ass admitted, and keep yourself there as long as you can, until you hear from me."

William shrugged. "Why?"

"Just do it. Believe me, the reason will be clear soon enough."

29

As Zac finished his own speech, Audrey stood in the back of the crowd, a bit stunned a bit at how effectively he had suffocated the goodwill Stephanie had built up just a few minutes earlier. It made her wonder if Zac was more devious than she'd previously thought. Or maybe a blindsided Stephanie just teed that up for him unwittingly. Either way, he seized the opportunity when he had it. Hers was an appeal to hope, community, and being positive in the face of adversity, while his was an appeal based upon fear. And Audrey knew exactly how powerful fear could be as a motivating factor.

She found herself studying the people around her during Zac's speech, and she saw lots of stiff shoulders, couples with their arms wrapped around each other and their children, and whispered talk. Because she'd stayed in back, most people hadn't even noticed her until Zac announced to everyone she was there; all those eyes on her hadn't been comfortable, but there was nothing she could do about it. She just had to stand and take it.

When Zac finished, there was none of the applause that followed Stephanie, but she figured he was probably okay with that. She would have been. It was a start of shifting people's thinking, and offering an alternative view.

Some people looked like they were preparing to come

over to speak to her, but her men stepped over and gave them looks that said to keep their distance. She glanced at George out of the corner of her eye.

"Walk with me, will ya?" she asked, over Nathan's shoulder.

"Of course, Ms. Reese. I'd be glad to."

George stepped around Nathan, and she looked at him with eyebrows raised. "I've told you, call me Audrey. I'm just another person trying to survive in this world, like you. I'm not your boss. There's no need for formalities."

"Yeah." George's eyes dropped. "I just...I have a lot of respect for the way you handled yourself previously. Law and order. Secure borders. Keep out those who don't belong. I'll always appreciate how hard you worked for us."

Audrey smiled and nodded slightly, then placed her hand on his shoulder. "Thank you for that. I do appreciate it. I made some mistakes, but I always tried to do what I thought was best for Alessandra. I'm glad some people recognize that." She squeezed his shoulder and pulled him in for a hug. After a few seconds, she gently nudged him back. "But I'm Audrey now, got it? Now, let's walk."

Audrey's men flanked her, one in front and two in the back, frequently checking over their shoulders. George walked beside her.

"What are your thoughts on Zac and Stephanie?" Audrey asked.

"Stephanie...well, she's nice. I think she does love Alessandra. And she's not a *bad* leader. I think some of the organization she's brought to tasks for the people of the town has helped to keep resources at the ready."

"But...?"

"But...Zac's right. The world is a dangerous place. I think Stephanie's been living in a bit of a wonderland, where the virus is eradicated, we've got a big fancy wall, and so everything's great. We can just have a perfect little democracy now. She wants too badly to please everybody. She's afraid to take a hard stand."

"Would you have let me back inside the walls?"

"Me? I absolutely would have. But it obviously wasn't my call to make. And, as glad as I am to see you again, part of me was hoping she'd turn you away."

Audrey looked at him, her eyes narrowed. "Why's that?"

"Because I was hoping she'd rise to the occasion and stand up to someone. I would have let you in, but we have a history going back a while. It doesn't make sense why *she'd* let you inside. She fought against you. She obviously thought you were a damaging enough leader that she needed to take you down. Why would you invite the wolf back into the chicken coop?"

"She'll face some criticism for letting me in, though."

"Sure." George shrugged. "But she can just insulate herself from the idle chatter that goes on around here. What she doesn't want is to tell someone *No* to their face, to be the bad guy who tells you, 'It's my job to protect the people of this town, and I can't do that with you inside.'"

Audrey nodded. "And what about Zac?"

"He's an interesting character. He seems confident. He reminds me a lot of your brother, which isn't necessarily a good thing. No offense."

She rolled her eyes and chuckled lightly. "No, I get it."

"Zac's a bit of a wild card. He makes some good points, and I think his vision of Alessandra is more aligned with mine than Stephanie's is. I'm just not sure if I trust him, in the end. He's ex-military, which counts for something. But is he smart? Competent? Will he make the right decision when it comes down to it? I just don't know. And so that's the difficulty there."

"How much of the town do you think is more or less

with you on Stephanie and Zac?"

"I'd say probably a good bit, from what I can tell. A *whole lot* with Zac. I think it'll be interesting to see if this speech moved that needle at all. On Stephanie, I don't know. Maybe it's close to fifty-fifty overall on support, but leaning toward her. Hope can be a powerful thing for some."

Walking up to her front porch, Audrey turned to George and extended her hand. He gripped it and shook.

"Thanks for your insight, George. Helps me get a lot better handle on the landscape here."

"Absolutely, Ms. Ree—Audrey." He laughed; she smiled and shook her head. "Yes. Anything I can do to help. Just let me know."

30

Under a single lightbulb dangling from the ceiling, flickering in and out from some solar energy gathered nearby, Zac looked around the basement at the men who'd been on his side for a while. It was a small group, standing in the shadows, waiting for what was going to happen next. Benjamin stood in front of him, back hunched, an uncertain look on his face.

Zac stared straight ahead, expressionless.

"I need you to hit me," he said to Benjamin, with the same passion he might reserve to ask for a glass of water. "And I need you to do it hard. For real."

Benjamin looked back and forth to the other men around him, but they had nothing to offer him. His eyes returned to Zac's.

"You want me to do what?" Benjamin asked. "I don't understand."

"I'm not sure how to be more clear. Hit me. Beat me. I need obvious bruises."

Benjamin's mouth opened, but nothing came out. He took a half step forward, then stopped.

"Is this…some sort of…test? Why do you want me to do this? It doesn't make sense."

Zac swallowed hard and shook his head.

"Does everything have to be a chore? You can't just do

what I ask? There are gonna be times when you just have to follow instructions. That's something you learn in the military. Commands don't have to make sense to you. You just have to trust that they make sense to your commander, so you follow them, immediately and without question, hurling yourself forward with everything you have. No matter what that order is. Because not only your life but the lives of many others may depend on you doing just that. I need men who are going to follow my instructions, not question them. If you can't handle it, there's a whole crew of men here. I'm sure one of them will step in if you can't."

"No. No," Benjamin's fists balled up. "I...can do it. I was just...surprised, is all."

"Well, are you done being surprised?"

Benjamin nodded. He took slow steps across the floor, getting within arm's reach of Zac. His head raised, and his eyes met Zac's.

"Okay, then," Zac said. "The face and arms, mostly. People need to be able to see it. Just don't fucking *kill* me, all right?"

Rolling his shoulders and neck, Benjamin stood up straight and pulled his right arm back, his fist pointing forward. Zac cupped his hands together behind his back and closed his eyes, his chin raised.

He felt the first punch land clumsily, glancing off his cheek and clipping his ear as it flew past.

"Oh, shit." He heard, as he grimaced and rattled his head a bit. He opened his eyes and saw Benjamin standing there, hands at his sides, his eyes wide.

Zac reached out and grabbed him by the neck, shoving Benjamin backward, his feet tapping awkwardly on the floor as he stumbled, held up by the throat. Zac drove him against a post in the middle of the room, dust splashing off its surface as Benjamin's back thumped into the black steel.

"Do you think I'm fucking around here?" Zac asked, his face getting hot. "I ask you to beat me, and you're pulling your fucking punch? You don't have enough sense in your head to realize that, if I'm asking you this, it must be *really* fucking important? You're a goddamn disgrace. Do you need me to fight back? Is that what you need? Because I'll gladly beat the shit out of you. You don't even *have* to ask me nicely. I'll do it just because."

Pressed firmly against the cold steel post, Benjamin's toes were barely touching the wood floor, his eyes wide and darting erratically as he looked down at Zac, whose hand squeezed just underneath Benjamin's chin.

Benjamin made some gurgling noises, spit trickling from his lips, and Zac let go. Benjamin's feet slid out from under him as his heels hit the floor, sending him crashing down hard, his head clanging off the post as his butt hit down with a thud.

He rubbed the back of his head, his legs splayed out in front of him as he sat on the floor, back against the post. Zac crouched in front of him, put two fingers under his chin and lifted it.

"Hit me," Zac ordered.

Benjamin's whole body seemed to shake for a moment, teeth chattering, shoulders convulsing. Then his arm lifted, and he quickly swung, his fist making contact with Zac's chin, causing his head to jerk to his right. Zac tumbled to the floor, then scrambled to his feet, stretching his mouth and rubbing his cheek.

"Okay. There we go," Zac said. "Now, stand the *fuck* up and finish me off. Do it!"

Benjamin grabbed the post to help himself stand up. The other men were cheering now, chants of "Hit him!" echoing through the flickering light of the basement, off the concrete walls and taking on a ritualistic quality. Fists raised in the air as Benjamin stood and looked ahead, eyes bloodshot and swollen, a red ring around the front of his neck.

Hunching forward, Benjamin charged toward Zac, taking three big steps and swinging his right fist wildly as he did, connecting with the side of Zac's face. Then a second blow came from the left, crashing into the side of Zac's temple. Zac closed his eyes, trying desperately to resist the natural instinct to defend himself. His head told him he could neutralize this threat without any problem, grab one of those flailing arms and twist it, maybe even break it as he turned around, putting Benjamin on the floor and stomping on his neck. In his head, Zac had Benjamin practically dead within ten seconds. But he needed to let this happen.

The hits weren't landing with the fury of a heavyweight boxer, but they were coming rapid fire and with passion now, mostly to his head, a few others doubling him over as they crashed into his midsection.

Blood spewed out as one blow hit a bullseye on the front of his nose, bringing with it a stab of searing pain in the middle of his face, then the metallic taste of blood streaming down his throat as more blows landed on both sides of his head. Nearly choking and paralyzed by the pain crawling up his septum, attacking his brain like a million spiders spreading across the ground, Zac fell to the floor and put up both hands.

"Stop! That's enough!" Zac felt like he was yelling, but it came out unintelligibly through a mouth brimming with blood that poured out as he tried to speak. He stopped and spit, sending blood splattering like a firehose, spreading out across the floor and Benjamin, who finally pulled up and took a step back, looking down at the mangled mess that lay before him.

Zac wiped his forearm across his mouth and spit again. The men were silent, looking on.

"That wasn't so hard, was it?" Zac said, leaning back on his hands, wincing with pain that came with each word. "You can wail when you get going. Good job. Everyone can await instructions. I'll be in touch again soon."

The men started filing out toward the stairs. Benjamin stepped hesitantly over to Zac and held out a hand to help him up; Zac waved his hand and shook his head.

"Go."

Benjamin stopped for a second, then turned and walked over to the other men.

Zac remained sitting as he watched the last of the men leave, the single light bulb directly over his head, the light still going in and out, darkness and light. He stood and grabbed the bulb, twisting it and pulling it out of its housing; the basement turned black as he threw the bulb across the room. He could hear it crash into something and shatter, shards of glass scattering on the floor.

Standing alone in the windowless dark, face crisscrossed with rivers of blood, Zac smiled.

31

"So, what seems to be the problem, Mister Greene?" Victor Davis, a Saint Francis nurse, asked, holding his wrist as William lay in a hospital bed.

"Um, I've been feeling tightness and some pain in my chest. Figured I should check myself in and make sure it wasn't something serious."

Victor scribbled in his notepad, then picked up his stethoscope, sticking in the ear tips. He lifted William's gown and reached underneath it to press the diaphragm to his chest.

"Take a deep breath for me, Mister Greene," he said, placing the diaphragm against the left side of his chest. "Okay, good. Exhale. Now, breathe in again."

He went through that cycle a few times, and then put the stethoscope away.

"Well, you did the right thing. Chest pains are nothing to mess around with. Have you had any other symptoms? Shortness of breath?"

"Shortness of…No. None of that."

"Have you been lethargic? Sleeping more than usual?"

"N-No. My energy has been fine. It's just chest pains."

"I see," Victor said, writing in his notepad. "Where exactly is the pain you've felt? Can you point to it for me?"

William hesitantly lifted his hand toward his chest, trying

to think of the most convincing place to point. If he were actually having chest pains that might be a problem, where would that pain be? He laid his finger on a spot on the right side of his chest.

"There?" Victor asked. "On your right pectoral?"

"That's right."

"That's good to know. Answer me this—Have you been carrying anything heavy around recently? Maybe straining a bit?"

William thought back to lifting Father Hayden out of his bed, forearms tucked into his armpits as he and Zac carried him down the stairs and through the kitchen to the back yard. He had been heavier and more difficult to manage than William would have expected. It was almost like death had weight. There was no way the nurse could know about that, was there?

"Why would you ask me that? That's none of your business."

Victor stepped back, a quizzical look on his face.

"I'm...just trying to help you, Mister Greene. These are standard questions, given the symptoms you're displaying."

"But what does my heart have to do with whether or not I'm lifting something heavy?"

"Well, I actually don't think this is your heart at all, so that's good news. It just sounds like a muscle strain. Lifting something heavy is a common cause. Heck, you might have just slept wrong. But I see no reason to think it's anything more serious than that. Your pulse is normal. If it was a heart attack, we'd expect the pain to originate on the left side of your chest."

William silently kicked himself for missing on a 50/50 shot.

"So what are you saying?" he asked.

"I'm saying you're fine. Try not to lift anything heavy for

a couple of days, and your muscle should recover nicely."

"Don't you want to run any more tests, or whatever? Just to be sure?"

Victor's eyes narrowed. "I…don't see any reason to. You're not exhibiting symptoms that would be consistent with anything more than a mild to moderate muscle strain."

William laid still in the bed, trying to think.

"But I haven't even been here an hour. That's not nearly enough."

"Not enough for what, Mister Greene?"

"No. I need to stay. Overnight."

"That's really not necessary. We could need the bed for someone who has a serious medical—"

"Look," William said, sitting up slightly, his eyes drilling into Victor's. "This is a big hospital, built to serve what? Five? Six counties? Now it's serving one town with way fewer people than it had when the place was built? There's no fucking way you're gonna run out of room tonight, of all nights. I know you *say* it's just a muscle strain, but what if you're wrong? Do you want to be responsible if go home and die of a heart attack tonight?"

"With all due respect, Mister Greene, there's virtually no chance that's—"

"With all due respect…" William looked at his name tag, "*Victor*, I'm sure you're a brilliant medical mind, but I'm just not willing to bet my life on you being right based upon pushing some metal thingie to my chest and asking me a few questions. If you want me out of this bed before morning, you're gonna have to go find some horses to drag me out."

They stared at each other for a few seconds, Victor's lips curled in something William thought approached a snarl.

"As you wish, Mister Greene. I'm not going to fight you," Victor wrote something else in his note pad, then turned and walked to the door. As he walked out, he said, "Dinner's at

seven," and William could hear the bitterness dripping in his
voice.

32

"I think it's time," Stephanie said, closing her front door behind Michael.

"*Time?* Time for what?"

Stephanie gave him a meaningful look.

"Nick."

"Whoa. Hey." Michael held up both hands as he backed into Stephanie's living room. "Let's not jump right to that. You're talking about having my best friend lie for us. A *big* lie that's meant to condemn a man."

"Yeah. And we already talked to him about it. He agreed. We *all* agreed."

"Right. But I thought we were talking about as a last resort. We'd exhaust every other avenue for figuring this out, and *then* we'd go to him if there was no other option."

Stephanie sighed and walked around Michael, nearly brushing his shoulder as she went to sit down in her recliner. He continued to stand where he was, looking down at her.

"What exactly are our other options right now, Michael? Tell me that. We have a dead priest on our hands here. How do you want to *prove* William did this?"

"Well, I...I don't want to prove *William* did it. I just want to be able to show *someone* did it."

"Oh, for fuck's sake, Michael. We both know William did it."

"He denied being anywhere near even Hank when I talked to him."

She leaned back and folded her arms across her chest. "And you *believe* him?"

Michael rolled his eyes. "I didn't *say* that. I'm just pointing out that I don't think we have him as dead to rights as you seem to think. Did he assault Hank? Probably. Sure. But is it at least *possible* Hank's wrong? Look, we may think he's credible, but Zac's not wrong that the blow to the head could bring his testimony into question. And he's *certainly* not wrong that it would give anyone who wanted to believe William an excuse to do so."

"It's the only lead we've got."

"So we beat the bushes for more. Talk to people. See what we can find."

"I've talked to plenty of people, Michael. What have *you* been doing? There's nothing. This is it. Stop thinking we're gonna magically find another explanation. William assaulted Hank. Then he jumped Derrick and killed Father Hayden. *That's* what happened, and *that's* what we need to demonstrate to the rest of the town."

Michael wrung his hands together and sat down on the couch.

"Why are you so desperate to pin this on William?" he asked.

"Why are you so desperate to defend him?"

"I'm not…" He looked at the floor and shook his head, then met her eyes again. "It's not about defending *him*. It's about defending a principle. I know this isn't exactly 'America' as we knew it, but don't we need to uphold some of the standards we admired about the old society? Innocent until proven guilty. Jury of your peers. Due process. That sort of thing. Shouldn't we push to keep those as the default standard we operate under? *At least* until we absolutely can't possibly do so anymore?"

Stephanie leaned forward and put her hand on Michael's knee.

"I'm sorry to break the news to you, but *that's* exactly where we are now. I admire your dedication to democratic principles and trying to maintain some semblance of what we used to have before everything broke down around us. But we can't afford to be naïve here. That world is gone. Dead. Buried. I'm not saying we go all Wild West. Ya know, anything goes, ends justifies the means, all that. We can do better. We're on the same page there."

She stood up and paced across the room, then stopped and looked at Michael.

"We're fighting for survival here, though. Think about what happens if we don't figure this out. The town's going to crumble. Forget about high-and-mighty principles. We won't even have a community to protect. Everything's going to dissolve around us. This needs to be solved. Not a month from now. Not two weeks from now or two days from now. *Today.* We have an opportunity to put this to bed. We can not only put people's minds at ease that the person who committed these awful acts has been exposed, but that their leadership is capable of keeping them safe. You said Zac was right about Hank's memory. Well, let's give Zac credit for one more—he's also right that people *need* to feel safe in order for a society function. There's just no way around that. And giving them this will accomplish that. We need to do it. And I need you with me."

She went back to the chair and sat down, reaching out and wrapping her hands around Michael's. He shut his eyes tight, took a deep breath and nodded. She leaned into him and wrapped her arms around his neck, nearly falling into his lap.

"You mean I'm going up on stage?" Nick said, walking toward the square, between Nick and Stephanie.

"Just for a few seconds, to tell people what you saw," Stephanie said. "We can't just tell everyone while you're standing there nodding. It needs to come from you to be convincing."

"You're gonna be fine, man," Michael assured him. "Remember when we were kids? You used to be great at just improvising shit in front of half the school. You didn't care. Just try to think back to that."

Nick grinned. "Man, drama class was a trip. Thought I'd hate that class, but then the lights went on and it was this huge shot of adrenaline."

Then his eyes dropped.

"Everybody liked me then, though," Nick said, his voice low, just above a whisper. "Everybody thinks I'm a freak now."

"They don't think you're a freak," Michael said. "They just think you've had a tough go at it lately. And you have. You've been through a lot. But this is gonna be a chance for you to start showing how far you've come. Ya know? You stand up there confidently and tell your story, and people will look at you differently."

Nick nodded, and the three of them walked in silence for another couple of blocks to the square. There were already a few dozen people there waiting.

"Nothing like a small town for being able to summon a crowd on short notice," Stephanie said. "Hank and some of my nurse friends volunteered to help spread the word. Shouldn't take much longer before everyone's here."

They went up the stairs onto the stage, and Stephanie picked up the bullhorn Zac had left at the back, laying it down underneath the podium. Hands on her hips, she looked out over the people as they found their spots, hoping this was going to put an end to the madness. Maybe they could put it behind themselves and move forward. She couldn't wait to see Zac's face when they revealed they had a witness.

"Thanks for joining me—us—again, for the second time in two days," Stephanie said, the bullhorn raised to her lips. "This isn't something I plan to make a habit of, but we feel like this is very important for you *all* to know, and we don't have TVs these days."

She could see everyone's face, the late morning sun behind her slicing a shadow diagonally across the crowd. All eyes were on her; she knew they were waiting for a message of hope, wanting for her to tell them they could stop being afraid. She wanted to see smiles radiating back at her.

"Before we get started, I want to acknowledge personally how much I respect and appreciate Zac's words yesterday. I recognize that he's passionate about this town, and he felt it was necessary to speak up. I want you all to hold me accountable, and tough words can sometimes be a part of that. We're always happy to hear from anyone who'd like to offer us feedback."

She saw a number of nods in the crowd. This was one more way for her to differentiate herself from Audrey. It also provided an air of honesty and transparency just before she was going to go the opposite way.

"Of course, you're all wondering about Father Hayden's murder and the recent assaults. First off, we welcome everyone to come to Saint Catherine's Church this evening, when we'll have a celebration of Father Hayden's life. Just listen for the church's bell to ring, and make your way there. Now, as for who did this to him...Michael and I have been looking into this for a few days now, since Hank's assault, following the bread crumbs wherever they'd lead us. After last night's event, we're happy to report that a witness came forward. Our own life-long Alessandran, Nick Dyerson, was taking a walk that morning and saw Hank being attacked...*by William Greene.*"

Stephanie heard a few gasps and chattering after she said William's name, and she paused for a moment to let the noise die down.

"Nick saw it all, and we believe that's plenty to justify severe punishment for William. But, with Derrick's assault coming so close on the heels of that one, and based on our previous absence of violence, we believe we have just cause to place William there as well. And that also puts him in Father Hayden's back yard the very morning that he was murdered. That's a heck of a lot of coincidence. I'm going to turn the bullhorn over to Nick in just a moment, so he can tell you his story himself, but I wanted to let you know that William can't go anywhere. He happened to check himself into the hospital with chest pains last night, and now he's locked inside a hospital room with no way to escape. He *will* face swift justice, up to and including the possibility of *banishment.* Now, let's hear from Nick."

Stephanie held out the bullhorn and motioned for Nick to come over to her. Hesitantly, he started walking, but then stopped. Michael put a hand on his back and whispered something into his ear. Nick turned and nodded at him, and continued heading over to Stephanie. He looked out at the people, took a deep breath, and raised the bullhorn to his mouth.

"Thank you, Stephanie. And all of you. This...isn't easy. I...have a hard time talking about it. You all know the...violence and horrible things I've seen over the past couple of years. It's been a traumatic time. I very much appreciate the support I've gotten. Seeing Hank being attacked really brought a lot of that flooding back—"

Nick stopped, as noise began coming from the crowd in

waves. Stephanie could see heads turning away from the stage and toward the street. She was a long way away from whatever they were looking at, but it was clearly a man walking in their direction. A late arrival? From people's reactions, she thought it was a good bit more than that.

Several people ran to him, urgency in their pace. The man put his arms out, motioning them away as he kept walking. Who *was* that? Stephanie still couldn't tell, even as he got closer. Was his complexion really bad? That couldn't be...*blood* all over his face? The crowd parted, and he was walking through it, making a beeline for the stage. It started to dawn on Stephanie what she was seeing; her stomach dropped, and she could feel her head swimming. She thought she might faint for a second, but she pinched her arm, willing herself to keep her feet.

She saw him coming up the stairs, slowly, each step meticulous, as if he might topple over at any moment. His face was crossed with jagged streaks of crimson and dark blue, his eyes swollen, nose askew. Stephanie could feel her mouth hanging open, but she had no words. Nothing could have prepared her for this, as she watched him take the bullhorn from Nick's hand, and turn to the crowd.

"In case you don't recognize me right now, I'm Zac Latham." His words were a mish-mash of garbled noises and liquidy muttering. He spit a dark maroon onto the stage. "Someone jumped me this morning and did this, in my own back yard. I never saw him. But, based upon what Stephanie said, there's one thing we know—it wasn't William."

He glared at Stephanie and then Nick. She thought she could see a small smirk cross his mouth, but it was difficult to tell with his mangled face.

"I don't know what else they're lying about and trying to spin in order to maintain power, but I think it's clear at this point that Stephanie and Michael are unfit to lead Alessandra.

I'd like to take this moment to call for a new vote. Let's see what the rest of you think. If Stephanie's as committed to 'transparency' as she claims, I see no reason not to allow it. Raise your hand if you agree."

Stunned, Stephanie turned and saw a sea of hands looking back at her from the square.

Looking out over the crowd, Zac wasn't sure if there had been a more triumphant moment in his life. Not the birth of his daughters or the day of his wedding. Not graduating high school or making Sergeant. Not that mission when he sniped seven concealed enemy troops, clearing a mosque in Afghanistan and helping his team return it to the citizens of Jalalabad.

Seeing those hands shoot up from so many of his fellow citizens gave him a feeling unlike any of those moments. This had been the result of a plan he'd devised and executed on his own, piecing together the map of how to get here from where he was, recruiting the men he thought could help him get there, making adjustments when the circumstances called for them, and taking advantage of opportunities when they presented themselves. This had been a war, against Stephanie, against the reality he had been faced with, and he'd won. Or, at least, he'd won to this point. It wouldn't be completely won until he was the one everyone was looking to for leadership, taking his rightful place in that mansion on the hill, taking the people of Alessandra where they deserved to go.

But, as of this moment, he couldn't ask for more. He'd deal with the searing pain from his face later.

"I don't think we need to do a headcount," Zac said, his garbled voice brimming with glee. "That's a pretty overwhelming statement in favor of a new vote. What do you think, Stephanie?"

She looked pale, her mouth agape, arms stiff at her sides as she stared out from the stage. Seeing Stephanie's reaction was almost as satisfying for Zac as watching the hands shoot into the air.

"Do you have any thoughts on this, Stephanie?" Zac said, moving closer and pointing the bullhorn at her; she jerked as if awoken abruptly from a dream. "I think it's clear what the people want."

He held out the bullhorn and let her take it from his hands.

"I'd...urge you all not to have a knee-jerk reaction here," Stephanie said, her voice trembling along with her shoulders. "I'm not..." She paused and swallowed hard, seeming to struggle for words. "I'm not saying I'll try to block a vote if that's what you truly want. I know I'm not perfect. I know I make mistakes. This is all new to me. I'm a doctor, not a politician."

She looked up at the sky, sucking in a deep breath. The crowd had settled down a bit, the hands coming down as Zac looked on.

"I just...I love this town, and I love you all. We've been through *so* much together. I want you all to remember what it was like before I stepped into this role. I want you to remember the lack of freedom, the lack of your own families. Recognize that, while I certainly have flaws, everything I do, every decision I make, is truly in service of you. It can get worse. It can get *so* much worse. And if you replace me, I fear that's the direction we're going to head in."

Part of Zac screamed in his head that he never should have given up the bullhorn, that Stephanie was a more gifted bullshitter than she gave herself credit for, and she could potentially talk her way out of this. But, for the most part, he was staying calm. Mere words weren't going to be enough for her today.

"We...want...a vote," Zac yelled, punctuating each syllable while waving his arms up and down to the rhythm. "We...want...a vote! We...want...a vote!"

Gradually, the crowd joined in, the chant picking up steam until it was echoing off the walls of the old city hall, rising into the breeze like a flock of birds. Zac went silent and just stood, soaking it in, letting the cadence wash over him like a waterfall, validating everything he'd done the previous few days. Whatever harm he had visited upon a few people was going to be worth it because a better Alessandra was going to rise from the ashes of all this. Their sacrifices would be remembered as the instigator of better times, the trigger point that ended Stephanie's incompetent, reckless reign.

Hanging her head, her face ashen, Stephanie nodded solemnly.

"I hear you," she said into the bullhorn, her voice cracking, and a tear trickling down her cheek; the chant began to fade. "Monday. That's five days from now. We'll get it set up."

Zac snatched the bullhorn from her hand and raised a fist in the air.

"A victory for democracy and the safety of Alessandra!" he said, and many in the crowd cheered. "Also, I think we should have a debate right here on this stage tomorrow around this time of day. Do you agree, Stephanie?"

She shook her head and sighed loudly. Then: "Sure. That's fine." She bit the words off like they carried physical weight, and Zac relished it. He laid the bullhorn and raised both arms, pumping his fists in the air as he walked toward the stairs. He was headed straight to the hospital. He figured he needed some stitches, a few pain meds, and to thank a certain heart patient.

33

"I'd like to be alone for a little bit," Stephanie said to Michael as they walked back toward their houses after leaving the square. "I just need to think and clear my head."

"Sure. I understand. We still have some work to do on finding the killer, but let's take a little break. We've been at it for a while."

Stephanie nodded, and they kept walking in silence for a couple of minutes.

"I was fucking *sure* it was William," she said, pounding her fist into her leg. "Absolutely *certain*. What happened to Zac doesn't make any damn sense."

"It makes sense if it wasn't actually William. Jumping the gun on Nick probably didn't help us much."

Stephanie stopped and looked at Michael, her lips pursed.

"What was that?" She saw Michael take two steps and stop, turning back toward her. "Did you have something to say to me?"

"It's fine," he said. "Let's just take a break for a bit."

"No, I wanna hear this." Stephanie stood in the middle of the street, arms folded tightly across her chest. "That sounded like the beginning of a critique."

Michael sighed. "Do you really want to do this here?"

"What the fuck do I care about where we do it?" she said, waving her arms. "I've just been humiliated in front of the *whole town*, not once but *twice* in the span of two days. What's a few gawking neighbors compared to that?"

Michael stalked over close to her and spoke quietly. "There's nothing for me to say I haven't said already. You know I wasn't in favor of going to Nick right then. I thought it was hasty. You overruled me. Fair enough. But that blew up in our faces. Maybe Nick's face too. You're entitled to a mistake, but that's what that was. Can we go now?"

Michael started to walk away, but Stephanie wasn't ready to let him.

"Maybe we wouldn't be in this spot if you hadn't let William and Zac trample all over you in that first interrogation session."

He stopped and spun around. "How would you know they trampled on me?"

"I talk to people. I've gotten a pretty consistent description of what happened in there. And everybody thinks you got played. It's part of why I was convinced William was the guy. Maybe a better questioner would have gotten him to own up to it right then."

"Oh, and you think *you* would have magically gotten it out of him?"

She shrugged and curled her mouth on one end. Michael took two big steps back to her and stood with their faces almost touching.

"If you were the world's greatest interrogator, maybe you should have done that job instead of going to have a friendly chat with Hank. If I suck so bad at it, take some responsibility for making a bad fucking hire."

He turned and quickly walked away, heading to his house a half block away, next door to Stephanie's. Still standing in the street, she didn't move, her feet in concrete, watching the door slam shut behind him.

She was too numb to feel bad about anything she had

said. He'd get over it. It wasn't the first fight they'd had, by any means. Somewhere deep inside, she still loved him, and she was pretty sure he felt the same way. And, in some twisted part of her mind, that gave her license to hurt him from time to time, because they both knew that, underneath it all, they cared about each other. That it wasn't coming from a place of hate but from a place of love.

Stephanie looked up into a blue sky with a few wispy clouds floating slowly past. An owl soared above, its wings spread wide as it glided onto a nearby tree and perched, its eyes staring into hers as if bearing a message. Those eyes looked intense, almost orange in color, the feathers forming a V shape between them that made them look lopsided. She wanted to know what it knew, see what it saw.

She felt a finger tap her shoulder and jumped, head spinning around quickly, heart pumping in her chest.

"I'm sorry. Didn't mean to startle you," Audrey said. "I just wanted to know if you'd be willing to talk for a few minutes."

"I…I don't know. I was kind of looking forward to being—"

"I promise I won't take up much of your time. I just saw everything that went down with Zac back there, and I feel like I can help. I've got experience with this sort of thing."

Stephanie let out a heavy sigh and looked around.

"Fine." She motioned down the street with her head. "Walk with me?"

They walked in near silence for a few blocks, just the sound of their feet tapping the cracked and buckling pavement. Audrey was biding her time, waiting for Stephanie to signal she was ready to talk. She knew Stephanie was stressed and needed to be eased into this conversation. Any sudden moves might scare her away.

Audrey thought today might be the day she could get Stephanie alone. And when she saw Stephanie and Michael walking away from the square alone together, something told her that was the opportunity she'd been waiting for. Then she'd heard their fight in the middle of the street, and she felt some sympathy for both of them. She knew Stephanie probably hadn't meant a lot of what she'd said to Michael, and he had to feel useless as Stephanie's inferior, knowing his opinions only mattered insomuch as he could convince Stephanie they were valid. And she was tough to convince.

But finally, Stephanie spoke up.

"So, how is it you think you can help?"

"Well, I know Zac a little bit, as you probably know," Audrey began, keeping pace to Stephanie's right. "He did some work for us when Paul and I were running things. Mostly Paul, but I've had a number of interactions with him over the years. He has some similarities to my brother, in that they both have a laser focus on what they want, and will steamroll over anything and everything in order to get it. The key is finding a way to stop that steamroller if you don't want to get run over."

"Okay. Do you know how to stop it?"

"Well, I can't *promise* anything, but I've got some thoughts on it. You agreed to debate him tomorrow?"

"I guess I did." Stephanie rolled her eyes.

"I'm not sure that's the best forum for you because it raises him to your level. It's going to have the effect of making it look to everyone in the crowd like you two are equals. Your *best* bet is probably to keep yourself above the fray and just let your experience and the respect people have for you speak for itself."

"I don't disagree with that, but I'm also not going to stand in the way of democratic processes if that's what the people want. I'm not a tyrant, Audrey. I'm just a doctor trying to help out."

"And I respect that. It's admirable. Maybe the very fact that you're doing this will gain you some votes too, from people who want to ensure that's the type of leader we have."

Stephanie stopped and turned to look at Audrey. "But you don't think that's enough?"

"Well, I'm not so sure." Audrey took a step forward, and Stephanie walked with her. "The people are feeling anxious and scared right now. You can see it in their faces. And, say what you will about Zac, he's smartly tapped into that. He saw an opportunity, and he grasped it. Now, he's got his shot. As long as you give him the forum to make his case, he's gonna try to bait you. His goal is going to be to make you seem at least as volatile and unreliable as he is. At that point, he makes it merely a referendum on the job *you're* doing rather than a question of who's the better leader. Or who's more intelligent and generally competent? Or who do I like the most? Those aren't questions he wants people asking when they go to vote, because he's going to lose that all day long. He only wins if people are saying 'I'm scared right now, and I'm willing to change anything if it makes me less scared.' He wants to stoke their fears so that all they have on their minds is how terrified they are that they—or their kids— might be next on this mysterious person's list of violence."

"So, then, I need to just not take his bait?"

"Right." Audrey wiped some sweat from her forehead. "But, more than that, emphasize your leadership experience. Speak in a calm voice. Exude competence and level-headedness. Don't let him get under your skin. You *want* that contrast. If they're thinking about being scared, you want them to say, 'Yes, I'm scared, but who's the better person to find a way to make me less scared?' He has no background in this. He can't point to anything he's done to execute policy, to improve people's lives. He'll try to point to his military experience, and that'll be impressive to some, but scaling that up to the size of a town is a monumental feat that he hasn't proven he can do. You've got a counter there. Use it."

Stephanie nodded, frowning a bit, then looked up at the sky.

"I want to show you something," Audrey said, pointing toward the lake to her right. "Walk down here with me."

They stepped off the street, over the curb and into the grass. There was a bit of a drop and then a gradual decline to just short of the lake. As they got far enough to see to the bottom, they saw what Audrey brought her over there for.

There were more than a dozen men—including the men Audrey brought—digging a trench and letting water flow from the lake through it, using old shovels, axes and buckets however they could to pull the water toward the town.

"Wow," Stephanie said, sitting down on the hill. "What are they doing?"

"They're digging channels from the lake that should help a lot with getting quick access to water within the town. One of my guys had the idea. This is the kind of thing they're good at. It should cut down a lot on the work to get clean water to the people who need it, and to shorten the time it takes for everyone to get water to their homes. The plan is to dig the trench almost all the way to the square. They've mapped out a route for it."

"A little civil engineering project…" Stephanie nodded. "I like it."

"I'm glad you approve. I said we'd earn our keep while we're here. But, more importantly, these are the people you're working for. What you're doing is important, and look at the work these men are willing to do in order to make Alessandra not fall apart. Zac isn't the person to lead them. You need to keep your cool, and make sure these people have a strong leader who has their best interests at heart. Don't let him get the better of you. You can do this. Okay?"

"I think I can do that." Stephanie smiled. "Thanks. I probably needed that pep talk more than you'll know. It's been a rough couple of days. And there's still some violent asshole out there somewhere."

"Well, you're not gonna catch any violent assholes on no sleep. I'll walk you home. Get some rest. Get ready for tomorrow. Let's hope the asshole doesn't do anything else in the next twenty-four hours, and then get back on that horse."

"Yeah. I'm gonna sleep pretty well. Thanks again."

"Absolutely. Least I could do. Let's get you back home."

As Stephanie curled up in bed, Audrey stepped lightly back out the front door, closing it quietly behind her. Walking back toward her house, Audrey noticed a man coming down the street in her direction. With the violence that had been happening recently, she wondered immediately if she should be concerned. But she figured she could take care of herself, and she also assumed that, no matter what she told them to do, at least one of her men was keeping an eye on her whenever they could.

As they drew closer to each other, their eyes met; it was William, likely returning home from his stay in the hospital. They stopped.

"Good to see you," Audrey said. "Been a while. I hope everything's okay with your chest."

"With my wh...Yes. Right. Yeah, clean bill of health. They think I might have just overdone it when lifting some stuff recently, and said to take it easy for a couple of days. What'd you do to your arm?"

Audrey glanced down at her forearm, covering it absent-mindedly with a hand.

"Oh. It's nothing. Just a scrape I got walking around by the lake earlier."

"Looks like it's bleeding. Cuts are no joke these days, Ms. Reese. You should get it checked out."

She nodded. "I've got some stuff back at the house. Thanks for your concern. Glad to hear you're doing better. How have things been for you lately? Are you still doing police work?"

He shuffled his feet. "That hasn't really…worked out with Stephanie in charge. It's been a little hard, to be honest. I *know* I can be useful. You and Paul knew that. Chief Bray knew that before he turned on you guys and got himself killed. That was sad. And I know you two were…close as well."

"Yes." Audrey bowed her head and swallowed hard. "Danny was a good man."

"There was just a sense of purpose, you know? A sense of making a difference, of being part of big things happening. That I was more than just a dumb cop. I was…*important*. And so I've missed that. What have you been doing for the past…however long it's been? It's crazy to see you back here. We all just assumed you were dead."

Audrey smiled. "Yeah, it's been quite a ride. I got lucky. Found another colony, a good ways from here. Not as organized or resource-rich as Alessandra, but it worked out for a while. That ran its course, though. I think I always knew I'd come back here one day. I was just hoping Alessandra would still be here waiting for me when I did. I'm glad to see Stephanie has kept things more or less running while I've been gone."

"She's done okay, in some ways. She doesn't even *have* a police force, though. No enforcers."

"No investigators to help her figure out this rash of violence either."

"Exactly. I don't know. Early on, she talked about the…'culture of the community' or some shit like that policing itself. That this town was small enough that people would hold each other accountable. I guess that idea has fallen apart, hasn't it?"

Audrey raised her eyebrows and smirked. "I see what she was saying, and it was an idea I considered, but I just didn't think it was sustainable over a long enough period of time. As far as I was concerned, as dangerous as we knew the world was, order was needed to prevent chaos. Always. Within these walls was a safe space, where you knew you could live, and you'd eventually be reunited with your children, once the virus was under control. There was comfort and hope there. I just wasn't comfortable with a more laissez-faire approach to governing. But different people have different styles."

"Sure." William rolled his eyes. "It's just that, sometimes I think she's trying to be the anti-Audrey, ya know? Like she's trying so hard not to be you that nobody knows who *she* really is. Does *Stephanie* want to govern this way, or does she just think it's the opposite of how *you'd* do it? She's clearly smart, but she's *doctor* smart, not necessarily *president* smart."

"And she wanted to nail you for this Father Hayden mess, too. Might have, if Zac hadn't gotten assaulted while you were hospitalized."

Audrey thought she saw a smile start to cross William's face, but then he bit his lip.

"Yeah, that's what they told me. That's why I'm out. Told me I was fine, and kicked my butt out the door." William laughed. "Not sure what they would have done with me if she'd gotten away with it."

"Pretty convenient that Zac got jumped at just the right time to clear your name, wasn't it?"

William paused and looked at Audrey, silent and blinking for a few moments, an almost undetectable grin on his face. Then he shrugged.

"I'm guessing God just wants the *right* person to be

caught for murdering one of the most loyal members of his flock," he said. "Eye for an eye, and all that. Ya know?"

"You think *God* had someone assault Zac?"

"He's done worse to get his point across. Just read the Old Testament. Violence is justified if the goal is righteous enough."

34

Walking up to the stage, Zac couldn't remember the last time he'd been in this high of spirits. This was going to be his moment, when he'd fully gain the respect and trust of the people of Alessandra, and then ride that wave into the mayor's mansion. He'd get to build the town in his image. Reward those who helped him, and punish those who opposed him. Rebuild the police force to keep the town safe from opportunistic criminals. Pour more resources into the wall and its security. Maybe he'd threaten to banish Stephanie but relent and allow her to return to Saint Francis to practice medicine and stay the hell out of his way.

But he really relished the idea of being able to choose Audrey's fate. He hoped everything that was happening would distract Stephanie long enough that she'd forget about dealing with Audrey. Her stay in town was supposed to be temporary—at least, that's what he'd been told—and he suspected there was an agreement to that effect between her and Stephanie. As long as Audrey was staying quiet and not making waves, though, he figured Stephanie had problems big enough that kicking Audrey out on her ass probably wasn't going to be high on the priority list.

And if that got postponed a few more days, it left the chance that Audrey would still be living in Alessandra when he took over. Maybe she'd see the writing on the wall and flee on her own, her tail tucked between her legs as she snuck out in the dead of night.

If so, so be it, he thought. At least she'd be gone. But he'd give anything to have the chance to finally do to her what he should have in that bedroom more than a year earlier. It'd be worse now, though. *So* much worse. Once Zac had full control of the town, no one could stop him from exacting his revenge. She had put him through the worst torture he could imagine for *years*, and that was his wish for her—utter, indefinite agony until she died, cold and alone. When she'd disappeared after the coup took place, he thought he'd never get the chance to make that happen. He thought he just had to settle for the high likelihood that she'd suffered and died in the forest somewhere, her stomach collapsing in on itself as she writhed in pain and the coyotes nipped at her bones.

She'd come back, though. It was a sign. A sign that this had all been fated, that he was going to rise to power and get the opportunity of his dreams. Once he had the throne, nothing would stand in his way. Audrey would be imprisoned by the very walls she built.

Stephanie sitting a couple of feet to his right, Zac looked out over the crowd and smiled, waving to a couple of friends who had just walked up. He'd shaken Stephanie's hand as she sat down, hoping a collegial display like that would help to make them look like equal choices for this role, and put everyone at ease with him. He quietly laughed at the idea that he was thinking like a politician already.

"Well, it looks like pretty much everyone's here, so we're gonna go ahead and start," Michael spoke into the bullhorn, standing behind the podium. "Because we only have one bullhorn, here's how we're going to work this. I'll pose a topic, then hand the bullhorn to either Stephanie or Zac.

There will be four topics, and we'll alternate who goes first. They'll each answer the question, and we'll go on to the next one."

They'd all agreed on the format and topics in a meeting earlier that morning, and Zac had been fine with it. It put them on a level playing field, and didn't allow her to just grandstand forever. He wasn't sure about Michael moderating, but he didn't know who a better option would be. All he'd be doing was asking initial questions, anyway. He'd sensed some odd tension between the two of them too. Something in the room just felt icy, particularly from Michael toward Stephanie. The way he angled his body away from her, and kept his space. He'd never seen them like that.

But, ultimately, Michael was all business, helping them work through the questions and figure out the best topics to hit on. Zac thought he had some good gut-level answers for them, and he was hoping Stephanie would overthink and then talk herself into knots.

"So, first question," Michael said. "We decided earlier that Zac would start it off, so this goes to him first. What do you consider to be your governing philosophy?"

Michael handed over the bullhorn, and Zac pushed himself up from the chair. He took a few steps, then paused in the front of the stage and took a deep breath before starting.

"Thank you, Michael. And thanks to everyone for coming out here…again. It's heartening to see everyone so invested in the future of our wonderful town."

He'd prepared that opening that morning, standing in front of a dirty, scratched mirror he found on the side of the road a year or so earlier. He wanted to sound magnanimous, friendly, and *presidential*. He knew his biggest hurdle was just getting the people to *see* him as the guy in charge, to envision themselves being subject to him. He was an outsider, and he needed to sell them on the need for that. The need for *him*. It was all part of the show.

"My governing philosophy is simple. In order for a society to thrive, its citizens must first feel safe and secure. Without that, nothing else matters. All the rest is window dressing. We might as well just be out in the woods, fighting off the cougars and the mountain lions, rubbing sticks together for warmth. Safety and security is the line that divides us from the animals, and from our early ancestors. It's why we built communities in the first place. To me, ensuring that comes first, and the rest flows from that. If people feel safe, they'll have children, growing the population. If people feel safe, they'll be more social, friendlier, and happier. You can see the difference lately, as that feeling of safety has eroded, and that throws a blanket over everything. Feeling unsafe negatively impacts *everything*. And my administration would be laser focused on returning you to a secure future, and an Alessandra where you want to raise your children."

There was a smattering of applause, and Zac was smiling wide as he turned to hand the bullhorn to Stephanie.

"Your move," he said, as she took it from him, and then he sat back down.

She stood and lifted the bullhorn to her lips.

"Thanks, Zac. Always good to hear from a citizen on what you think. And, of course, I echo Zac's thanks to all of you for coming out. Great to see you all. So, what's my governing philosophy? Well, one thing I've learned very well over the past year or so is just how much easier it is to *talk* about a governing philosophy than it is to actually put one into practice. Heavy hangs the head that wears the crown and all that. This job is the most challenging I've ever had, and that includes being the only doctor in the emergency room at one a.m. in Atlanta when I was in school. That's because I know that every decision I make impacts hundreds of lives, and the future of one of the last organized colonies of people on Earth. Think about that for a moment. Think about our place in this world. It's kind of amazing."

She paced to her right and stopped closer to the front of the stage.

"So, back to the question…What is my governing philosophy? Empower the people, and be transparent in what you do. In that sense, this debate is awesome, because I'm given a forum through which to directly communicate with you all, and help you understand my decision-making process. Does safety matter? Of course. But is that a governing philosophy? Haven't we seen what happens when some subjective idea of 'safety' becomes the North Star by which we guide everything we do? I have faith in the people of Alessandra. I have faith that you want more for yourselves than to have your present and future shaped by someone's sense of what makes you feel safe. You want freedom. You want to have rich lives, and a sense of community. You want your leader to behave with integrity, and trust in you to be a part of the solution instead of just a cog in a big wheel. That's why I believe in Alessandra."

Zac didn't think that was a surprising answer, and he was pretty pleased with it. Stephanie had basically surrendered the "safety and security candidate" mantle to Zac, and he'd wear that badge with honor. For those Alessandrans who were concerned with the direction of the town, and the ability of Stephanie to keep them safe—and he was betting there were a lot of people like that—he was the candidate who was most focused on changing that.

"Okay, on to the next question," Michael said. "What would go into your decision on whether or not to allow particular migrants to stay and live in Alessandra? Stephanie, you're first this time."

"Thanks, Michael. I think the answer to this question says

a lot about who we are as a community. What are our values?
What do we believe in? The Alessandra I know opens its
arms wide, even in the most difficult of times. We don't turn
people in need away if we can afford to take them in. We
know that new people and new perspectives contribute to our
great town, that diversity is a strength and not a weakness. I
look, of course, for need first. I then try to evaluate what this
person can add to our town. Do they have a particular skill
set that we could use? Can they do carpentry, like Tyrone and
Cherie, who came to our gates around this time a year ago?
Are they knowledgeable about gardening, like Emily? Can
they build and landscape, like Derrick, who's lying in a
hospital bed right now? These people can bring more back to
us in work than we give to them in resources, in addition to
being peaceful additions to our community."

Zac nearly leaped out of his seat to get the bullhorn,
snatching it out of Stephanie's hands. He didn't bother to
notice what her reaction might be.

"Look, no offense to people like Tyrone and Derrick, but
we need to get our own house in order before we start taking
others in. Now, I'm not saying they did it or anything, but
these murders weren't happening before Stephanie started
letting outsiders in. I'd keep that gate locked until we feel
confident that Alessandra is on the best footing it can be.
Personally, and I don't think I'm alone, I think we have to
acknowledge that this is a dangerous world, and we can take
care of each other far better with that gate locked than if we
keep opening it to every random person who wanders up to
it. Stephanie is willing to put you in danger in order to appear
to be the good guy, but she's clearly not ready to defend you
against those who would hurt you."

Another fractured round of applause met Zac's words,
though he thought it seemed less enthusiastic than the first
one. He wasn't sure if that was just in his head. It wasn't like

everyone was going to burst into cheers and carry him off to the mayor's mansion on their shoulders, whatever his fantasies might be, but he wished he was getting more of a positive vibe from the crowd. He handed the bullhorn to Michael.

"Next question," Michael said. "What sorts of punishments do you think are appropriate for people who behave in ways the people of Alessandra find to be wrong? Zac, you're up."

"Dead men commit no crimes," Zac said, a grin crossing his lips. "I think we have to accept that the death penalty is an essential—*extreme*, but essential—part of any rational punishment policy. It's the only foolproof way of dealing with those who commit unacceptable sins. They have to be dealt with harshly, both to prevent them from ever doing it again, and to provide the ultimate deterrent to others who might be tempted to do the same. Of course, there should be tiers leading to that most final solution—ration reduction, house arrest, a jail at the mansion, and banishment would be among them. But, frankly, some people forfeit their right to life with their behavior. And we treat them with kid gloves at our peril, while cheapening the lives of those who've earned the breaths they're taking each day. We can't hesitate to act without mercy when the time comes that mercy has become unworkable. We must pluck out the eye that saw evil. We must take their heart, to let the rest know that they cross Alessandra with the guillotine hanging over their heads."

Zac practically bowed after finishing, but even the scattered applause didn't come. Were they just waiting for Stephanie's rebuttal? He thought he'd nailed that answer, but the response wasn't what he'd hoped again. He laid the bullhorn on the stage and walked swiftly back to his chair, brushing Stephanie's shoulder as he did.

"While I certainly understand the primal appeal of the

death penalty, especially in today's world, I think we need to understand just *how* final it is," she said, walking slowly toward the front of the stage. "We have virtually none of what used to be 'modern' investigative methods here. Even *with* those, there was no way to be a hundred percent certain someone committed a crime. That's a large part of the reason the bar was set so high for juries, to have to find criminals guilty beyond a reasonable doubt. Defendants were found guilty or not guilty, *not* innocent. That was purposeful. Once we kill someone, we're righteously saying we're infallible, when we know we aren't. This is why I'm even uncomfortable with banishment, as it's essentially a death penalty we can just pretend is something else. I firmly believe that social forces will prevent—and *have prevented*—the vast majority of crimes in a town of our size. Yes, there have been recent problems. But keep in mind that those problems are as troubling as they are in large part because they've been *so rare*. Over the five seasons or so I've been leading this town, the crime rate has been virtually non-existent. Social pressures and incentives can accomplish a hell of a lot in Alessandra. If you prove yourself to be untrustworthy, people won't want to be friends with you, or work beside you, or live near you. Becoming a pariah is a real risk, and there's nowhere else for you to go. If someone shows that won't work for them, yes, I agree that house arrest could be worthwhile, perhaps even ration reduction and, on the most extreme end of the scale, banishment. But my experience tells me that's needed only in the rarest of cases, and we should admit our own imperfections before judging others so harshly."

Zac found himself analyzing the crowd closely, stretching his neck to see every head nod and whisper to a friend standing nearby, wondering what they were saying. He didn't want to obsess over it all, but he was struggling not to let it distract him.

"Now for the final question," Michael said. "Stephanie, this is for you first: Under your leadership, in ten years, what do you think will be different and better for Alessandra? This will also serve as your closing statement."

"Okay, great. I hope you can see some of the changes starting already. In ten years, I expect to continue much of what I've begun. I think Alessandra will be a kinder place, a safer place, and a more *free* place than it is today and than it's been in its recent past. I plan to make further strides toward making Alessandra more diverse and more accepting of all of our differences. I look forward to leading you into recreating technologies that we had in the pre-virus world, doing a better job of farming and preserving food, increasing rations in the process as we improve sanitation and means of communication. Alessandra is in a position to be one of the founding democracies of a new world, and I take that responsibility seriously. I know you do too. The next decade—forty seasons—will tell quite a tale when it comes to how far we can go. I can't wait to walk shoulder to shoulder with you there. Thank you."

Zac had wanted to pull her down into more divisive rhetoric, but it seemed like she'd stayed her course, remaining calm and together, exactly what he hadn't needed. The question for him now as he took the bullhorn back and walked to the front of the stage was whether he could beat her in a competition of calm leaders, or if he needed to veer off course.

"You all have heard a lot of words from Stephanie today—words I think most of you know don't sit well with the reality we're living in. People are being murdered in this town, and her priorities are diversity and kindness? I don't know about you, but I feel like that's about as tone deaf as it gets. How will Zac Latham take Alessandra into the next decade? With a fucking *forceful hand*, that's how. I don't have the first clue as to whether or not Alessandra will be more diverse, but it'll be a damn shade safer, I'll tell ya that much. We won't have to lock our doors, or worry that our children might be raped in the street. We'll know our neighbors. We'll have common ground, and a shared set of values. We'll strike back harshly against those who wrong us. And if that includes Stephanie herself, then she'll be imprisoned, banished, or killed just like the rest of them. *Nobody's* immune. We're going to take back Alessandra. Thanks."

35

Nick winced and slammed his shot glass on the bar, then slid it across to Walt.

"How'd you think it went?" Nick asked.

"Politics is bullshit, is what I think," Walt spoke through gravel, wiping the glass with a dirty rag and pouring another half glass of his moonshine. "I thought we'd left that shit behind in the old world."

He poured a second glass and pushed one of them over to Nick, who wrapped his fingers around it.

"It was always bound to come back." Nick lifted the glass to his lips and paused. "Do you think we'll have a new leader by next week?"

"The only fucking constant is change." Walt tossed back his shot at the same time as Nick, and then wiped his sleeve across his mouth. "So either she'll change, or we will. That little dog-and-pony show ain't gonna change shit with me. I'm still gonna be right here, pourin' this stuff for whoever stops by."

"Hey, Nick," Hank said, sliding into the barstool next to him. "It *does* seem like a good time for a drink, doesn't it?"

Hank raised a finger to Walt, who grabbed a glass and reached behind the bar.

"Don't ask Walt about the debate," Nick said. "He has no opinion, as usual."

"Ah, Walt. Always the diplomat."

"A good rule of thumb for life, boys." Walt slid a shot over to Hank, then another to Nick. "Don't make fun of the man pouring you free shots of hooch."

Hank raised his glass and motioned for a toast. Walt snorted and walked to the other side of the bar to help someone else; Nick tapped his glass to Hank's, and they both drank. Hank squeezed his eyes tight and rattled his head back and forth.

"God damn," Hank said. "What does he put in that shit?"

"Nobody knows. It's probably slowly killing us all."

"Could be worse."

Nick laughed and nodded, banging his glass on the bar and beginning to feel the effects of the alcohol. He'd been drinking here for years and had developed a solid tolerance for whatever it was Walt was pouring, but his head started swimming around the fifth shot. He was still deciding how drunk he was going to get this particular day.

"Thoughts on the debate?" Nick asked. "Is it gonna be Stephanie or Zac?"

Hank laughed. "Well, this is Alessandra, so anything can happen. Hell if I know. But I was standing next to Leslie and Quinn during the talk, and neither of them was buying much from Zac. It all just seemed either over the top or weirdly restrained, like he'd rehearsed in order to look less nuts. Talked to a few other people between the square and here. Only one or two sounded like they were considering Zac. This whole 'Safety is the only thing that matters' argument just isn't going to work today. We're more resilient than we were a couple of years ago, ya know? And this is coming from a guy who's still healing from a concussion and a couple of broken ribs. If *I'm* not willing to turn my life over to a crazy guy in the name of safety, who will? Back when the virus was still a big threat, I think we were more susceptible to an argument like that. It was our survival as a species at that point. But today, I just don't see it working. Maybe that's the only way he thinks he can take down Stephanie, though."

"Right. I trust Stephanie. What reason do I have to trust Zac? He talks like the world's about to end and he's the only one who can save us. He's more than a little out there."

"Look who's fucking talking." The voice came from behind Nick, and he swiveled around to see who it was. He saw Benjamin and Andy standing there. Nick ignored them and turned back to Hank.

"Yeah, I'm talking to *you*, Nick," Benjamin said, nearly yelling. Nick bowed his head and sighed, hearing their footsteps coming closer. "You calling someone else crazy is pretty rich. Ever check out a mirror?"

Benjamin and Andy stopped next to them, both glaring at Nick.

"We're just having a conversation here, guys," Hank said. "We don't want any trouble."

Nick noticed Benjamin's right hand was wrapped tightly in bandages that spots of dried blood had soaked through.

"Why'd you insult Zac?" Andy asked. "He's our friend, and he's trying to protect this town. We don't think he deserves that."

Nick raised both hands up in surrender. "Hey, look, guys. Hank's right. We don't want any trouble. I was just expressing my opinion. We're still allowed to do that around here. Sorry if it bothered you. But this is a fucking *bar*, okay? We're drinking and talking about shit that's happening around town. What the hell else is there to do?"

"Oh, I don't know," Benjamin said. "I bet you wouldn't mind fucking Rachel right about now. I sure enjoyed the hell out of it."

His body starting to shake violently, Nick leaped off the stool and pressed his chest to Benjamin, who stumbled backward.

"Whoa, guys," Hank said, trying to grab Nick by the shoulder. "Let's stay cool. Come on, Nick. We can go."

Nick barely heard him, his eyes locked on Benjamin's, breathing heavily into his face.

"I'll give you one chance to take that shit back." Nick bit the words off like snapping twigs.

"Did you think you were the only one who got a piece of that ass?" Benjamin said. "Get real, man. She banged every guy in Towns County."

Nick shoved Benjamin back, then launched himself forward, driving his body into Benjamin's and crashing into a cluster of tables, sending a group of drinkers scrambling. Nick threw a couple of wild punches, neither landing with much force. He felt Benjamin trying to kick him, and he pressed Benjamin's legs to the floor with his knees. Benjamin was grabbing Nick with his left hand, seemingly trying to hold their chests close together; he tried to hit Nick with that hand a couple of times, but he hadn't been very effective with it as his right hand lay limp on the floor.

Connecting with a couple of punches to Benjamin's cheek, Nick felt like he had him stunned for a moment. Nick rolled off to the side and let all his weight fall hard on Benjamin's right hand. Benjamin screamed as loud as Nick had ever heard a man, a piercing, pitiful yell that jammed into Nick's ears like an ice pick. Nick felt a shove from behind; he fell forward onto Benjamin's face and then spun around to look toward the ceiling.

He caught a glimpse of Andy holding a barstool in his hands, and then the stool hurtling toward his face. That was the last thing he remembered before he was knocked out.

36

"You can't possibly be serious!" Zac said, pacing his living room. "Are you sure?"

"I mean, we're not professional pollsters. This is all pretty informal," Andy said meekly, Benjamin standing next to him clutching his right hand. "But, from the people we talked to, opinion's running something like five to one for Stephanie right now."

A bang rattled through the room as Zac slammed his fist into the far wall, leaving a small dent in the plaster. He shook his head, his face still scratched and heavily bruised.

"I just don't fucking *get* it," he said. "What do they want? After all of this, they're still considering going with that woman? What more would they have to see to understand that she has no idea how to keep them safe? She's just grasping at goddamn straws. Do I need to remind them that Father Hayden is *dead* because of her? Jesus."

"We totally agree. You've been making sense from the beginning. That's why we're here," Andy said. "I'm just not sure what the next move is. Has the previous violence not been enough? Do we need a bigger statement?"

It had certainly been on Zac's mind. The original plan had been to sow more violence, and he guessed he still could. The problem was that people were paying attention now. His rhetoric had served to basically put everyone on edge. That meant more people would be watching for suspicious behavior and reporting anything remotely unusual they saw. He had been able to catch the town napping for a bit, but that wouldn't last much longer. Every criminal act they committed would increase the chances he'd be caught. And given that he was running against Stephanie and people already didn't seem to trust him, he'd be a logical suspect in any violence that occurred from this point.

He also had a lot more to lose now. Before he had been on that stage with Stephanie, what was she even going to do to him if she found out he was responsible for the attacks? Rely on some sort of "social" consequences? He'd be a pariah or something? He could have lived with that. Now, though, he was *this close* to the throne he wanted. He just needed to convince a few more people. It was a small town; the vote could shift on something small. He needed to figure out what that might be.

"I don't know. A bigger statement might be too much of a risk at this point," Zac said. "It's tough to go much bigger than Father Hayden, anyway. If that didn't move the needle enough, we may need a different tactic altogether."

"We're hearing that people want to be safe, but they still seem to think that Stephanie is the type of steady leader who can get them there," Andy said. "They're still skeptical of you, with no real leadership experience, and they think you seem volatile."

"Fuckin' A…Volatile." Zac laughed, shaking his head. "Does my military experience not help? I was a fucking sergeant. That's not nothing. Does no one remember any of that?"

Andy shrugged.

"Lots of shit has happened since then," Benjamin said, pushing himself off the wall and wincing. "I think they think you're a different man. Maybe they're right. I don't really know. I just wish they could know the real *you*. I wish they could truly understand how passionate you are for this town, and how much you want to make it great. You're willing to sacrifice everything for them, and I think that's noble. It pisses me off when people suggest otherwise."

Zac nodded and looked away, then glanced back.

"Is your hand getting worse? Did you somehow get hurt more from punching me in the face than I did from being punched?"

Benjamin held his hand against his body, stepping back toward the wall. Andy walked over to Zac.

"We got in a bit of a fight with Nick and Hank over at Walt's after the debate," Andy explained, in a low voice. "They were shit talking you. We just couldn't take it any longer. Benjamin was pretty damn brave, jumping in there with his hand in the shape it was in. But Nick got him on the ground and jumped on it. Probably did more damage to it. It's been bothering him pretty bad on the way here, but he refuses to go to Saint Francis. Says it could raise suspicion about where your bruises came from."

Zac looked over Andy's shoulder at Benjamin. "That certainly *was* true, but maybe that fight could give him an excuse to get the hand checked out. Take him over there. Tell 'em about the fight. That sort of shit happens. How'd you leave Nick and Hank?"

Andy smiled.

"Unconscious on the floor when we walked out. And it wasn't from the moonshine."

"That's fantastic." Zac laughed loudly, then slapped Andy on the shoulder. "Appreciate you guys. I'll remember it when I'm on that throne."

"We know you'll take care of us. Do you have any idea of what you can do from here? Did the polling help?"

Zac's eyes dropped, and he scratched his head, then ran

his hand across his hair, grabbing the back of his neck.

"You say they want to feel safe and secure, but they also want someone they feel is steady and experienced to get them there? Is that about it?"

"Like I said, our methods are far from perfect, but we talked to and eavesdropped on as many people as we could after the debate, and that's pretty much what we heard."

Zac took a deep breath and exhaled, his eyes closed.

"Then I've got an idea." He opened his eyes and looked at Andy. "I'm probably crazy for trying it, but it may be the only chance I've got."

37

Stephanie nudged the door open with her left hand and peeked her head around the corner into the room, Michael waiting behind her.

"Knock knock," she said. "You awake?"

Derrick's head turned away from the window.

"Yeah, I'm good. Come on in. I always struggle to sleep when it's light out."

She walked over next to the bed while Michael sat in a chair against the wall.

"You look great!" Stephanie said, and she meant it. Compared to her first visit, Derrick looked like a new man. He was barely conscious the previous time, and she could tell he was in a lot of pain. Now, he appeared rested. "I talked to the doctors. They said you could be out of here in a day or two."

"Yeah, that's what I hear. It'll be nice to get back to my lumpy mattress at home."

"You never know what you have until you lose it, do ya?"

He laughed. "I think we're learning that's true on a lot of levels these days." He pushed himself up into a sitting position on the bed, his head resting against the wall behind him. "So, why are you guys stopping by?"

"First off, obviously, we wanted to check in and see how you were doing," she said, folding her hands in her lap. "I had heard a few things from the people I know here, but I had to see it for my own eyes. It really is great to see, Derrick."

She reached out and lightly patted his shoulder.

"Beyond that," she said, "I don't know if you've heard much of what's been going on out there."

"You mean about Father Hayden?"

She pressed her eyes shut and lowered her head.

"Well, there's that. So you heard? I'm so sorry, Derrick. I know you two were close."

"Yeah." Stephanie could hear his voice catch a bit, and he looked back out the window without speaking for a few seconds. "When I first got to Alessandra, he gave me work before anyone else would. He embraced me as a brother and a neighbor, without question. That meant a lot to me. And it was like that gave other people the permission they needed to treat me like a friend too. Father Hayden was a good man. And I can't help but think about how he'd still be alive if…"

He trailed off and looked at the ceiling, tears escaping his eyes and hitting his cheek. Stephanie laid her hand on top of his.

"I think about how he'd be alive if they hadn't gotten me, ya know?" He looked back at Stephanie, his voice choked. "Maybe I wasn't careful enough. Maybe they followed me, stalked me over there. I brought those guys to his door, and then I let myself be knocked out so I couldn't protect him. I don't know if they'd planned on hurting Father Hayden from the start, but maybe he just happened upon them. Maybe if I'd fought them off, or if I'd paid more attention, he'd still be alive."

Derrick shook his head, his eyes closed. Stephanie pulled a tissue out of a box by his bed and handed it to him. He took it and nodded, wiping his face.

"I'd give anything to have five minutes alone in a room

with whoever did this, once I'm better," he said. "I'd make them pay for this. They deserve whatever they get."

"You *can't* blame yourself. You don't know what their plans were, and you couldn't have known they were coming. It wasn't even fully light out, and you were focused on your work. You were doing a good thing; I'm certain Father Hayden wouldn't blame you even a little bit."

Derrick nodded slightly and blew his nose into the tissue.

"But 'whoever did this' is sort of where we come in," she said. "I hate to tell you that we still don't have that answer. I really thought we had William. Hank identified him as his assailant, and I know some of his tendencies from before, but I'm just not sure anymore. I'm not a homicide investigator, though. Neither is Michael. That's just not a skill we have in plentiful supply in Alessandra. I'm doing the best I can, but finding useful evidence is tough. It would really help if you remembered something. *Anything.* Maybe you glimpsed someone out of the corner of your eye, or heard something distinct."

Balling the tissue up in his fist, Derrick lolled his head to the side. He looked like he was thinking hard, trying to will a memory into his head.

"I mean, I *want* to remember something," he said. "I really do. And, hell, I could lie to you and say I did. But I don't want to punish the *wrong* man here. The worst thing would be to go nuts on the wrong guy while the guilty man still walked the streets, waiting for his next opportunity to hurt someone."

Stephanie nodded. "Yeah, and that's sort of where we are now." She glanced back at Michael, who raised his eyebrows. "I was sure it was William until he was up here when Zac was assaulted. So, we either have a copycat, or—"

"Zac?" Derrick's eyes perked up, looking at her.

"Zac. Yeah," she said. "I was giving a speech in the

square, and Zac came wandering up the street with a bloodied—"

"I think I remember something."

Stephanie's heart skipped. "What? About your assault?"

"Yeah…Yeah!" His eyes were darting around the room, like a memory was trying to fly away and he didn't want to lose sight of it. "I was pretty out of it after getting knocked down. But…okay, so I was a little in and out on the ride up to the hospital. It's fuzzy, but the ride was rough. I was lying down, bouncing around. It was like the world was barely there, ya know? Like my mind was in another place, and I couldn't bring it back. So, at some point—we must have been pretty close to the hospital—I fell and hit the ground fairly hard. It's where I got these scratches."

Derrick lifted his right arm and draped it across his body to show Stephanie some scrapes along the underside of it.

"That jarred me a bit, and I had just the slightest bit of awareness of someone struggling to lift me off the ground, yanking at my arms, then one leg, then another. I was still groggy, but my eyes opened briefly. I'm sure he didn't notice. The guy was Zac. I'm sure of it."

Stephanie gasped, stumbling back a step. She heard Michael jump up from his chair.

"*How* sure are you?" Michael said. "This is important."

"A hundred percent. Stake my life on it. It was him."

Stephanie's heart was pounding fast.

"Is there anything you can think of that we could get for evidence? We trust you, but having more than just you saying so would help a hell of a lot."

Derrick paused for a moment. "Check with the hospital. Find out if they're missing a gurney. If you can find their missing gurney at Zac's place, that may be enough."

"I'm on it," Michael said, darting out of the room.

38

Hands and crooked elbows raised in the air, Zac stepped off the curb into Audrey's yard. As he did, two of her men stepped out the front door onto the porch. He could see one of them holding a baseball bat.

"It's fine, guys," Zac said. "I'm here in peace. I recognize that I've been wrong."

The men said nothing, just stood on the porch, arms hanging at their sides.

"I was hoping to...um, get an audience with Audrey this afternoon." Zac took a few steps closer to the house. "I'd like to apologize to her for my behavior, and make her an offer of peace. I think we can help each other."

If the men even heard him, there was no way to tell. Were they deaf?

"You guys aren't the talkative sort, are you?"

Behind them, the door opened, and Audrey stepped out, wearing faded, tattered jeans and a grey blouse that looked like it was too big for her.

"You came here looking for peace?" she asked. "Why should I give it to you?"

"Look, I get that I was wrong, okay?" Zac was standing at the foot of the porch now. "I understand why you had to do what you did before. It was a hard decision, but it's the type of decision I'll have to make once I'm leading the town. The

JEFF HAWS

closer I get to that position, the more I get how hard it is. You have to make hard calls every single day. Sometimes, those may even mean that a few have to lose in order for the town as a whole to win. Of course, I wish my wife and daughters hadn't been on the wrong side of that. Surely you understand why I took that personally. But I get it now. I was just being emotional. You were being smart. I'm sorry."

He looked up at Audrey, hoping that was enough to get her on his side. Supplicating himself wasn't easy, but he thought it might be his only chance to get inside. As he said it out loud, more of it felt plausibly true to him than he thought it would when he rehearsed it on the way over. Had she *actually* been right to do what she did? The fact that he couldn't completely rule it out if he looked at the situation dispassionately bothered him.

Audrey nodded and turned around, stepping back through the doorway. The men stood to the side, and one of them motioned for Zac to come inside.

"So, what is it I can do for you, Zac?" Audrey sat in a brown wicker chair, on a burgundy cushion with tufts of cotton poking through the threads. Two of her men flanked the chair, while Zac settled into the ragged couch across the room from her. "This is certainly an unexpected visit."

"Yeah. It's just something I've been thinking about a lot lately, even since before the debate. There might be a mutually beneficial arrangement you and I could work out."

"And how's that?"

"Well, what I'm seeing is that the people seem to agree with my general idea that safety is the most important thing, but that they still trust Stephanie more. She's just…more experienced, more generally respected. You probably know I'm not the most popular guy around town. I haven't made a ton of friends. But I'm *right* here, damn it. I fear that

Alessandra is in the middle of a full-blown crisis and, instead of fixing the wound, they're holding a fucking popularity contest. I fear for us, Audrey. I fear for our town. If Stephanie survives this challenge, I shudder to think what it's going to actually take to dislodge her from power. She tries hard, but she's incompetent at this job."

Audrey listened to Zac, barely blinking. "I'm not hearing anything about me yet," she said, a slight edge to her voice.

"We both have something the other wants. You don't want to leave here. And don't give me that shit again about it being temporary. I know you enough to know you don't want to walk back out of those gates. You don't want to wander the woods and mountains, barely surviving on fruits and nuts until you eventually wither away. You know you have more to offer than that, and you want to do that here. You wanna stay. But, right now, Stephanie holds the key to that. And, from what I hear, she's threatened by you, and she's not inclined to give you permanent residence."

Zac paused for a moment, taking a breath.

"What I want is to be where Stephanie is, which would mean I would be the one deciding on your fate. I could, of course, banish you the same way she's planning to do. On the other hand, if you were to publicly endorse me, talk me up as a leader to other people in the town, I'd owe you something when I got elected."

"And that something," Audrey said, "would be my permanent residence."

"Exactly. Look, you have what I don't and can't buy— political experience, respect among a large portion of the town, name recognition, and you're smart. You know what people need to hear in order to vote for me. You've run a bunch of campaigns before. This is in your wheelhouse. And let's face it, you agree with me a lot more than you agree with her. I'm a far better person to carry your legacy forward. I admire what you did for us. You kept us safe. This town hasn't been the same since you left. I want to bring that philosophy back."

Audrey considered what he was saying. He wasn't completely wrong. Was this a partnership that could work? She had been mostly laying low since she'd arrived, but she wouldn't mind doing a bit of canvassing. She'd be back in her comfort zone. And if it helped her keep her comfortable bed, it might very well be worth it.

"Can you give me a little while to think about it?" Audrey finally said. "This is a big decision. It'd be a public rebuke of Stephanie, so I have to think about how to navigate that if I choose to do it."

"Of course. Yes. Just…keep in mind that time is short. The vote's in just a few days. The sooner we can get going on this, the better our chances are of making it work."

"I'll come visit you to give my decision by tomorrow morning. How's that?"

"Perfect," Zac stood and extended his hand. Audrey stood part of the way up and shook it. "Looking forward to hopefully working with you again."

39

"Do you see anything?" Michael asked, standing on Zac's front porch.

"It's quiet as far as I can tell." Stephanie crouched beneath Zac's front window, peeking her eyes just high enough to see between the curtains inside. "If he hasn't answered after knocking three times, he's probably not here."

"I guess we can give this another shot later."

"Maybe he's out hurting someone else." She stood and walked toward the porch.

Michael shook his head. "Hopefully not. We could always just wait for him. Sit right here on the porch."

"Seems a little obvious, don't you think? Everybody's gonna see us out here. He might even see us before we see him, know something's up, and then take off. You really think he's just gonna stroll up to us and welcome us in for some tea and cookies while we snoop around to figure out if he's a murderer?"

"Fine. Then we come back later. Get him when he's inside and can't just run."

"But we have no idea when that could be. We're just gonna keep coming back here every hour or so until he's home?"

"You've got a better idea?" Michael leaned against the side of the house and folded his arms.

"Look, if he's got a gurney that's big enough to lug Derrick up to the hospital, he's probably not keeping it inside the house. It takes up too much space. Doesn't this place have a detached garage out back?"

Michael looked up, his head bobbing for a moment. "I...*think* so."

"Uh-huh. And that's where the gurney is. Let's just go back there and check."

"You want to break into his house?"

"His *garage*. Not his house. This is about catching a killer. You said yourself, he might be out hurting someone else right now. We're gonna let some informal idea of privacy violation keep us from investigating that and maybe putting this crap to bed?"

"Maybe. I'm just not—"

"Michael...think about it. Not only would this mean we've caught the killer, but it would also extinguish this idea of Zac leading the town. You know as well as I do what a nightmare that would be. This would end it all. If you feel strongly enough that you need to leave, I won't hold it against you. But I'm going back there. I'd like you to come with me."

Michael looked down and scratched his forehead. He closed his eyes and breathed deep, then leaped off the porch and followed Stephanie around the side of the house.

"Well, it's locked," Michael said, jiggling the doorknob to the garage. "I guess that was predictable."

Stephanie walked around the left side of the garage and saw a high window. Even standing straight up, she couldn't see through the bottom of it. There was enough of a lip on the concrete for her to get her hands on there and pull herself up; she held there for a couple of seconds, peering inside. On a quick glance, she could see maybe half of the garage. It looked pretty cluttered, with shelves littered with various rusty tools and rags, paint cans strewn on the floor and even an old lawnmower.

"What could you see?" Michael asked, peeking around the corner.

"No jackpot yet, at least in the part I could actually see. Lots of junk. But there weren't a ton of cobwebs either. That makes me doubt this is a time capsule or anything like that. I think he uses it."

"Okay, good. That's a start. Any idea how we get in?"

Stephanie walked around to the back of the garage and pushed some overgrown weeds out of the way to reveal a plain concrete wall. The other wall was right up against a picket fence.

"No dice in back, unless we've got a tank." She walked back to Michael, who was looking up at the window Stephanie was peeking through earlier. "The window here is pretty high. If we found something to break it with, one of us might be able to boost the other one up high enough to get through it, then unlock the door from the inside."

"Yeah. But it's also high enough that it'll be hard to get all the glass out. Good chance we get cut. And getting cut is bad news these days. Lots of risk of infection, especially with what's probably an old, dirty window."

Stephanie nodded. "Ya know, there may be one other possibility…"

She walked around to the opposite side of the garage and looked down the fence line. As she'd guessed, there was also a window on that side. Same size and height, but the opposite corner. She guessed the picket fence was maybe two feet shorter than the bottom of the window.

"Michael, come check this out." He came around the front of the garage and walked over to her. "What if I went into the neighbor's yard there and climbed up on the fence? If I could balance myself on that horizontal board, I'd be high enough to break the glass with…something. Maybe we can find a big rock. Then I'd probably be able to clear all the glass off there and just climb inside."

"It's probably a delicate fall to the floor going through there head first."

"If I can get my skinny ass through there, I'll figure that part out."

"Think there's any possibility he notices the broken window and knows someone's after him before we can get to him?"

Stephanie stopped for a second and thought.

"I can't imagine he's out here all the damn time. It's a small, old garage. We'll hide the broken glass as much as possible. I'd be surprised if we don't have him in custody before he has a hint anything's up."

"It will be important not to tip him off, though. If we find this gurney, we plan to come back tomorrow morning. Give him a chance to get home, settle in, and think everything's fine. Wait until just after daylight, and we should have him. Now, let's find something to break that damn window."

They spread out across Zac's back yard, Stephanie heading toward the overgrown half near the back fence and Michael searching closer to the back porch.

It was challenging to care for a yard these days, and Zac wasn't the only one who didn't put much effort into it. Weeds had long ago taken over what Stephanie remembered as a fairly well-manicured lawn in the old world. Back before Zac's wife and daughters had died, they'd had occasional barbecues or other parties and invited most of the town. She'd been over a time or two, and remembered them as a happy, seemingly normal family. Had this evil always been inside him and he'd just hidden it from everyone, or did losing his family trigger something inside of him? Seeing the previously nice lawn overtaken by angry, invasive weeds made her wonder how it all had changed so much. It was sad, thinking about what might have been, and the toll this virus had taken on so many.

"Stephanie!" Michael's voice snapped her back to the present, and she swung around. His obvious excitement suggested he'd found something more than a rock. "You need to come over here now!"

She jogged in his direction; when she got about halfway there, she could see it barely showing through a maze of vines and bushes—a blue tarp. Michael was yanking them apart, snapping vines.

Stephanie rushed over to help him clear away the shrubbery, revealing more of the tarp with each vine she pulled away. It didn't take long before they were both standing there, breathing heavily, staring down.

She looked at Michael and smiled. They grabbed the tarp and pulled it to their right, spreading it across the ground.

Stephanie's heart jumped when she saw it.

"Holy shit, we got him," she said. "We fucking got him. And if he did this, does this mean he killed Father Hayden too?"

"If not, that's a crazy coincidence that he was there the same morning."

She turned to Michael. "Unless someone was with him. But—"

A wailing noise began to slowly creep down the street in front of Zac's house, and Stephanie's back stiffened.

"What the hell is that?" Michael asked.

"I think…it's the siren on the hospital's electric vehicle. Shit. That's not good."

Stephanie turned and started running.

"Where are you going?" Michael yelled.

She stopped and turned back. The siren was very close

now.

"Cover that thing up. Get everything back as close as possible to how it was before we got here. I need to check on this. It's an emergency, whatever it is."

Stephanie ran around to the front of the house and saw the hospital's electric SUV coming fast down the street and quickly past her. Its tires squealed to a stop three houses away, at the Brownings' home.

She saw two people wearing hazmat suits jump out of the vehicle and run toward the house; her heart sank, and she felt a sudden nausea. Instead of going to the front door, she approached the driver's door of the vehicle. She knew the driver would stay there and keep the engine running so they could move fast.

She banged on the door and saw the driver was wearing a gas mask. He swung toward her, startled, then pushed the button to roll down the window.

"What's going on?" She felt like she was screaming.

"You need to get out of here!" the driver said, his voice wobbly and a little ominous through the amplifier. "It's not safe without protection! Go!"

"I'm Doctor Sloan," she said, attempting to stay as calm as possible. "I need to know what the situation is!"

He glanced back at the house; no one had come out yet. He turned back to Stephanie.

"Tyrone has boils on his skin. We're not sure how many yet."

Stephanie stumbled and nearly fell backward. The driver reached out to grab her arm and steady her.

"Are you okay?" he asked.

She pressed a hand to her forehead and closed her eyes, then nodded.

"You need to go now, before they come back," he said firmly. "Get inside somewhere if you can."

She started to leave and felt dizzy, putting a hand on the side of the vehicle to keep herself upright. Then she heard screams coming from the house. They were coming out the front door.

"Now!" the driver said. "Go! Run!"

And she did.

40

"Shit, you're here," Zac said, looking around into the dark beginnings of dawn behind Audrey, standing on his front porch with her arms crossed. "I didn't think you'd come. Did you hear about the lockdown?"

"Of course. In fact, that's a big reason why I came. The stakes were just raised. No time to mess around."

"Um…yeah. Sure. I'm just barely awake, and it's dark in here. Come on in. Let me grab a few candles. Go ahead and find your way to the couch if you can see it."

Audrey hadn't been able to sleep much since Stephanie's voice had boomed through the bullhorn, announcing a possible new case of the H6N1 virus, and that everyone should stay inside their homes until further notice. She didn't say who it was, but Audrey knew that would leak out soon enough. She did say they'd successfully quarantined the person at Saint Francis, and they'd provide an update after they knew more.

Up until that moment, it'd been easy to think the virus had been eradicated. It'd been a long time since any new cases of it had arisen. Having a regional quarantine and research center at Saint Francis had probably been what insulated Alessandra from the first, most deadly attack of the virus; it had given them somewhere to immediately take victims and seal them off from the rest of the population.

Many towns didn't have that and tried to make do with locking doors and closing windows. But, as people continued to get sick and die drawn-out, painful deaths, suicide had become almost as common a cause of death as the virus.

Audrey knew this had to feel ominous—and familiar—for the town. The last time, though, she had been isolated up on the hill in that big mansion, secure in her distance. Now, though, she was right there with everyone else, so she had to be more careful. Hell, it hadn't been long since the entire town had been gathered in the square. Whoever was showing symptoms of the virus was almost certainly there. Did they already have it then, and just didn't know it yet? Was everyone a ticking time bomb?

"Here we go." Zac returned to the living room carrying two thick red candles. He put a plate underneath them on the coffee table in front of Audrey and struck a match, lighting them both. "That's better. So, I'm hoping the fact that you're here so early means you have good news for me?"

"Hopefully you'll see it as good."

Zac sat back in his chair and folded his arms across his chest. "Okay, then. Whatcha got?"

Audrey had been thinking about this for much of the night, and had rehearsed her opening a few times. She wanted this pitch to go well, because she didn't like the alternative. She leaned forward, her eyes tight on Zac's.

"I do appreciate the value of your offer. I want you to know that. Your read on me is, honestly, pretty good. I *do* want to stay here. I'd like my men to be able to stay as well. Clearly, Stephanie's got bigger things on her mind right now, and I don't think she's itching to boot us, so there's a solid chance we get more than just the week she said she'd allow us. But the clock's ticking. And going out into the woods will almost certainly be a death sentence for at least one of us, with no logical direction to head in."

"That's what I could step in and prevent," Zac said. "So does that mean I have your endorsement?"

Audrey took in a deep breath.

"I'm not high on Stephanie's priority list right now, but what happens if I come out and publicly, loudly endorse you? She's done me a pretty big favor in letting us back in. That's practically spitting in her face. Maybe that spurs her to action, saying I've overstayed my welcome."

"I don't think she'd—"

"You saw her stand Nick up there to lie for her as well as I did. Don't give me some bullshit about her being ultra-virtuous. She may not be a ruthless politician, but she's got an instinct for survival. If she feels threatened, she's not above doing something underhanded. I just think it'd be too much for her to stand there and take."

"So…I still haven't heard what you're actually proposing."

"A spot in your administration. Deputy mayor. Or whatever you'd plan to call it. But your right hand. I'd be your top advisor and execution person, while you'd be able to think big picture. I'd help to realize your vision for the town, and offer my counsel from the inside. Think about it. We have similar enough philosophies that it should be a good fit. You need somebody like me. And then you could tell people you were planning on that. That'd help alleviate some of the concerns, I think. They'd know someone with more experience would be there with you. A stabilizing force, if you will. I'd talk about how I was flattered by the mention, but never confirm it until—"

"And what happens when you get tired of taking my orders?" Zac asked, his face stern.

"When I what?"

"I've seen the way you work, Audrey. I've seen what you'll do to maintain power. We all have. Can you honestly tell me this isn't your move to try to get back into that mansion, and then have your goons take me out the first chance they get?"

Audrey rolled her eyes. "That's not fair, Zac. I'm offering you the help you need. Just in a different way, but also more long term. I think this is a better offer than what you asked for."

"Only if I trust you. And what reason would I have to trust you? The offer I made was an exchange of your help to get me elected for me helping you stay in Alessandra. You instead want to change it to me making you the second-most powerful person in the world, and I'm supposed to thank you for that?"

"Yes. Because, otherwise, Stephanie's gonna wipe the floor with you. She's a damn *research doctor*, Zac. If this really is H6N1, how are you gonna compete with that? You were already losing ground over trust and stability. Now, you think you can beat a medical research specialist in the face of a virus that could kill everyone in the town if they don't figure out how to suffocate it? You need someone with experience dealing with this."

Zac looked at the far wall and shook his head.

"You're trying to bullshit me, Audrey, and I'm not falling for it. I'm not as naïve as you think. I know how to make sure people are quarantined as well as you or Stephanie does. You want to have me within arm's length so you can drive a knife into my back the first chance you get, and I'm not gonna let that happen. Rest assured, no matter who wins, you and your gang of mutes are gonna be on the first ticket out of Dodge. And we'll all be better off when that happens. This conversation is over. Get the hell out of my house."

Audrey closed her eyes, her head hanging toward the floor.

"I *strongly* encourage you to reconsider."

"Reconsider?" Zac laughed loudly. "Was I not clear before? Get the *fuck* out of my house! Do I have to physically throw you out?"

Audrey stood and sighed, shaking her head slowly as she turned to head for the door.

41

The sun's first light cresting the mountains in the distance, Michael twisted the knob on Stephanie's front door, kind of glad to feel it hitch. He hoped it wouldn't be this way much longer, but she was right to keep it locked for now. He inserted his key and unlocked it, then went inside, closing and locking it behind him.

"I'm here, Steph." He raised his voice loud enough for her to hear back in her room. "Come on out when you're ready."

As he crossed the living room to the couch, he could see some light coming from her bedroom; it looked like the door was open. It was unusual for her to sleep without the door closed. Maybe she was already up?

He stood still for a moment, listening for any sign of her moving around. No footsteps. No floorboard creaks. Slowly, he began walking down the hall toward the bedroom, past pictures hanging on the wall, one of the two of them at the Grand Canyon. He always liked that picture, her shoulder-length hair blowing in the breeze, silk scarf hanging loosely off her neck, one arm draped across his shoulders as she strained to get them both—and the canyon—in the shot. He remembered it must have taken her at least five tries to get the picture she wanted. By the time she took this one, they were both laughing uncontrollably, a moment of pure pleasure, looking out over one of the most beautiful landscapes on Earth. He sometimes thought about how the canyon was still out there, unchanged through all that had happened in the years between then and now, and what all he'd give to be able to go back, just to bear witness that some things were still static in this world.

He craned his neck to look around the corner into her room. It was silent, the bedsheets rumpled and slept in, an indent still lingering on one of the pillows. Where was she? The sun was barely up, and there was a quarantine on. Michael was trying to think where she might have gone, and one part of his mind wondered if he should care.

His discomfort with the fight they'd had after the debate was still there. He couldn't seem to fully shake it. They'd had their share of arguments over the years, but he couldn't help but feel like this was different. He was still going through the motions of being alongside her, but sometimes he resented that she felt like she could say whatever she wanted to him, and he'd just take it. There were no repercussions for her. She knew he'd come crawling back. Because what else did he have, really? Being with her gave him status and something like a purpose. What was he going to do? Walk away, back to his life of obscurity, trying to make sure people showed up in time for their shifts at the furniture factory when they didn't get paid a dime? What was the point of any of that? Of course he was going to come back. They both knew it. And so their relationship devolved into a cycle of periodic sex and resentment. Until here they were, him standing in her bedroom wondering where she'd gone without leaving so much as a note.

Then the silence was broken by a noise from the front of the house. A clicking, maybe. The doorknob jiggling. Then the door swung open, and he scampered back into the living room.

"Oh. Shit. You're here," Stephanie said, standing just inside the front door, wearing shorts and a maroon tank top, sweat beading on her forehead. "I just…squeezed in a jog and was hoping to get back here in time to wash up a bit."

Michael shook his head and walked toward the couch.

"I assumed you'd be locked up inside. Isn't there a quarantine on?"

"It's just a quick jog, Michael. You know I like to get these in to start the day."

"Sure." He was a little annoyed at her ignoring her own order, but there wasn't much point in arguing again. "That's fine, I guess. I just didn't know where you were."

"Well, now you do. I'll be fine after I get cleaned up."

"All right. Go for it."

He sat down on the couch, and she walked past him toward the hall.

"We'll pay Zac a visit after you're ready?" Michael asked.

She stopped, his back to him, and paused a few seconds.

"Yeah. I guess we do owe him a visit, huh?"

Thirty minutes later, Stephanie emerged from her room, wearing faded jeans and a flannel shirt with a frayed collar.

"I slept like shit." She draped her arm across her forehead as she flopped onto an armchair. "My mind just keeps swimming around everything."

"I know what you mean. And now we're basically stuck inside until we hear something from Saint Francis."

"Nah. That doesn't apply to us."

"We can't just keep acting like the quarantine doesn't matter. What if someone saw you jogging this morning? Or sees us just walking around like everything's fine? They're going to think they can too, and the virus can spread more quickly. We need to be careful."

Stephanie spun and went back to her bedroom; when she

came back out, she was carrying two gas masks.

"Grabbed these when I was at the hospital last night. They said they could spare a couple, as long as they got them back."

"Shit. Are we sure those work against the virus?"

"Well, we're really not even certain how H6N1 spreads. But it's pretty safe to assume there's some airborne component to it. These are N95 respirators, which should block virtually all airborne particles."

"So they're safe?"

"As long as they're worn properly, I'm confident in them. Wouldn't want to wear them for a long time or go run a marathon in them or anything. They're not exactly comfortable. But we should be good for a short walk down to Zac's place. I'll help you put it on."

"Where the hell is he?" Michael hissed through his respirator, peering in Zac's window. "I don't get it."

Stephanie knocked on the door a few more times. "Maybe he knows who it is, and he's ignoring us? Or just ignoring everybody?"

"I don't know. But the sun hasn't been up long. Seems like he should be here. Pretty sure we'd know in this town if he had a girlfriend."

Michael got as close to the glass as he could, cupping his arms around his mask, trying to cut off the glare of the early-morning sun behind him and get a clear view of Zac's living room. There was an old, brown cracked-leather couch on the left and a matching chair sitting next to it. Nothing he could see appeared out of the ordinary. The chair looked like it was in an odd position, not quite perpendicular to the couch, like maybe it'd been jostled a bit, but it was barely worth noting.

Scanning the room, he noticed two red candles on the coffee table. Neither was lit, but he squinted to look at them more closely. As the sunlight glanced off them, he could see there was a pool of wax glistening in the middle of them, suggesting they'd recently been lit. He couldn't say with any level of certainty *how* recently, but he'd burned enough candles in recent years to guess it couldn't be more than a few hours. The previous night, maybe? Perhaps. Or even more recently. And that meant Zac had almost certainly returned home between when they'd been there the previous afternoon and now. So was he just asleep and not hearing the knocks? Ignoring them and hoping they'd go away? Or did he come home and then leave again really early? When he'd attacked Derrick, it was right around this time.

"We need to get inside," Stephanie said. "If he's not here, we need to find him. He's dangerous, and there's a good chance he had an accomplice who's out there too."

"What's he going to do if he *is* here, and we just walk in?"

"He's a fucking murderer, Michael. I'm not worried about decorum at this point."

"It's not about decorum. It's about not overstepping our bounds. We aren't—"

"I'm trying the doorknob."

"What? We shouldn't just open his door and walk in. What if he's sitting in there with a gun or something? What about the law?"

"Jesus, Michael. We *are* the fucking law." Stephanie grabbed the doorknob, twisted and pushed. "Oh, look. The door just nudged open on its own. Did you see that? Might as well go inside and check it out."

Michael glared at Stephanie as she crept into the foyer, stepping lightly to avoid creaky spots in the floorboards. He jumped up to the porch and went in behind her, shutting the door. She peeked nto the living room, and he craned his neck to see around her.

From this higher angle, he could see he'd been right

about the candles. They were definitely freshly burned, the paraffin still floating thick within the candle husk, light bouncing off it like a wobbly mirror.

He took a step forward, onto the carpet. He also had a better angle at the chair now, and it had recently—perhaps *very* recently—shifted position. He could see the marks on the carpet where it had been sitting for what appeared to be some time, and they were still very clear.

Staying on the balls of his feet, Michael took another big step around the coffee table, and now could see around the wall into the kitchen with its black and white tiled floor that seemed like it was out of another era. He thought it could use some mopping, but was that worth using water for? He heard Stephanie trailing a few feet behind him.

Then, going a little further, he could see around the chair that there was something on the floor. Had he spilled someth—

"Shit." The words tumbled out of his mouth in a quick breath. "That's blood!"

He ran past the chair and saw Zac's body lying on the kitchen floor, blood still trickling from his neck, which had been sliced open all the way across. He fell to his knees and felt his muscles start to tense up. Stephanie ran over and was standing next to him.

"This is fresh, Stephanie." Michael looked around, his face feeling hot. "*Really* fresh."

"It looks that way." She crouched down and took a closer look, placing two fingers on his neck. "A couple hours, maybe."

"Jesus. Is he…?"

After a few moments, she shook her head. "Nothing."

Michael's mouth hung open inside his mask, his eyes unblinking. He took a deep breath, trying to calm his pounding heart. Stephanie pulled Michael's mask toward hers, making eye contact, then pointing at the back door off the kitchen.

"We need to go." She carefully moved her lips to the words without saying them, tilting her mask to make sure he could see. He knew she was right. Whoever had killed Zac, they hadn't missed him by much. And he wasn't sure they'd missed him *at all.* If the killer was still inside the house, he might not hesitate to take out two witnesses.

"Now."

42

Lying in bed, Audrey turned over one more time. She never had been able to sleep well when the sun was bright, but today was especially hard. She'd pulled her curtains tightly together, but it wasn't helping much. The mid-afternoon sun still found a way through, and there was no way to hide from its spotlight.

She didn't know what else to do now that the virus was potentially back. There just wasn't much she *could* do until the lockdown was lifted. Part of her was glad they might be back to fighting the virus. That was a reality she was used to at this point, and desperate people made desperate decisions.

Then she heard the voice booming through the bullhorn from the street, near her house.

"This is Doctor Frank Lawry, from Saint Francis," the voice radiated around her. "I'll make this announcement several times. If you aren't hearing well, just wait where you are, and I'll come closer to you shortly."

Audrey braced herself; she was about to find out where the town stood. Had they been able to contain the spread? People were going to be nervous for a while, no matter the outcome of this. Audrey was nervous, but she felt like she was ready for anything.

"The most important thing for you all to know right now is that we see no reason to maintain a twenty-four-hour lockdown. The town doesn't need to come to a full stop. If there's work to be done, please do it. But we're leaving a pack of surgical masks on your front porch. If you do go outside, wear them until further notice. And if you don't need to leave the house, please do stay inside, and keep interactions to a minimum.

"As for Tyrone, we regret to announce that he has tested positive for H6N1. We don't yet know how it got into his system, but we're working on understanding that. His wife is not exhibiting symptoms, but she's also tested positive, as have their two children. Their immediate neighbors have also been tested, but those came back negative, which is encouraging. We're doing everything we can to see if we can hold the virus at bay for Tyrone's family, but we don't expect him to live past another forty-eight hours.

"I can't stress to you enough that care must be taken now that we know the virus is active in our community. Over the coming days, we'll keep Tyrone and his family in our quarantine bay at the hospital. But we still don't know with any certainty how the virus spreads. All we know is that it's extremely contagious, and extraordinarily deadly. There is no vaccine, or cure. As far as we're aware, the survival rate is zero. We will have doctors come to each of your houses in the next twenty-four hours and test everyone for the virus. In the meantime, for the sake of you and your community, please be careful. Thank you."

As the announcement ended, Audrey felt a lump in her throat—This was it. Alessandra was either going to survive this challenge, or it wouldn't. Even in the worst and most fearful of times during the virus's initial strike, it hadn't breached the town's walls in this way. No one in the town had officially been diagnosed with it; they hadn't watched one of their own die, scratching madly at their skin and choking on their own blood until they collapsed from respiratory failure, but they had seen a number of suicides in anticipation of what was coming.

She'd never forget the chaos and exhilaration of those months, commissioning the wall and watching the town come together to erect it while the hospital worked to quickly isolate and process H6N1 victims from around the region. She'd never been prouder to lead a team of people than she'd been then, seeing Alessandra rise up and beat back the virus that destroyed the world they knew.

This time, though, the walls weren't enough. The virus was here. Instead of playing defense, they'd have to play offense to a greater extent than they had before. This was bound to be the biggest, most important fight any of them had ever known.

Audrey cracked her front door open to grab the pack of surgical masks when she heard a different voice booming through a bullhorn. She looked up and saw a masked Stephanie walking down her street.

"People of Alessandra, thank you for your cooperation with Doctor Lawry's advisement. That's the best recommendation we can follow right now. I also have an important announcement that you should hear. Zac was found dead in his home early this morning. We're still working to determine the cause of death, but it definitely *was not* virus-related. That much, we know."

Audrey slipped a mask on and walked down her front porch toward Stephanie, who had turned and was facing away from her as she spoke.

"What we also know is that Zac committed the assault against Derrick, and likely also killed Father Hayden; Derrick positively identified him, and then Michael and I found the gurney he used to wheel Derrick up to the hospital, hidden in his back yard. So, there is good news in all of this—the man who had been terrorizing our town is dead. We can move forward. In light of his death, and the immediate urgency of H6N1's threat, I'm going to cancel—"

Audrey tapped Stephanie on the shoulder, and she pivoted around, her eyes wide. Audrey shook her head, a slight smile on her face.

"I'll take his place," Audrey said.

Stephanie's forehead creased, and her eyes darted left, then right.

"You shouldn't even be outside, Audrey. What do you mean about taking his place?"

"You were about to cancel the vote because you don't have a competitor. People know me. I'll step in, so there's no need to cancel."

"What? But no, you're just a temporary—"

Audrey reached for the bullhorn, which Stephanie was holding loosely at her waist. Stephanie tried to snatch it back, but Audrey got her fingers wrapped around the handle, yanking it in her direction and wrenching Stephanie's shoulder as she cried out in pain. One more hard tug, and her grip loosened enough for Audrey to get the bullhorn; she lifted it to her lips.

"People of Alessandra, this is Audrey Reese, your former mayor, and I'm pleased to announce that I'll be stepping into Zac's place as a candidate to be your mayor again. I hope to fill his shoes adequately, and do everything I can to earn your vote."

As she spoke, she could see some people's faces appearing in windows, surprised by the news. She handed the bullhorn back to Stephanie.

"Here ya go," Audrey said. "Let's keep walking. We've got some more announcements to make."

43

Stephanie pounded the wall in her living room, her hand stinging with each impact, but she couldn't help it. She needed to feel something other than the constant frustration and helplessness that had fallen over her like a heavy blanket in recent days. Happiness and relief would be welcome. Absent that, pain would do.

"Come on, Steph," Michael said. "It's gonna be fine. Who's gonna vote for her anyway? After everything she did before? We practically fought a war to pry her out of that mansion before. People aren't gonna want to go back to that. Too much was lost. Too many died for that cause."

Stephanie's forehead rested on the wall, her hands laying flat against it.

"I want to think that's true. I'm just not sure."

"Why not? You're always confident in yourself. You've already been a big part of defeating her once. Why don't you think you can do it again?"

She backed off the wall and sat down on the couch next to Michael. Her head was pounding, and she could feel tears stinging the surface of her eyes.

"It's not that I *can't*. It's that I'm not sure the people look at us overthrowing her in the same way *we* do. We were immersed in that. We were active participants, coming up with plans and executing them. Hardly anyone even knew what we were doing until we played that video in the square. That awakened people, jarred them out of a sort of resigned stupor they'd been in. But even then, I'm not sure they understood exactly what they were doing when they dropped their rings to the ground. Hell, we didn't either. None of us expected the officers to just start indiscriminately firing on people. It was horrifying. We lost friends. Others lost family—mothers, fathers, children. It was a massacre I'm not sure we ever fully recovered from, as a community.

"And then Audrey was gone, her reign turned off like a light switch. We know everything that went into it, all the plotting, all the work. But to everyone else, I'm just afraid it seemed like Audrey was the unquestioned leader one moment, then disappeared the next. Where was she? What was her explanation for everything that happened? What would come next? Nobody knew. And while we were certain it was the right thing to do because of how deep into everything we were and how much we were aware of, I'm not sure everyone in the town feels the same way. I think some still find comfort in the old way things were done."

Michael placed his hand over hers. "But do you really think there are enough people like that to give her a majority?"

She lowered her eyes and looked at Michael, swallowing hard.

"Maybe."

"Well, okay," he said. "Let's say you're right. Let's say that there's a sizable chunk of Alessandra who would be eager to return to Audrey's world. What do we do? Do we have another debate? Or just put both of you on stage in front of the people and let you make your cases? Can you outsell her? Convince those people not to go back?"

Stephanie looked at the floor and shook her head, then looked back up.

"I think there's only one thing we *can* do."

"And what's that?"

"I eject her."

Michael took his hand away and leaned back.

"You what? What do you mean?"

"Banish her. Kick her out of the town. And her men, I guess, though I'd be willing to keep them if I thought they weren't so loyal to her. They're good, strong for—"

"What are you saying? You're gonna kick your political opponent out of Alessandra so that you don't lose a vote?"

"She was on a temporary stay, anyway. I'd just be accelerating that by a little bit. Nothing was guaranteed to her, Michael. *Nothing.* I agreed to take her in on a temporary basis. I extended her a hand, and she just took a big fucking bite out of it. This is a betrayal. She tried to act friendly, like she'd changed. She even came by to offer me advice. Once she saw an opportunity to strike, though, *bam!* She's a viper. And you can't allow a viper to live among us."

"But it's an awful look, Stephanie. *Terrible.* Everyone knows Audrey just announced she's running against you. It'll look like—"

"I don't give a shit what it *looks* like, Michael. At this point? I don't care. I'm trying to run a town here. A town, mind you, that has people being murdered when they're not contracting a virus that killed all of fucking humanity and wrecked our goddamn world. You're gonna have to forgive me if I stop caring about how my decisions look, and just do what I need to do. Hell, what are you upset about? You practically begged me not to let her in in the first place."

Michael was staring at her, his face pained. He stood and walked across the room.

"What's the matter with you? I know all this is stressful, but that's the kind of thing I would have expected to hear from Audrey. Yes, I disagreed with allowing her in from the start, but that decision's been made. This would just look like you were trying to make an authoritarian play for the town. I *need* you to reconsider, Stephanie. This can't be who we are. What happened to our ethics? What happened to freedom to choose, and all that?"

"Wartime versus peacetime." Stephanie stood and faced him. "This is wartime."

"Yeah, well, if your so-called ethics only apply during the best of times, they're not ethics. They're just a convenience. Anyone can be ethical in peacetime. The test is if you can still do it in war."

"During war, the ethical perish. We've seen that plenty. I'm preparing for war. I hope you'll be with me, but I'll do it with or without you."

Turning onto Audrey's street, Stephanie could see her house just a few away now. Stephanie was keeping her head up, striding with what she thought looked like confidence as she approached maybe the most consequential act of her leadership. George walked beside her, a loaded handgun tucked into his waistband just in case. Michael had refused to come, and she figured having George there to escort Audrey and her men to the gate would be appropriate anyway. Showed she meant business. She hadn't told George yet who they were going to see or what they were doing, but she figured he'd probably guessed by now.

Was Michael right? Would she get some blowback for this? Probably. But she'd given up on playing it safe for the sake of having people like her. She was ready to do something bold. The people might even respect that she'd done something that went against her principles because she felt strongly enough that it was in the town's best interest. There's something honorable about that. She was making a sacrifice. It wasn't selfish, even if Michael couldn't see that at the moment. She was working for the people. Michael could seethe about ethics all he wanted; he wasn't the one held accountable for the decisions.

As they stepped onto the front yard, two of Audrey's men came out the front door and stood on the porch, staring down at them, masks over their mouths. They were intimidating, she'd admit. Tall, broad shouldered, draped in black, their bulging arms stretching the sleeves of their too-small T-shirts, hands crossed at the wrists in front of them.

Stephanie stopped ten feet or so shy of the stairs, trying to deepen her voice as she spoke.

"We need to see Audrey," she said, emphasizing the "We" to suggest she wasn't alone in this. "We'd prefer to discuss this inside, but we'll do it out here if we need to."

The two men looked at each other, then back at Stephanie. Neither moved beyond that.

"So, can we come inside?" Stephanie demanded. "Or can you get her for us? This is urgent."

They stared ahead, saying nothing. She was trying to tell if they were blinking. If it weren't for the scars on the one man's cheeks and neck, Stephanie would have wondered if they were actual cyborgs.

The door opened slowly, and Stephanie could see a feminine hand pulling on the doorknob. Then Audrey emerged onto the porch.

"Good to see you, Stephanie." Audrey looked at her for a few seconds, then shifted her gaze to George; Stephanie thought Audrey's eyes lit up a bit. Did she know what Stephanie was planning here? "George." Audrey nodded, and turned her gaze back to Stephanie. "Come inside. Both of you."

Stephanie climbed onto the porch, and she could feel the men's eyes boring into her as she walked between them, George close behind her. It wasn't a comfortable feeling. The thought crossed her mind that, if they chose, those men could probably kill her and George without a thought. She hoped George wouldn't have to take his gun out. If Audrey and the men would just surrender peacefully, it wouldn't be necessary. Maybe Audrey would see there was no swaying Stephanie, and decide it wasn't worth the fight. This was Stephanie's town now; Audrey had abandoned it once, and there was no getting it back.

When Stephanie came into the living room, Audrey was sitting in a wicker chair, a long tan robe fluttering down to the floor.

"Sit down," Audrey said, motioning toward the couch. "What can I do for you?"

"Nice robe," Stephanie said, sitting down with George next to her.

"You think? It was left behind by whoever had this place last. It's a little itchy, but I'm actually okay with that."

Stephanie nodded and looked around. The men stood like mountains on either side of the room. They were probably trying to look inconspicuous, but she doubted either of them had been inconspicuous for at least a couple of decades.

"Thank you for having us, Audrey. We appreciate it," Stephanie said. "First off, I wanted to follow up to gauge how serious you are about running against me for leadership. I have to admit, that caught me by surprise, considering I was kind enough to let you into the town, and you know you're just here as a *very* temporary resident."

Audrey's eyes never wavered as Stephanie spoke. There was something unnerving about that. She leaned back and crossed her left leg over her right.

"Oh, I'm completely serious. And I intend to win. Look, Stephanie, don't think I don't appreciate that you chose to let us inside. That made this whole thing far easier. But let's be honest...I was finding a way in here regardless. I mean, did you think I was just gonna walk away quietly if you said 'No'? After coming this far? Come on. You're smarter than that. In fact, I assumed that was why you decided to just let me in. That at least gave you something to hold over me, just like you're trying to do now. I thought it was an interesting strategic play—let the devil in, and keep him close enough to have eyes on him. It might have worked if Zac had beaten you, because we'd have had a common enemy. But it was a tough needle to thread, I admit."

Stephanie could feel her stomach tightening as she listened, the discomfort growing with each word.

"You think you'd have found a way in regardless? Doesn't say much for your wall."

Behind the mask, Audrey was clearly smiling.

"I *built* that wall, Stephanie." She raised an eyebrow. "There are things about it I know that you never will."

Stephanie blinked and then looked at George, who just shrugged. Did he know what she was talking about? If so, he hadn't discussed it. That wasn't important at the moment, though. She just needed him for what happened next. Then she'd have to address any weaknesses in the wall after Audrey was gone.

"Okay, then," Stephanie said. "You've got that on me, I guess. And you probably think that gives you an advantage. But it's important for you to recognize that no vote has happened yet. And no vote *will* happen unless I authorize it. I already let you inside; now you expect me to also provide you with the opportunity to take this town back under your rule? Why would I do that? Why shouldn't I just squash this vote and go forward?"

"Because, even if that would work at this point, you care about what people think of you. You're not a politician. You're just not. You're not built for this. I could have seen all this coming from miles away. You're a doctor. That's where your skill set is best used to help Alessandra. Instead, you're out there chasing killers and making chore schedules. It's not you. I'd counter with, not only should you not try to kill the vote, you should just step aside so I can take it over. Stop standing in the way, and let us both do what we do best."

"You're wrong if you think I can't do this job. I've been doing it, in my second year now. Have we had bumps in the road? Of course. You think your reign was perfect? You got fucking coup'ed. By *me*, in case you forgot." She hoped Audrey noticed her smile there. "So I'm up to this. I've never failed at anything in my life, and I don't plan for this to be the first. I'll do what I need to do. And in the interest of that, I've got a proposal for you."

Audrey sat forward and brushed her hair back, her eyes bright with interest.

"I want to think we can co-exist," Stephanie said. "You and your men *do* have some value to me and this town, as long as you know your place, which is not in that mansion up there. Not again. So, here's my proposal—You announce publicly that you've had a change of heart, and you fully endorse me continuing as mayor. In exchange, I remove the 'temporary' tag from your citizenship and agree to let you stay indefinitely."

"And if I decline?"

"These terms are non-negotiable."

Audrey shifted in her chair. "What does *that* mean?"

Stephanie sucked in a deep breath.

"It means that, if you choose not to accept my offer, you'll be banished. You and your men."

Audrey's head turned, and her back stiffened. To her right, Stephanie noticed one of the men move for the first time during the discussion, his arms uncrossing and then crossing again.

"*Banished?* You don't have the guts."

"It's your choice to find out."

"When?"

"Today. Now. George is here to facilitate it. If you refuse my offer, he'll escort you all out the gate, then help me shore up the wall to ensure you can't return. If you find some way back in, there'll be guns pointed at you. We'll shoot on sight."

Audrey stared at Stephanie for a few seconds, and then turned to George.

"Is this true, George? You've agreed to this?"

He scratched his head. "Well…This is the first I'm hearing of *this*," he said, turning to face Stephanie. "You…Stephanie, you never told me you were planning to kick Audrey out of the town. For what? Just for being your opponent? You're a tyrant."

"No," Stephanie said. "No, wait…It's not just because she's my opponent. She's—"

"Then why? What's she done that was wrong?"

"She's *dangerous*, George. Look what she did before. She's a threat to Alessandra. And you work for *me*, not her. *Me*. If you won't do this, I'll find someone else who will."

"I won't! What…I just don't understand what's happening with you, Stephanie. You can't do this."

"Then you're relieved of your command, George. If you can't be loyal enough to follow simple orders, I need someone else manning the gates."

"And I'm gonna make sure *everyone* knows exactly what you're doing!" George rose to his feet.

"I'd be careful here if I were you, Stephanie," Audrey said, leaning back in her chair, arms resting lightly on the armrests. "George is right. This is a pretty tyrannical move, disposing of your political opponent. And you don't have a police force to intimidate anyone. You do this, and everyone's gonna know. People are gonna hate you for it. Even people who would have voted for you. And someone else is gonna rise up to take you on. If you keep killing votes, they'll eventually just kill *you*. The people *will* rise up, Stephanie. No one knows that better than I do. If you do this, you'll regret it very soon."

Stephanie looked at George, still standing and staring, his eyes blazing. She turned back to Audrey, who appeared relaxed. Stephanie wondered if she appeared as stiff and nervous as she felt. Her breathing picked up.

"Now I've got a proposal for *you*," Audrey said. "As of right now, everything that's been said here is in this room. It doesn't have to leave here. I'm willing to chalk it up to a bit of an emotional outburst. George, do you agree?"

They both looked at George, who nodded.

"It's understandable," Audrey continued. "You've been under a huge amount of stress lately. It's a tough job. Lots of responsibility. Seeing the virus come back, Zac being killed, it all just came bubbling up. We get it. So, we tell *no one*..." She looked around the room, pointing at George and her men. "...about what was said here today. It's forgotten. In exchange, you allow the people to have their vote. That's all. I ask for nothing more. I don't expect you to just step down; you seem determined to stay. So I'll give you a fair shot. Beat me, fair and square. Then I guess you'll have the power to do with me as you please."

"As you will with me, if it goes the other way," Stephanie stated gravely.

Audrey nodded.

44

Audrey knocked on the Miller family's front door, then paused a beat before she began.

"This is Audrey Reese; I hope you heard that I'm running to be your mayor in the vote that's taking place tomorrow. You don't have to open the door if you don't want to. Just come peek out the window so I know you hear me."

She spoke at a volume just below a yell, puffing out her chest and projecting. It was a skill she'd learned from Mayor Handy many years earlier, because you never knew when a microphone might go out, or you might not have one. That couldn't be an excuse not to get your message to the people. You needed to expand your diaphragm, stand up straight, and let your voice reverberate from your lungs. If she didn't talk herself hoarse, that was going to serve her well as she went door to door over the course of the day.

After several seconds, Theresa Miller's face appeared in the window to her right. She gave a slight nod.

"Okay, great. Thank you, Theresa. I'm leaving two pieces of cloth on your front porch: One red, and one green. Tomorrow morning, you'll hang one outside a front-facing window. It'll be red to place your vote for me, and green for Stephanie. You can remember red because my last name is Reese. Audrey Reese. If you want to vote for Stephanie, you'll hang the green one. This will keep everyone from having to venture away from their homes unnecessarily. Be sure to have it up shortly after sunrise. If it's not, your vote may not get counted. That's it for the election logistics, unless you have any questions."

Audrey waited, listening for anything to be yelled from inside the house. This was the eleventh house she'd stopped at this morning, and there hadn't been any questions yet. But she and Stephanie had agreed to give people time just in case. Once Stephanie backed down from her demand and accepted Audrey's terms, this had been the voting system they agreed upon. It seemed straightforward and simple, while also allowing people to stay safe.

Audrey honestly didn't know who the people of Alessandra would vote for. She'd been through many campaigns over the years, and you typically got a lot of face-to-face interaction, shaking tons of hands—and using tons of hand sanitizer. You looked people in the eye and did a lot of nodding. You smiled until your face muscles ached, and you kissed babies on the forehead. And you grabbed sleep where you could over those weeks and months, often in one-hour or two-hour increments. Quick breakfasts grabbed on your way out the door. Late nights looking at polling and strategizing. A buzzing team of mostly twenty-somethings wearing buttons with your name on them.

This time, though, the whole thing was going to happen in one day, and she was just talking to doors. She'd told herself she'd work tirelessly on this day, knocking on every door, trying to get her voice heard by every single person in town so she could make her case. Stephanie, Hank, George, and a few others were helping to distribute the voting cloths, so she didn't have to go to every house, but she sure as hell was going to anyway. Fortunately, she already had plenty of name recognition. But so did Stephanie. With such a time crunch, Audrey felt like it was a toss-up.

"Now, let me tell you quickly why I want to be your mayor again. Alessandra has always been in my heart. You probably remember that my last stint as mayor didn't end in the way I would have liked. My brother, Paul, let the power go to his head, and he corrupted my administration from the inside. I admit, I probably had a blind spot for him; he was family, and that's important to me, as I'm sure it is for you, especially in these difficult times. I thought I could lean on him. I thought we had the same values. But, by the time I accepted that we didn't, and he was engaging in horrifying acts in order to cling to power, it was too late to stop it all. That train was running downhill. For that, I apologize, and I've grown to be a better woman. A better leader.

"It's important to know that Paul wasn't from here. He didn't have Alessandra in his heart, deep within his skin, in the very blood he bled. Not like you and I do. So, there will be nothing but native Alessandrans in my administration. We will fight for you and your safety every day. It's unfortunate what happened to Zac, as we've never had more reason to cherish all life that stands before us, even life that's made some mistakes. And we'll punish whoever did it to the fullest extent of the law. You should know I don't shy away from making the difficult choices your leader needs to make in this world. Zac was not a good man, and I condemn his violence against those men, but he did bring up some important issues during his time pressing Stephanie for answers. He was right that Alessandra isn't as safe as it should be. Too much immigration is part of that. We need to band together as a town, as a community, and rise up against the outside threats that could take us down. Nobody knows that better than I do. I *built* that wall. We can bring Alessandra back to what it once was. I hope I'll have your vote to do that. Thank you."

Michael wasn't sure what to do with himself. After

refusing to go with Stephanie to tell Audrey she'd have to leave, he didn't hear anything about what happened. When he walked next door to ask Stephanie about it, she'd tried to wave him away, shutting the door in his face, but he blocked it with his foot. She was clearly upset, and wouldn't tell him anything beyond the fact that Audrey was staying, and the vote was on. Eventually, she screamed at him to leave. So he did.

Now, he sat in his house, trying to make himself read a book, but he couldn't concentrate. When he heard a knock on his door earlier, he'd hoped it was Stephanie coming over to apologize, but it was Hank, dropping off cloths he could use for voting the next day. Now the red and green cloths sat on his coffee table, staring back at him. Who would he vote for? How could he possibly vote for either one?

Michael wondered if he was overreacting. Stephanie was still the woman he'd known for so many years, right? She was still the woman he'd married, surely. But *was* she? The way she'd been acting recently was *really* troubling. It seemed like she'd become more distant, more willing to cut corners in the name of maintaining power. Was power just inherently corrupting? Was it something you eventually couldn't avoid? If it'd even wrapped its tentacles around Stephanie, Michael wondered if there was anyone who could resist.

Deep in thought, Michael was startled by another knock on his door. His heart jumped. Maybe this time it was Stephanie?

As he cracked the door open, he quickly saw it wasn't her.

"Hi, Michael," Audrey said. "Figured I'd find you here."

"Where else would I be?"

He felt a tightness in his gut, and his head was starting to pound. Memories were flooding back. He hadn't had a real conversation with Audrey since that day up at the mansion, when he'd tried to tell her why it couldn't have been Nick who killed Trevor, that Zac had the motivation and opportunity. She tried to treat him like he was crazy, then kicked him out. That made him think he couldn't trust her, and set in motion the events that would include dozens of deaths and Audrey being unseated. It was a traumatic time in his life, and he didn't relish re-living it.

"I think we should talk," she said. "I know it's been a while."

"It's…not a good time, Audrey. I've got a lot of things to do. We have a killer to find, in case you forgot during this whole campaign thing."

He ducked back into the house and pushed the door, but he felt it hit her hand.

"That's exactly what I want to help you with." Audrey peeked her head through the crack in the door. "I think I know who killed Zac."

Puzzled, Michael pulled the door back open a little further.

"How would you know that?"

She looked around. "I'd prefer not to talk about it on the front porch like this. Let me in, and I'll tell you everything. I think we can help each other, Michael."

Michael closed his eyes and took in a sharp breath, then motioned for Audrey to come inside.

"You have a nice place," Audrey said, sitting next to Michael on his loveseat with notches for the rings cut into the back. It appeared to be the only sitting furniture he had. The living room was plain, with white plaster walls and tan crown molding at the ceiling. "Not sure I've ever been inside before."

Michael blinked, not really acknowledging the compliment.

"You think you know who killed Zac? We found enough

evidence to pin him for Derrick's assault, which puts him in Father Hayden's back yard the morning of his death. So our assumption was that Zac did both, but I'm not sure what to think at this point. Do you think William helped him?"

"That's pretty heavy talk to start with, Michael. Can we at least—"

"It's been a long few days, Audrey. I'm not looking for idle chit-chat. If you have information that could help us find out what's going on, I'd love to have it. Beyond that, I'm just too tired."

"Why aren't you helping to distribute the voting cloths? I assumed you'd be out there."

Michael sighed. "I was never asked. Didn't know it was happening until Hank brought me mine."

"But I assume you know Stephanie paid me a visit yesterday?"

Michael was silent for several seconds; Audrey crossed her legs and waited.

"I'm aware." His reply was curt.

"I thought it was odd that you weren't there with her. You two are partners in leading the town, right? That seemed like a pretty important meeting. Why didn't you come?"

Michael pursed his lips, his eyes narrowing. She could tell he didn't want to answer.

"I've always liked you, Michael. I think you have a lot of great leadership qualities, and I think they're being wasted to some extent. My guess is that Stephanie told you why she was going to talk to me, you guys fought over it, and you told her you wouldn't have any part in it. Am I close?"

He crossed his arms and looked away.

"That shows a lot of character," she said. "You didn't want me in here in the first place…"

Michael swung his head around and looked at her with a sideways glance.

"Yeah, I could tell." She smiled. "It was obvious you were fighting for her to make us keep going instead of letting us inside the gates. Yet, when she wanted to banish me, you were against that too. You have principles, Michael. That means something. I respect that. You were the one who stood up to me about Trevor's murder, and tried to make me see what was right there in front of my face, but I stupidly dismissed you. I was wrong. You were right. I got caught up in what I was doing, and wasn't thinking straight. I should have listened. For what it's worth, all this time later, I'm sorry."

Now he was looking straight at her, and he nodded.

"Look, if I win this vote tomorrow, I'm gonna need people like you, people who have the respect of everyone in the town, who understand how Alessandra operates, who are principled leaders. I saw that in you years ago when I made you the head of our Watch team. If I win, you're the first person I'm coming to and ask if you'll be my right-hand man. You don't need to give me an answer now. Sleep on it. But, unlike Stephanie, I'd give you an actual say in what happens. You'd have a strong, important voice in the future of Alessandra. I hope you'll consider it."

"I…I don't know what to say." He rattled his head back and forth. "I never expected that."

"No rush, Michael. If I win, the offer's there. Just think about it."

Audrey started to stand up.

"Wait," Michael said. "What do you think happened with Zac?"

"Oh, yes. Look at me getting distracted from the main reason I came here in the first place."

Audrey sat back down.

"So, the way I see it, there's one person who had the right motivation and timing to do it. I think it's obvious."

"Yeah?" Michael moved a little bit closer to Audrey. "Who is it?"

"I'm surprised you haven't thought of it yet, honestly," Audrey said. "One person stood the most to gain—Stephanie's the one who killed Zac."

"Can I come in?" Michael said, looking at a weary Stephanie through her cracked-open front door. She walked away from the door silently, letting it stay open, and he stepped inside, shutting it behind him. He paused for a second, then reached back and locked it.

He came into the living room, where she was sitting in her recliner, brown liquor in a glass cradled in her right hand. She was swirling it around just a bit.

"What are you drinking?" he asked, surprised.

"Some of Walt's hooch." The way her words slurred just a bit suggested this wasn't her first glass. "He gave me a little to take home. Maybe that means he's voting for me. Or he just pitied me."

"Damn, Steph. You pretty much never drink. The last time I saw you take one shot of Walt's stuff, you nearly spit it out on the bar."

Her head lolling forward, she gave a loose shrug. "You get used to it."

Michael sat on the couch and turned to face her. "You never came and saw me today. Is this what you've been doing?"

"This?" She looked into her glass and turned it in her hand. "Nope. Just a busy day."

"I heard what happened with Audrey. I heard you tried to go through with banishing her, but George refused to help, and you backed down. Is that true?"

Her head jerked up, and she made eye contact with Michael for the first time since he'd arrived.

"What? Who told you that?"

"George. He stopped by this afternoon. Looked like he was going door to door." This wasn't exactly true, but Michael didn't want Stephanie to know he'd learned that from Audrey. While he did see George knocking on doors, he skipped Michael's house.

"God *damn* it!" Stephanie slammed the glass down on the arm of the chair, splashing half the liquor onto the floor.

"Is it true?"

"Shit." She looked away, slowly shaking her head. "If that's all he told you…yeah, it's true. He turned on me."

"It wasn't the right thing to do, Stephanie. I told you that before—"

"Oh, sure. 'I told you so' is *so* what I need to hear right now, Michael. Tell me more about how you knew all along what would happen, and how you'd have done it better."

"It's not about knowing what would happen. It's about doing the *morally right* thing. I used to always know I could count on you at least doing *that*. Now, something's changed."

"Well, I'm fucking sorry I let you down, all right? I'll try to do better."

He couldn't tell if that was sarcasm or just the liquor talking.

"Hey…I need to ask you something. It's important. It's a hard thing to ask, but I need to know the answer tonight."

"Okay. Go ahead and ask, then."

Michael shifted in his seat, moving closer to her.

"Seriously. You need to look at me for this. I want to look into your eyes."

She hesitated, then raised her head, eyes shut, then open. "Fine. This better? Now, ask."

This wasn't an easy conversation to have, and Michael had debated how—or even whether—to get into it with her. But after what Audrey had said, he eventually decided he had no choice. If nothing else, it was their responsibility to try to figure out who killed Zac—and if that person was also involved with Father Hayden—and this was effectively a lead. It seemed that, whoever won, Michael was going to have an opportunity to have a prominent role in the administration, so he needed to keep an eye on this situation.

Also, the more he thought about it, the more Audrey's point made sense. Where had Stephanie been when Michael showed up at the house? During a quarantine with a deadly virus spreading in the town, she felt like she just *had* to take a jog? And Zac happened to end up dead at the exact same time? It was quite a coincidence if she had nothing to do with it. And she had proven by trying to kick Audrey out of the town that she was essentially willing to kill in order to get a threat to her power out of her way. After all, there was little doubt that sending Audrey and her men away without adequate supplies of food and water was the equivalent of a death sentence. If she'd do that, would she also kill Zac? Especially when she thought that would be the end of any challenge to her power?

He wanted to say the answer was No. A week earlier, it never would have even occurred to him to suspect her, jogging session or not. Now, though, he wasn't sure, and it was eating away at him. He needed to ask the question. He took a deep breath.

"What were you doing the morning of Zac's death?"

Her eyes narrowed, and an answer didn't come right away.

"What was I *doing*? I already told you I was jogging. You and everybody else knows I go for a jog around that time of the morning. What are you trying to ask me?"

"I'm asking you what you were doing. Were you really out for a jog?"

"Don't treat me like I'm an idiot, Michael. If you're

leading where I think you are, just fucking get there."

He looked away, then back.

"Just…This is hard, Steph. Just help me out. Where were you—"

"You know where I fucking *was*, Michael. What do you want? You want some corroboration for me jogging? Well, it's too goddamn bad, because I was alone. Somebody may have seen me out their window. I don't know. Wanna go poll the town? Maybe if you ever got off your ass and exercised, you could have come with me. But no. *Now* what?"

"Did you do it?" he asked.

Her head tilted, and he thought she almost smiled.

"Do *what*?"

"You know what. Did you?"

"No, no, no. That's not how this works. You have to say the words. If you're gonna accuse me of fucking *murder*—"

"I'm not *accusing* anyone of *anything*!"

"Then what are you saying? No dancing around this shit, Michael. You wanna be a big-boy detective, you have to go all the way."

He shifted uncomfortably, then saw something out of the corner of his eye, a glint from behind the couch. He pulled his chair out of the way and climbed back toward it.

"What are you doing?" Stephanie asked.

Michael moved the couch away from the wall a few inches and bent down to get a closer look. He reached down and pulled out a serrated knife. As he raised it up, holding it delicately with two fingers by the handle as if it was infected, Stephanie's jaw fell open.

"What is this doing here, Steph?" Michael asked, getting a closer look at it as he lifted it. He could see there were flecks of color on the blade. "I'm pretty sure that's blood, but you tell me."

"I…What the hell? Since when have I had a knife like

that? Jesus. I don't know where the fuck that came from!"

Michael's mind was swirling. He'd never wanted to believe it, and he was trying to excuse this in his head. But the astonished look on her face made it hard to excuse it away.

"What am I supposed to think about this?" he asked. "Honestly, Steph. Give me *something* here."

"Michael…" She moved closer to him, her hands clasped in front of her chest. "You know me. You know I'm not a goddamn *murderer*, okay? This is ridiculous."

"Then what about the kni—"

"I don't fucking *know*, okay? I don't *have* any knives like that. Maybe it's been there for years. Whatever's on the blade could be pasta sauce for all I know. I have no idea what's on there. And, honestly, Michael…If I had a bloody murder weapon, why would I just toss it carelessly behind my couch? Wouldn't I throw that shit in the lake or take it deep into the woods? Do you think I'm an idiot in addition to being a murderer?"

"I just…I don't know, Steph. You're drinking a lot lately. Maybe you were drunk, and weren't thinking straight. Maybe—"

"Get the *fuck* out of my house! Right now. I'm totally serious."

"What am I supposed to think? If you'd banish Audrey, how do I know you wouldn't hurt Zac?"

"Because I'd send away a potential tyrant who you never wanted to let inside in the first place, why wouldn't I also slit the fucking *throat* of a man? Well, of course! Now that you put it that way, it makes perfect sense! What the hell is *wrong* with you?"

"You've been acting weird lately. Maybe you didn't *intend* to kill him. You just went over there, had a fight, and he got the worse end of it. I don't know. I'm just trying to understand."

"Just get the hell out. Seriously. I can't deal with this shit."

"You're not gonna answer—"

She shoved him, and he stumbled backward toward the front door, dropping the knife. Stephanie scrambled over and grabbed it, holding it in front of her face.

"Go! Fuck you. Go. Leave. I can't look at you right now."

He looked her in the eyes, and felt a little bit scared of her for the first time. Did she kill Zac? Michael still wanted to believe she couldn't do it, but he wasn't sure.

Silently, he turned and walked out.

45

"Can we talk alone?" Michael asked, as Audrey opened her door. "I need some advice."

Audrey looked at her men on her right and gave a slight nod. They went out the door, and she motioned for Michael to come inside. She closed the door behind him, then walked ahead of him into the living room and sat down in her chair. He paused to sit, but began pacing instead, eyes fixed on the floor.

"I found something," he said, sweat beading on his forehead.

Audrey nodded. "Okay. You found something. What did you find?"

Michael paused and looked up at the ceiling, then started pacing again. "Do you really think Stephanie killed Zac?"

"Well, as I told you before, I think it's a distinct possibility, but I couldn't possibly know for sure."

"I found a knife." He stopped and looked directly at Audrey. "Behind Stephanie's couch."

She leaned forward in the chair. "Really?"

"And it had...*something* on it."

"Something?"

"Yeah. I don't know. It...might have been blood. Or something else that sort of color. I'm not sure."

"That's incredible, Michael. That's a *great* piece of

evidence!"

"Is it?" He began pacing again. "Am I just trying to make the facts fit some narrative that was planted in my head? Audrey, I've known Stephanie for a *long* time. It's just hard for me to wrap my head around the idea that she'd be capable of murder. No matter what. But…"

"But the knife?"

"Right." He sighed. "The knife. And the fact that she wasn't there when I got to the house that morning. She usually does go jogging, though. Is that *every* morning, like she said? I guess. But that's an awfully convenient excuse. Kill him during your normal jogging time, in your jogging outfit, and that's what people will think you were doing at the time. I don't know what to think."

"What about the knife? Did you take it with you when you left?"

"No. I dropped it, and she got ahold of it."

"Well, shit," Audrey said. "You know we'll never see that knife again. She's gonna clean it, and then get rid of it."

"That's probably true."

"But *you* saw it. You held it in your hands."

"Yeah. It just isn't possible, is it?"

Audrey leaned back.

"I don't know. You know her far better than I do. I'm not trying to tell you what to think. But I certainly know first hand what power can make people do. It can be intoxicating. And I don't doubt she's a good woman. I think she means well in whatever she does. But if she was convinced in her head that Zac being out of the way was a net good for the town, might she have decided it was worth it? And no one would suspect her. She wasn't expecting you to be at the house when she got back. She wasn't expecting you to find that knife. She thought Alessandra couldn't afford to have Zac end up as the leader, so she took drastic measures to prevent it. You can see the internal logic working."

"I mean, there's a certain logic to it, I guess. It's just hard for me to accept."

"I understand that it's hard. But you're the only one who can attest to either the fact that she wasn't home during the time Zac was killed, or that there was a bloody knife in her possession. The question is what you want to do with that. The election is tomorrow. Do the people deserve to know all this before they vote?"

"What do *we* even know? Whatever we told them would be my word against hers."

"I know that's hard to think about," Audrey said. "If you want to go door to door, I'll back you up. I'll stand right there beside you and vouch for what you're saying."

"But you're running against her. Then it just looks political. She denies it, and we both look bad. And I..." Michael finally collapsed onto the couch, drained of energy. "I don't want people to be as confused as I am going into this vote. It's too important. We'd basically be playing judge and jury, trying to convict her of murder in the court of public opinion without leaving her any time or forum for defending herself. Maybe there's a totally reasonable explanation for the knife that we haven't thought of yet. And maybe she really *was* jogging. It's one thing to say we have enough evidence to launch an inquiry into whether or not she was involved in Zac's death. It's another to tell everyone we found a possibly bloody knife in her house and they should weigh that when considering their vote."

"Okay, Michael. I'll trust your judgment. We'll keep this quiet for now, and see how tomorrow's vote goes."

He nodded. "I appreciate it. I'm confident we're doing the right thing. And now, I think I've taken up enough of your time. I'm gonna head back and get some rest."

He stood and walked toward the front door; Audrey

followed him and held the door as he stepped onto the porch.

"Have you given any more thought to my offer?" she asked.

"About being part of your team?"

She smiled. Michael was silent for a moment before speaking.

"It's on my mind. No decision yet, but I won't make you wait if you win."

"That's all I can ask."

46

Saint Francis looming just up the street behind him,
George was the first to arrive at the spot where they'd agreed
to start the vote count, working their way from Hickory
Avenue, nearest the hospital, and finishing up on Kimsey
Street.

From where he stood, he could already see several green
cloths hanging out of windows along Hickory, fluttering in
the breeze. Within another hour or so, they'd know who the
next leader of Alessandra would be. He was anxious to get
started with the count, but he was the only one there. He sat
down on the curb to wait.

Just then, he saw Stephanie coming up the street. When
they made eye contact, she seemed to pick up her pace. She
stalked within a few feet of him, and he stood.

"Why the hell did you tell everyone about what happened
with Audrey?" Stephanie seethed, her teeth clenched. "That
wasn't supposed to leave the room. I thought we'd agreed."

"That's information about you the people deserved to
know. Audrey kept her promise, but there was no reason for
me to."

"It's not right, George. It's a betrayal. Remember, you're
still *my* security director. You don't work for fucking Audrey,
all right? You work for *me*. And you don't backstab me like
that."

"*Backstab* you? You *fired* me, don't you remember? Ya know what? Screw you. If you didn't want people to know you did that, you shouldn't have done it. I didn't lie to anyone. I told them exactly what you *actually did*. If the truth is that damaging, you probably should have made a different decision. Nobody made you do that. You chose to."

"Just like you *chose* to tell everyone!"

George sighed and shook his head.

"And I'd goddamn do it again too." He stood up straight and looked hard into Stephanie's eyes, their faces just inches apart. "Good fucking luck finding a new security director. I'm sure there are lots of qualified people around for you to choose from. That is, if you're still in charge in a few hours. I have a hunch Audrey will rehire me pretty quickly."

Stephanie's eyes were on fire as they stared a few more seconds, before they both saw Audrey coming and swung their heads toward her. Stephanie backed away.

Pencil and paper in hand, Stephanie and Audrey walked the streets of Alessandra, red and green cloths draping down the sides of homes, each one drawing another dash on their notepads. George followed them in order to moderate any disputes and keep his own count just in case, though Stephanie had her doubts about how neutral he could be if the time came.

The colors made it almost seem like Christmas, in the cool, dewy spring mountain air that Stephanie loved. It was helping to nurse her hangover, a feeling she hadn't had since college, as far as she could remember. Back then, she'd roll out of bed at ten and chug a bottle of Gatorade, maybe drop in some Pedialyte and get a big, greasy breakfast biscuit from some shitty fast-food restaurant to get herself ready for the day. Now, she didn't even feel like she could drink too much water because she didn't want to use up her ration. So she suffered. Jackhammers ringing out in her head, her skin a tint of grey, she continued on.

Four streets in, the vote was close—Audrey was ahead 32-28—and Stephanie thought she might have a couple of strong streets coming up. That was especially true for Pine Street, where several immigrant families had congregated— the Vicarys, Pellicos, and Mayeses seemed like sure Stephanie votes, given her support of them and the rhetoric coming from the other side. There were 127 people of voting age in Alessandra, and it seemed like most were voting. Stephanie found it mildly amusing how few houses hung two different-colored cloths. Husbands and wives were, for the most part, voting hand in hand for this election; there were only a couple of split houses so far on the walk.

Given how close the vote was, Stephanie wondered how much of an impact George telling everyone about her failed gambit with Audrey was going to have on the outcome. She had been afraid when this count began that she might just see a sea of red before her as they walked, but that hadn't been the case. Lots of people were still sticking with her, despite what she assumed they now knew. Did they think she'd done the right thing? Or did they think the other good she'd done outweighed one mistake? She had no idea, but even a small number being swayed against her could be enough to swing it to Audrey.

And did Michael tell anyone about the knife yet? Who would he even have told in such a short period of time? However tense everything had become the previous day, she saw no way he actually believed deep down that she killed Zac. He couldn't possibly believe that. Not with everything they'd been through. Not with all they'd meant to each other since they were barely adults. Ultimately, they'd move past this. If she could just get through this election and maintain her hold on leadership in this town, she'd apologize to

Michael and convince him there was nothing to the knife. It wouldn't take much; she knew he wanted to believe her. She could tell him she'd been stressed from the election, and everything would be back to normal. *Tomorrow*, she thought.

Two more streets counted, and Audrey's lead held at 46-44. Pine Street was next, and she felt good about that one. And her street would be the last they'd hit; that one was mostly single-person homes. She was starting to think she had a real chance to win this, which she would have been far less sure about an hour earlier.

They walked in silence, just their footsteps along the wet, cracking pavement of the street and the morning birds to keep them company. Stephanie wondered what the others were thinking. Was Audrey starting to count the votes in her head and wonder if she had enough on the remaining streets? There was still William to count. She knew Andy and Benjamin were close with Zac, so they'd probably go for Audrey, if they voted at all. Nick's vote was already in for Stephanie, and she'd run up some quick early numbers when the first street they counted was the one where several of the doctors and nurses lived, closest to the hospital so they could stumble back there to sleep in their own bed when possible.

Stephanie kept looking for some reaction out of Audrey, but she wasn't seeing it. The woman would just look around and calmly make a slash in her notepad. Nothing seemed to faze her, including fluttering green cloths. Stephanie was trying to keep a poker face of her own, but she wasn't sure if she was able to keep quite as composed. Every red cloth she saw was like a knife driving deeper into her. She was trying not to think about who was hanging them. *Just look at the color and jot it down, Stephanie. Don't even register whose house it is. Don't think about what street you're on. Just count the vote.* But whatever she told herself in her head, it was *so* hard. She didn't want to think differently about the people who had voted for Audrey, or to want to punish them if she won, but the temptation was going to be there, as long as she knew.

Just as she anticipated, Stephanie cleaned up on Pine, taking all the immigrant votes and nearly sweeping the street to take a 57-56 lead going into her own street. Thinking of Kimsey Street in her head, there were no more than eight votes left. Going in with a one-vote lead, Stephanie needed three votes to clinch a tie, and four to win, if everyone on the street voted. Given that she felt certain of getting at least three with her, Hank, and Michael, that just left one more to put Audrey away. This was within her grasp.

As they turned the corner onto the street, her first glimpses of cloth were red. It was a tree-lined street, so she couldn't see the votes very far into the street. Some of them, you didn't even really have to walk down; you could spot all the bright cloths hanging from the corner. But they walked them anyway just to be certain. On Stephanie's street, though, there were several front-yard trees with limbs and young buds that obscured the view of the cloths people hung. They'd have to walk this one.

The first two houses were for Audrey. *Don't think about who lives in them. Just count the votes.* That put Audrey in front 58-57. Stephanie, Michael, and Hank were all toward the end of the street, so Stephanie knew she was essentially still up 60-58, but she wondered if Audrey had that figured out. They walked on, and two more cloths emerged from behind the trees—red. Both of them. The official count put Audrey in front by three, which meant it was basically a tie at 60 with Hank's ex-wife Leslie as the wild card who could swing the vote either way. Stephanie never would have thought it would be this close. All along, she'd figured the people of Alessandra would coalesce around one candidate, and it'd be a decisive victory for *someone.* But to see the town this divided was borderline shocking.

Leslie's house came up next. In her head, Stephanie knew that was going to decide it. Counting Hank, Michael and her own vote, Leslie was the one nobody could be sure about. Stephanie had never been especially close to her, but they were neighbors who were reasonably friendly. Sometimes, Stephanie worried that she didn't have any friends outside of the hospital. She'd spent so much time building her career and driving herself to be the best at what she did that her life had almost been on pause. She liked Leslie, but when was she going to find time to build that relationship? Between twelve-hour shifts and trying to get a couple of hours of sleep in? Maybe a few more conversations, time spent sitting on their front porch with drinks in their hands, something more than just a quick wave as she went to work would have made her feel better about this one. But, craning her neck around the newly budding tree in Leslie's front yard, she hoped. Maybe whatever she'd done had been enough. Maybe Leslie would want to give her a renewed chance to lead.

Then, fluttering in the slight breeze, she saw it—green. Relief washed over Stephanie like a warm shower on a cold morning. She closed her eyes and took a deep breath, a smile crossing her lips. That should do it. She was going to survive. They pushed past a cluster of trees, and the last houses were coming into view behind them. Stephanie first glanced right and saw the green cloth hanging from Hank's window, bringing her to within one vote of Audrey. She smiled as she turned to her right, but then heard Audrey scream and saw her raise her arms in the air. As Stephanie swung toward her own house, she caught a glimpse slightly ahead. The green cloth hung from her living room window, where she'd put it before she left the house that morning.

One house past it, though, hung a red cloth. Michael. Stephanie fell to her knees, her notepad wet on the pavement.

It actually happened. Audrey's long-term vision when she left Graysburg carrying only what her men could grab from the house before they fled had come to fruition far faster than she'd expected. Her greatest triumph. Her destiny. She thought it might take years. When the opportunity presented itself, though, she pounced. If there was anything she knew how to do, that was it.

Between offering Michael her respect and him finding that knife, he'd apparently had enough doubts to swing to Audrey. She was glad she'd found a way to bring him to her side. Give him something tempting, and see if it sways him. That's how politics gets done—Carrot and stick. You needed to have both. She knew she'd have plenty of stick.

But, right now, standing there looking at the red cloth hanging from Michael's window, Audrey was reflecting back on the hardships she'd faced to get there. The endless winter nights in the forest, desperate for the warmth of a fire but concerned about the attention it might bring them. The aching hunger pangs, trying to drag them down to the ground, hold them in place, sated only in the most minimal way by the occasional nut or small fruit picked off the forest floor. The brutal climb in elevation—more than 1,000 feet over the 100-mile hike—that made the walk feel two or three times as long. There were moments she thought they'd never make it, that they'd just collapse and die, one by one, left for the bears and the wolves to pick over their bones. Belief in her destiny was probably what kept her moving, taking one step after the other, driving forward through it all. For this. She was back.

She saw Stephanie crash to her knees on the pavement, and scrambled to help her. Audrey recognized how difficult this had to be for her. A week earlier, Stephanie had no inkling this could possibly happen, and now her world had changed in a morning. She was out of power, and she'd have to submit to Audrey's rule again. The people had spoken, and handed her a rebuke she hadn't seen coming. And one of those people had been her own co-leader and ex-husband, who had stuck with her through everything until this moment. With what he knew, she had to wonder what came next for her too.

Audrey reached out to help steady her, but Stephanie quickly swiped her arm away, then buried her head in her hands, tossing her mask onto the street and weeping. Audrey thought it was best to let her be.

There were so many decisions to make. George walked over to shake her hand and offer congratulations, and she wondered if he'd be up for building and leading the police force she knew she'd need. She owed him something big. Had he not stood up to Stephanie and refused her order, there's no telling how ugly that situation might have gotten. Audrey had been ready to do what she needed to do in order not to get sent away, and she knew her men would follow her lead. George's loyalty was commendable, and she'd reward him for it.

To her right, Audrey noticed movement; she turned and saw the front door of Michael's house open, and he stepped outside. Coming down from his front porch, he walked across his yard toward them.

Stephanie lifted her head from her hands and looked up, seeing Michael and screaming. It was a scream not of fear or pain but betrayal, a banshee wail from within the deepest part of her, guttural and deep. Stephanie rose to her feet and sprinted to her house. Michael stopped and watched her disappear through her front door. For a moment, Audrey thought he might follow her, try to apologize, maybe even beg to change his vote. But then he continued walking toward Audrey.

"Congratulations," he said. "I feel bad about Stephanie. I

still don't know if I think she killed Zac, but I've got too
many doubts to give her my vote right now. I'm putting a lot
of trust in you. I hope you can prove me right."

She nodded. "I certainly plan to, Michael. I appreciate
your support. Looks like I needed it."

He looked at her notepad, and she pointed to the final
vote total.

"Damn." Michael took a sharp breath. "That may help
explain Stephanie's reaction."

"That's some of it, yeah."

"What's gonna happen to her now? Will you let her go
back to the hospital and work? Are you gonna put her on trial
or something?"

"I haven't decided how to handle her just yet. She could
be useful to me. Well, to *us*. You could have a real say in
Stephanie's fate, along with the rest of what we do. I need
you. What do you say?"

"I want to see her treated fairly."

"I know you do, Michael."

They stood shoulder to shoulder, looking silently at
Stephanie's house.

"I'm in."

They smiled and shook hands; George slapped them both
on the back and laughed.

"We're gonna do some great things here, guys," he said.
"We can make this town better than it's been in a while."

Audrey noticed another door opening, this time across
the street. At first, she didn't see anyone, just an open door,
revealing a dark hallway. Then she saw a foot, stepping
weakly, wobbly on the front stoop. Hank walked out, his
arms held stiff at his sides, palms pointed outward, his eyes
held high toward the rising sun. His chest rose, and then he
fell forward, tumbling to the ground, his head hitting the
pavement.

They all ran to him. As they approached, Audrey could clearly see them—boils covering his arms and the back of his neck. She stopped and threw her arms out.

"Don't get any closer!" she yelled, her heart pounding in her chest. "Look at the boils. He's got the virus. George, get to Saint Francis as soon as you can. We need him in quarantine ASAP. And fucking *find out if there are more!*"

47

"Should I be worried about you?" Walt poured another couple fingers of his moonshine, the late afternoon sun casting jagged light into his bar. "This isn't like you. Second time in two days?"

"I'll be fine. Hair of the dog, right?" Stephanie said, watching the dark brown drink splash into the glass. Her hair looked like she hadn't brushed it in days; her eyes were tender and puffy. She pushed her mask up and took a sip. "Hell, maybe this'll be better for me. Ya know?"

"How ya figure?"

"Well, once I emerge from this bender, I'll be sort of a butterfly coming out of its cocoon. I can return to the hospital. They've kept my old office unoccupied all this time. My name's still on the door. You know that?"

Stephanie saw Walt's cheeks rise in a smile behind his mask, while wiping a glass clean.

"So, fuck it. Ya know? I can just throw myself into that. Plenty to research, with H6N1 lingering around here again. Three more cases just this morning. It's spreading. But that means plenty of live virus to study. Actual people still alive who we know are carrying it. If I can develop something that could help, that'd be a hell of a legacy. Don't ya think?"

"Better than the legacy of leading the town through it?"

She looked away and ran her fingers through her hair,

which felt to her like sticking her hand in a pile of straw.

"Maybe I'm just not cut out for that. It's not me. I tried to be as fair as I could be, and it got me in trouble for not being tough or decisive enough. Then I tried to do what needed to be done, and Michael turned on me because he thought I lost my integrity, or some such bullshit. Oh, and he wanted to know if I fucking killed Zac. Do you goddamn believe *that*? Michael asked me about that, just before he voted for fucking Audrey."

Walt wiped down the bar and tossed the rag by the sink, as Stephanie took another sip.

"Well, I've never known you to kill a man, Stephanie. But Zac *was* a pain in the ass."

"Not only was he a pain in the ass, but he was the one who attacked Derrick. Which also means he almost certainly was at least involved in killing Father Hayden. And a couple of years back, we're fairly certain he killed Trevor. Remember that guy? Then, one night, he stalked me onto the back dock of the hospital, I think with the intention to kill *me*."

Opening another bottle, Walt took out a glass and poured himself some of the moonshine, pulled the mask aside and threw it back.

"And who else do you think it was who took that shot on Doctor Giles?" he said.

Stephanie's eyes grew wide.

"Damn. You're fucking right. Wasn't he a sniper or something like that in the military?"

Walt nodded. "And he owned some sort of stupid gun he didn't need. He's come in here braggin' about that shit. 'Fin Fall' or something like that. I don't know shit about guns, other than the three-fifty-seven I keep back here in case there's trouble. But it sounded to me like he babies that thing, and it's got some crazy range on it. Who else had the training and equipment to take that shot?"

"Son of a bitch. So much was going on then that I never had time to pursue who shot at us that day. I was just thinking about getting the hell out of there without getting shot myself so I could keep Michael alive. And that was the night Zac tracked me to the hospital."

"The way I look at it," Walt said, leaning against the bar and looking hard into Stephanie's eyes, "whoever killed Zac did us all one hell of a favor. If it had been you, I'd raise my glass to you right now."

Stephanie took a drink and then looked around the bar. She was the only one there. With four people having contracted the virus—one dead and three fighting in quarantine—who was going to risk going out? Other than her, anyway.

The door to the bar burst open, sunlight drowning out the long shadows, and three silhouettes stepped through the doorway.

"Stephanie Sloan, you're under arrest," George said, as he walked forward, revolver pointed toward her. He was flanked by William and Andy. "I'll put the gun away if you'll agree to come peacefully."

Walt stepped back from the bar, and Stephanie hopped off her stool.

"What the hell am I under arrest for?"

George glanced at Walt, then back at Stephanie, gun still held firm.

"We'd prefer to go over the charges privately at the compound. Will you agree to come with us peacefully?"

"No, I want Walt to fucking hear this. Tell me what you're arresting me...what *Audrey's* arresting me for."

George licked his teeth and took two steps closer to Stephanie.

"You're under arrest for the murder of Zac Latham, attempted murder of Audrey Reese, and abdication of duty as—"

"Murder? Abdication of fucking duty? Is this the way Audrey is running things? You're okay with this, George? This is the type of administration you want to work for? You arrest your political opponents?"

George's eyes narrowed. "You wanted to banish your political opponent to die a slow death in the woods, and you slit the throat of your other one. With all due respect, you have no moral high ground here."

"I *did not* kill Zac!"

"Ms. Reese believes you did, and she said she has evidence to prove it. I'll ask once more, will you come peacefully?"

Stephanie's mind raced, thinking of what her options might be. She could just go. She got basically half the votes in the town, despite everything. There was no way they'd stand for her being arrested on trumped-up charges like this. She was a native Alessandran and a respected member of the community. They'd rally to her defense.

On the other hand, she had no expectation of being treated fairly by Audrey. She probably wanted to extract her pound of flesh to get back at Stephanie for trying to have her ejected from the town. Whatever awaited Stephanie up at the compound, it wasn't going to be pleasant.

Stephanie spun on her heel and began running toward the back of the bar, but she slipped a bit, and felt a rough hand grip her wrist, twisting her around as her shoulder hit a bar stool and she collapsed to the floor. A knee drove hard into her back, and she screamed as her arms were wrenched backward, cuffs slapped forcefully on her wrists. She felt her body being lifted and carried through the front door and into the light.

"What'd you do with Stephanie?" Michael was out of

breath as he burst into a large, wood-paneled room that Audrey seemed to be turning into an office. "Are you locking her up?"

Audrey stopped pulling things out of boxes and walked toward Michael.

"It's okay, Michael. It's just due diligence. She's a key suspect in a murder, and my men were able to find the knife in her house. We're gonna need to have some law and order around here. It's standard procedure to bring in felony suspects to at least see what they know. We can't just let them stay out there and possibly commit more crimes, can we?"

He shook his head, not wanting to simply accept this. "It just doesn't feel right."

She touched Michael's arm. "I understand. You two are close. I get that. George is going to personally ensure her comfort while she's here. And if we find she didn't do it, if the knife turns out to be nothing, she'll be released immediately. Does that sound fair?"

"Just…Don't hurt her, okay? I'm trusting you that this time is gonna be different."

Audrey smiled. "And your trust will be greatly rewarded."

She walked out of her office and down the hall to the left, motioning for Michael to follow her. She opened the next door he saw, and led him into a room very much like her own office next to it.

"What do you think?" she asked.

Michael looked around, taking in the deep brown of the wood, and a large, uncovered desk sitting in the middle.

"It could use a good dusting."

Audrey laughed, a deep sound that seemed to come from her gut and echoed through the room.

"You're right about that." She nudged past him into the hall and clapped three times, then came back inside. "But do you like it?"

"Well, yeah. It's nice. Almost like a cabin."

"It's great, isn't it?" Audrey came closer to Michael and put her arms out. "And it's yours. I want this to be your office. It was Paul's old bedroom, but I think it'll work great for you. And if you want to live here, there are plenty of rooms. We can set one up for you, and bring all your stuff."

Michael was having a hard time taking this in. Stephanie had barely given him a voice in anything that was happening, but Audrey wanted to give him a beautiful office and even a new place to live. He'd never had a big office before. This would give him a place to work, and a feeling of belonging again. He'd be important.

"Pardon me." He heard the voice come from behind him; it was one of Audrey's men, looking enormous up close. Michael realized this was the first time he'd heard any of them speak. The man laid down a box he was carrying and extended his right hand. "Nathan Partridge. Nice to meet you."

They shook hands.

"Michael Sloan. Same."

Nathan put the box in the corner and pulled a duster out of it, then started brushing it on the desk's surface. Had Audrey really summoned this giant with just a few short claps?

"So we're good?" Audrey asked. "Ready to get to work?"

"Yeah. What's the plan?"

"Well, as you know, we have three more cases of H6N1. It's tragic. We're going to lose three more good people, and it continues to spread. We're isolated pretty well up here, but the people down in the rest of the town, they're stuck in a petri dish. I'm afraid they'll all die if we don't take swift action. We tried things Stephanie's way, but I think it's pretty clear that experiment failed. Would you agree?"

Michael wanted to reject that idea. It hadn't failed. They

all thought the virus was behind them. Nobody could have seen this coming. But the fact was this had happened on Stephanie's watch. The murders. The virus's return. It couldn't be ignored as part of the legacy of what freedom and democracy ultimately brought to Alessandra. And if they weren't decisive now, it could lead to the end of the town itself.

"I guess that's hard to argue against," he said. "She was trying to do the right thing. At least, up to the end."

"I know she was, Michael. She's not a bad person. Power can just lead some people astray, and the best of intentions don't always lead to the best results. She tried. But we have to move in a different direction. We need to go back to what we know works, if we're going to get Alessandra back to being the amazing community we know it can be."

Michael nodded, willing to give her ideas a shot.

"Wonderful!" She walked over and put her hands on his shoulders. "Come with me."

Deep in the basement of the mansion, Audrey threw open a large wooden door and stepped into an enormous storage space with a cold concrete floor and flipped on a flashlight. Her footsteps echoed alongside Michael's as they walked, her light dancing on the floor in front of them.

"My men found this room when they were doing a sweep of the place a few days ago," she said. "There's something pretty interesting down here that I think will be useful."

Michael said nothing, but kept pace with her as she walked past several thick pillars spanning high to the ceiling above them. They couldn't see anything her light wasn't shining on, including each other.

Finally, she stopped and turned her flashlight on Michael.

"Are you ready?" she asked.

"Go for it."

She smiled, knowing he couldn't see it yet. Then she swept the flashlight across the back wall and around behind her, shining it just in front of what she wanted Michael to see.

"Come closer," she said, and walked in that direction, her flashlight still fixed on the floor.

They stopped where the beam of light was pointing, and she waited another couple of seconds before lifting it.

There before them were the steel rings, piled high and haphazardly, some spilling onto the floor. Someone had tossed them back here, perhaps hoping no one would find them.

She reached out and touched them, caressing the cold, hard steel, remembering the weight of them, the sense of power that came with their size and shape.

"We kept the virus and crime at bay before with these," she said. "We have to bring them back. It's time, Michael."

Audrey turned and shined the light on Michael. He blinked, and ran his hand through his hair, scratching the back of his neck.

"What do you need me to do next?"

She handed him the flashlight and clapped three times.

ACKNOWLEDGMENTS

It never fails to be rewarding to get to this point. Each of these novels is another mountain to climb, and every one of them presents a different path to the top. But it's always fun getting there. At the point where it's not, I guess that's when I won't do this anymore.

But I couldn't do any of it without the support of so many individuals who provided the time and energy needed to bring this story to life. First and foremost of that group is my wife, Jamie, who accepts all the time that I put into this over the course of a year or so, listening to my ramblings about plot holes and character challenges, offering her own thoughts, and being my most important first reader. I don't think there'd be single book without her cheering me on.

On the beta reader crew, Jamie was joined by my long-time friends Emily Landers, Bryan Nale, and Mike Holcomb. They absorbed the brunt of whatever stupid early mistakes I made, slogging through a draft that only I had looked through, and dealt with the loads of errors I undoubtedly missed. Their contributions were essential to getting this book to where it is now. They were the first eyes other than mine to dive into the story, and I'll always be grateful for their help.

To take the story the rest of the way, I had to turn to a professional who could help me mold this lumpy ball of clay into something great. For the second straight book, that was Julie Tibbott. I feel really fortunate to have found Julie online, and she's been such a good fit for what I need in an editor.

She's thorough, insightful, and patient, finding those little language and plot manholes I had no idea I'd left behind. She's a terrific guide for helping me get the most out of whatever writing talent I have, and it's been a great relationship working with her these past two projects. All errors left behind are, as always, on me.

And then, of course, there's the cover. Monica Haynes has been such an amazing, talented find through three books for me now. My covers are starting to have a consistent feel that comes from her incredible sense of design and the message I'm trying to convey through the cover. It can't be all that common for an indie writer to have a cover designer who's also an early reader of the story and a real fan of the writing, but I've found that in Monica. I consistently get compliments on how my cover design looks, and I have pretty much nothing to do with it. Monica makes it all happen.

And thanks to all the family and friends who've been behind me from the beginning on this journey into novel writing. It'd be so much harder to do if the people around me weren't so supportive and encouraging for me to take this path. Hopefully, I can keep letting that motivate me to continue for decades to come. Can't wait to see what comes next. All I know for sure is there's a Book 3 on the way.

MORE BOOKS BY JEFF HAWS

Novels

The Solitary Apocalypse (Book 1 of The Alessandra Chronicles) — Along with the rest of a North Georgia town that survived a deadly worldwide plague, Michael's forced to wear a steel ring around his waist wherever he goes. He's seen cohabitation banned. Marriages dissolved. Families torn apart. But he's a good soldier, supporting the leader's draconian policies — until he learns an explosive secret about her that threatens to destroy the delicate balance they've achieved between safety and order. Now, Michael must enlist help to confront the awful truth about the town of Alessandra, and the fate of what may be the last human colony on Earth before he's silenced by the people who don't want anyone to know what they've done.

The Little Tragedy — For the past twenty years, every child has fallen into an endless coma on the night of their 10th birthday. Families are broken apart. Society is forever altered. And now, the human race itself is marching toward extinction. Until Kevin Fraser wakes up. With one Fraser child awake and the other rapidly approaching his 10th birthday, his family -- and the world -- holds its breath. Is this the sign of the plague finally ending, or will the walls start closing around the Frasers as the burden becomes too heavy for them to bear?

Killing the Immortals — Would you murder for god? Would you stand in the way of those who would? Cain and Hannah have to decide what side they're on in this fast-paced thriller about the dangers of fanaticism in a world where people are living indefinitely.

<u>Novellas and Short Stories</u>

Tomorrow's News Today — When Walt suddenly discovers that anything he writes at his small newspaper job will come true, he believes he has the power to reshape his crumbling marriage and career. But he also has the tools for his own destruction. Which path will he choose?

The Slingshot — Taylor's a typical geeky teenager who just wants to fit in with the cool kids for once. But soon, events spiral out of his control, and his moment of mischief threatens to tear apart his life, and his family's along with it. His older brother is the only one he can trust to save him.

FREE WITH NEWSLETTER SIGNUP

The Trolley Problem — Andrea will do anything for her son. She wants what's best for him, so she's doing her best to work a custody arrangement with her husband, and juggle a relationship with her new boyfriend. But now her ex wants to cut her out of her son's life, and she has to decide how far she's willing to go to keep her boy in her life.

REVIEW AND RATE *LET THE DEVIL IN*

Now that you've finished *Let the Devil In*, please consider posting a review and rating on Amazon and Goodreads. This serves both as invaluable feedback for the author, and as social proof to other readers that this book is worth their valuable investment of time to read. Also, if you liked what you read, follow Jeff on Amazon and Goodreads to interact, and be among the first to know when he writes something new.

ABOUT THE AUTHOR

Jeff Haws is a long-time journalist who has turned his writing eye to fiction. This is his fourth published novel and sixth published book. The first novel in this series, *The Solitary Apocalypse*, was published in 2017. Over the past 20 years, his writing has appeared in the *Washington Post, Atlanta Journal-Constitution, Miami Herald, Arizona Republic, New Orleans Times-Picayune*, and many other publications. He lives with his wife in Atlanta, Georgia.

SIGN UP FOR NEWSLETTER FOR UPDATES: jeffhaws.com/newslettersignup
TWITTER/FACEBOOK/INSTAGRAM: @ByJeffHaws

www.ingramcontent.com/pod-product-compliance
Lightning Source LLC
Chambersburg PA
CBHW052035240626
47153CB00006B/2089